Adrift
in
Iceland

Victoria Walker

For Beth
Because thirty-five years ago we both adopted a whale,
it feels like this story is ours.
(Even if you can't remember your whale's name)

x

1

Leifur Magnússon sat on the edge of the harbour in Hafnarfjörður, his legs dangling over the side, staring down past his boots into the cold water, looking for answers. He'd probably spent more time in this harbour than anywhere else in his life, and that was of some comfort, even today. His fishing boat, *Brimfaxi*, was moored next to him and shifted from side to side in rhythm with the gentle waves that lapped at the harbour walls. Except she wasn't a fishing boat anymore. Right now, he didn't know what she was. It would break his heart to let her go. She was the only thing he had left of his family's fishing legacy, and that weighed heavily on him.

He drew his gaze up beyond the harbour wall and out to sea. The North Atlantic. The sea that had been his livelihood and that of his family for so many years had nothing left to give him. He knew what he needed to do, but for a proud, knowledgeable fisherman, it was hard to bear thinking about. And that was how he found himself sitting here. Maybe there was another option that he hadn't thought of. But he knew there wasn't. He'd already spent countless hours sitting right here, contemplating the future, and this was the only way. Today, he was going to cast off, sail around the peninsula to

Reykjavik and, for the first time in his life, ask someone for help.

He sighed, stood up and stretched his arms over his head, moving his hips from side to side in an attempt to work out the kinks in his lower back. Although it was a life he loved — the only life he'd known — fishing was tough on a person's body, and Leifur, at thirty-six, was feeling it. Maybe there was a silver-lining in all of this after all.

After he climbed on board and made some preliminary checks, he radioed into the harbour master and then set his course. He pulled in the ropes, settled himself in the wheelhouse and guided *Brimfaxi* out of the harbour and onto the sea. It was a grey day, and as soon as he was in open water, the wind picked up and rolled the boat back and forth as it smacked across the white-tipped waves. Leifur grinned. He loved this. The motion of the boat on the sea made him feel truly alive in a way nothing else did, and it was a timely reminder of exactly why he'd done whatever he could to keep *Brimfaxi* and forge a new path for both of them. The sea was part of him, and he couldn't give that up without it tearing a part of his soul out at the same time. Asking for help was hard, but not as hard as the alternative.

Once he rounded the peninsula, Leifur radioed the Reykjavik harbour master asking for a mooring in the Old Harbour, the area closest to the city centre and where he'd arranged to meet Jonas Einarsson.

Leifur and Jonas had been at school together, albeit Jonas was a few years younger. They weren't exactly friends but if they saw each other, they'd pass the time of day, and Reykjavik is a small place, so Leifur knew Jonas ran a successful tour company. He also knew that Jonas didn't currently offer boat trips, and he hoped he could offer him the opportunity to tap into that market, with the fact they already knew each other working in his favour.

'*Hæ*, Leifur!' Jonas called out as he approached the harbour entrance. He was carrying two coffees and handed one to Leifur.

'*Hæ*, Jonas. *Takk*.' He shook Jonas's hand and took the coffee with a small nod of gratitude. 'Thanks for agreeing to meet.'

'It's an interesting proposition,' said Jonas as he followed Leifur back to *Brimfaxi*. 'What made you decide to stop fishing?'

Leifur stopped walking, wishing that hadn't been the first question.

'We rely on landing capelin, and last year there weren't any.' It was the simplest of explanations and had been the catalyst for their family fishing business failing almost overnight. It was unprecedented that there had been no capelin in Icelandic waters last year, and with the quotas of other catches already spoken for, there was nothing they could do.

'I heard about that. I'm sorry. And you don't think there's any chance of that changing?'

Leifur shrugged. 'I can't take the chance. I can't support my family on hope.' Since his father had died almost fifteen years ago, he had to support his mother. His younger brother had been all too happy to join a larger boat working for a big industrial fishing company, which although it felt like a betrayal at the time, meant that Leifur didn't have to worry about supporting him too.

Jonas nodded, his expression full of understanding. It was well known that the fishing industry in Iceland was changing. Small fishing businesses like Leifur's were being bought out by large companies, which were stiff competition for anyone not wanting to go down that road. The lack of capelin was not the only problem.

'She looks like a fine vessel. Permission to come aboard?'

Jonas asked with a grin as they reached *Brimfaxi*.

'Permission granted,' Leifur said, breaking into a rare smile himself.

They stood on the deck, which aside from the room taken up by fishing equipment, was expansive but open to the elements.

'What changes would you need to make to get her up to scratch for excursions?' Jonas asked.

'I have a friend who is a boat builder. He suggests taking the fishing equipment out, fitting railings around the deck, and putting some seating in the middle.'

'We'd need a platform for the tour guide to stand on so that they have a good view of the water all around the boat.'

'That's no problem,' said Leifur, hoping that was true.

'Is there anything that can be done to make any undercover space?' Jonas asked, nodding towards the wheelhouse that housed the controls, which was only big enough for a couple of people.

Leifur reached down and opened a large hatch. Steep metal steps led below deck into the hull of the boat. 'Follow me,' he said, jumping down while Jonas took each step carefully.

They were standing in a small space which, although it was head height, wasn't usable at the moment.

'We can make the hatch bigger and fit proper stairs,' Leifur explained. 'We'll remove the fish holds, and then this will be almost the same size as the upper deck. We can fit windows and install comfortable seating. The galley and forward berth are through here. We will refit the galley to make it larger so we can serve hot drinks, soup, that kind of thing.'

'That's a lot of work. And presumably will cost a lot of money,' Jonas said.

'It's an investment for sure, but my friend can turn it around in a month and will do the best he can on the cost.'

'It's an exciting idea. I'd love to offer boat excursions as part of our summer programme. We lose the northern lights tours by April, so this would fill that gap. Have you thought about how you want this to work?'

In that moment, Leifur knew he'd done the right thing in approaching Jonas. He could have gone into it by himself; there were plenty of ex-fishermen who had made the move into the tourist industry, but being part of an established brand like Iceland Adventures from the start would make all the difference. He appreciated that Jonas didn't wade in and call the shots, knowing he had the upper hand. That didn't seem like Jonas's style.

'I want to pay for the work the boat needs, but I don't have the money.' He had to be honest. Jonas had probably guessed anyway. 'If you're willing to loan me what I need to get the work done, you take all the profits and I will work for an hourly rate until that's paid back. Then afterwards, perhaps we could work on a profit-share arrangement?' Leifur held his breath. This was his ideal scenario, and he didn't expect Jonas to go for it. It was just the beginning of the negotiations.

Jonas gave a thoughtful nod and was quiet for a moment. 'Do you have a quote for the work needed from your friend? How long do you think it would take to pay back the loan?'

Leifur led the way into the galley and took a seat at the small table, gesturing for Jonas to do the same. He reached inside his coat and pulled out the pieces of paper that held the plan for the only future he could contemplate; one that meant he could still work on the sea on *Brimfaxi*. He'd spent hours crunching the numbers, knowing that if he was making a business proposition of this nature to someone like Jonas, he needed to be prepared. Hopefully, he'd thought of every single thing. He laid the sheaf of paper on the table and spread the sheets out.

'We can do three tours a day with thirty guests. It is weather permitting, so I have factored that in. This is what I think we can charge,' he said, pointing to the figure and looking at Jonas, who nodded his head in agreement. 'This is the cost of the work, so I think in three to four months I would pay back the loan. That means if we start sailing in April, even if we can only fill two tours a day to begin with, the loan would be paid back before the end of the season.'

'We have to factor in extra staff costs and equipment, but even so, I think you're right.'

'Extra staff costs?' Leifur said with a frown.

'You can't do everything. We'll need someone to help with the guests on top of a marine biologist to guide the whale-watching. You can't sail the boat and point out what they're looking for at the same time. And you can't serve coffee while you're sailing,' Jonas pointed out.

Leifur was annoyed with himself. He had thought through everything but this. He'd been concentrating so hard on getting to the point where *Brimfaxi* would be an excursion boat, he'd overlooked what running an excursion would look like from the point of view of a guest.

'I'm sorry. You're right. And this is your area of expertise.'

'Don't worry,' Jonas said. 'It won't impact the timeline for paying the loan back by much. We can work on this plan together. Refine it. But at first glance it looks good.'

Leifur looked up in surprise. 'Really? You think it can work?'

'I do. Yes, it's a busy market, and we'll need to make ourselves stand out with a point of difference. You can leave that for me to think about. But what you have here is a solid business plan. Something I can buy into.' Jonas had a twinkle in his eye.

'So we have a deal?' Leifur said, unable to keep the surprise out of his voice.

'We have a deal,' Jonas said, standing up and holding his hand out.

Leifur ignored Jonas's hand and hugged him instead. 'Thank you. You have saved…' My life, is what he almost said, but it felt too raw. 'You have saved *Brimfaxi*. Thank you.'

'Believe me, you're doing me a favour as much as I'm doing one for you. It's easy to be lazy when things are going well and forget that every business needs to evaluate what it's doing every so often. Make sure it's staying relevant. This is just what we need. A new challenge, a new adventure.'

Even if Jonas was just saying that to make him feel better, Leifur didn't care. He felt as if he could breathe again. The future was there again, looking different from how he'd expected, but it was there. Replacing the void, the unknown and easing the sense of failure he'd felt for the past few months.

Leifur rummaged in one of the galley cupboards and pulled out a full bottle of rum and two plastic tumblers. 'We should have a toast.'

'Ah, a sailor through and through,' Jonas laughed, as Leifur poured a small amount into each cup.

'*Skál*!'

'*Skál*! Welcome to Iceland Adventures.'

2

At around the same time, Astrid Jonsdóttir was sitting with her legs dangling over the edge of a different harbour, in Tromsø, Norway. If it wasn't that she had just emerged from a ridiculously hot sauna, she might have been feeling chilly, wearing only her swimming costume and woolly bobble hat, but she was relishing the sensation of the cold air biting at her skin, and biding her time until the moment she would plunge into the freezing water in front of her.

It had been a strange day. After four years, her contract at the Atlantic Marine Mammal Council had ended. If she were honest with herself, she'd been burying her head in the sand, hoping that someone would simply decide they couldn't live without her and extend her contract for another four years. But that hadn't happened. It was part of their ethos, an attempt to offer opportunities to young scientists and keep things fresh. Of course, Astrid knew that. She had benefitted from this herself, so she shouldn't be annoyed by it. But she was devastated that she was going to have to leave Norway. Four years had been enough time for her to fall in love with the place. It wasn't so very different from her homeland of Iceland, but coming to Tromsø had been a milestone in her career and, on some level, she felt like a failure having to return to Reykjavik.

Astrid lowered herself off the dock and into the water, managing to keep her head out and her hat dry. Although it never failed to make her gasp, it put a big smile on her face, and suddenly the fact that today was the end of everything as she knew it didn't seem so bad. She swam to the steps that led back up onto the dock where the wood-fired sauna floated in the harbour, decorated with fairy lights to stave off the late afternoon darkness of the late Arctic winter, hauled herself out of the water and hurried back into the welcoming heat of the sauna.

'Hey, Astrid. Do you want me to come to the airport with you?' Sofie was a colleague and had become one of her closest friends. She still had two years to go on her contract and was sad to be losing Astrid back to Iceland.

'No, thanks. It's better if we don't have to say goodbye at the airport.'

'True. If you're sure. Or I could make Aksel go with you?'

Aksel was Sofie's on-again/off-again boyfriend. A great Norwegian Viking of a man who would make easy work of carrying all her luggage, but Astrid preferred to say her goodbyes before the very last moment, even to Aksel.

Astrid shook her head and moved up to the top bench in the sauna, where it was hotter. 'No, I'll be fine.'

'Do you have a plan yet?' Sofie asked.

They'd talked about it a handful of times, and it was always Sofie that brought it up, never the other way around. Sofie couldn't understand how Astrid could contemplate going back to Iceland without having a plan. How could she leave Norway with nothing in place, not even anywhere to stay?

'I'll talk to my sister and hopefully I can stay with her to begin with.'

Gudrun was four years younger than Astrid and had lived

in Norway for a while herself while she was establishing her career. She, like Sofie, was a planner. She was settled in Reykjavik with her long-term partner, Olafur, and was manager of Snug, a homeware shop that specialised in sourcing its stock from local producers and craftspeople.

'She'll be able to give you some work, I expect,' Sofie said, as if this was a good thing.

'Probably,' said Astrid, wanting to say whatever Sofie needed to hear to put an end to the conversation. 'I'll definitely ask her.' She definitely wouldn't. The last thing she wanted was to be stuck indoors day after day like her sister, selling pointless things to tourists. The past four years at the AMMC had established her career as a marine biologist and a respected expert in North Atlantic marine mammals, and she intended to continue on that trajectory. Somehow. The downside of having buried her head in the sand was that she had left herself with no time to look for suitable roles in Iceland, or anywhere else, and there wasn't much around. Admittedly, it was a niche career, and her next job could take her away from Iceland again. She didn't mind. Her love of these graceful, magnificent creatures meant she was willing to go wherever she had to go to work with them. Her work at the AMMC had been her first proper job after years of working on short-term contracts and volunteering to get the experience she needed. She specialised in tracking and monitoring particular individuals and groups of mammals, building up pictures of their habits and migratory patterns. Although she was based in Tromsø, she'd had the opportunity to be out at sea for weeks at a time on research vessels with other scientists. Another thing she'd miss. At least staying in Reykjavik with Gudrun would give her half a chance of finding work of some sort. Maybe even in her field, if she was lucky. Anything but working in a shop would do.

'I'm going in,' said Sofie.

She pushed open the sauna door and left. Astrid watched out of the tiny porthole window as her friend plunged straight into the dark water without even taking a moment to think about it. Astrid laughed, thinking how much she'd miss her. Although she loved the career she'd chosen, it wasn't great for maintaining close friendships or relationships. It was too transient, often too remote, in places where there were more whales nearby than there were people. Sofie was a rare find. A person Astrid genuinely liked as well as being a colleague at a similar stage in her career.

She watched Sofie climb back onto the dock, walking nonchalantly back to the sauna without a hint of desperation to be back in the warmth.

'You'll miss this,' she said as she settled herself next to Astrid on the top bench. The cold coming off her skin briefly cooled the surrounding air before the heat of the sauna obliterated it.

'I will,' Astrid agreed. 'We're into warmer water at home, so I'm looking forward to that. I've missed it.'

'Hot springs, you mean?'

'Yes, but the local pool is just as good. And sociable too.' She'd forgotten how much she used to enjoy hanging out in the hot pots at the pool, chatting to whoever else happened to be in there. More often than not, it was someone she knew, or they turned out to be a friend of a friend. Maybe she'd forgotten lots of other good things about living in Reykjavik.

'I'll come and stay with you when I'm in the depths of a Tromsø winter and even the sauna isn't working for me.'

'You're welcome anytime,' said Astrid, hoping that she'd be in a place of her own before Sofie visited because there wasn't much room at Gudrun's.

When their time was up, they dried themselves, dressed, and strolled through the quiet streets.

'See you tomorrow,' said Sofie as they hugged goodbye when they got to her building.

'It's pastry day tomorrow.' Astrid had promised a box of pastries from Backstube as a going-away gift for her colleagues. Boxes of the mouth-watering pastries from the bakery on Storgata were purchased for every occasion from birthdays to retirements and everything in between.

'My mouth is watering already,' Sofie said before she waved and disappeared inside.

Astrid continued on the short walk to her own building. Her flat came with the job. It was cosy and made the most of what little light there was at this time of year, with windows in the main living area that faced south. She felt lucky to have landed a place to live on the main island that formed part of the city of Tromsø. It had the convenience of the city on her doorstep and beautiful views across the fjord to the other part of the city, where the Arctic Cathedral soared into the sky and the cable car ran up the mountain.

She took her layers off and jumped into a hot shower before dressing in jogging bottoms and a soft sweatshirt. This was her last week at work, and although in her mind she was going back to Iceland to stay with her sister, she hadn't got so far as to actually ask her. Suddenly, having no solid plan past the next few days was overwhelming. She sighed and picked up her phone.

'*Hæ!*'

Astrid grinned. She tended to forget how enthusiastic her sister was.

'*Hæ.*'

'How's things?' Gudrun asked.

'Good.' Astrid curled herself into the corner of her sofa. 'I'm coming home for a while.'

'Oh my god! For a holiday? How long for?'

'Not a holiday. My contract's ended, so I'm at a bit of a

loose end for now.'

'Are you going to Mamma and Pabbi's?'

Astrid had been hoping Gudrun would assume she needed to stay with her. It felt awkward to ask.

'Only joking,' Gudrun said, laughing. 'You have to stay with us. You'll be desperate to leave Iceland again if you have to live at home.'

Astrid laughed. 'Thank you. If you're sure you don't mind?'

'Of course I don't mind. I can't wait to see you! When are you coming?'

'This weekend.' Astrid braced herself.

'And you're asking me now? This is so typical, Astrid. You are leaving Norway after four years, and you are telling me now. Five days before.'

'I don't know what I'm doing next. I was waiting to see if anything came up here.'

Gudrun harrumphed in reply. 'It's lucky for you that I'm such a forgiving sister. So what are you going to do?'

'I'm still looking. I'll sort something out. I have enough saved to see me through a couple of months.'

'Hang on,' said Gudrun, and put her finger over the microphone.

Astrid could hear muffled talking. She was probably speaking to Olafur.

'It's your lucky day. Olafur thinks they could use a marine mammal expert at Iceland Adventures.'

'It's not certain yet,' Olafur said in the background. 'The boat isn't finished yet, and I'll need to ask Jonas.'

'It's okay,' Astrid said. 'Don't make him ask Jonas.' Astrid knew Jonas and knew he was a soft touch who would probably give her a job even if he didn't need anyone, especially if Olafur asked him.

'He doesn't mind. Or you can work in the shop with me.

We're coming up to the busy time. I always need extra staff.'

'Honestly. It's really kind of you, Gudrun, but I'm not ready to go straight into anything. I'm happy to use the time to have a break. Catch up with all of you.'

'Okay. You're right. You need a break. I know you, Astrid. You will have bottled up all your feelings about your contract ending. You love that job,' she said gently. 'It will be difficult to leave, and it'll take you some time to come to terms with it.'

Astrid sniffed and blinked away some tears. Trust her little sister to put into words the feelings she couldn't acknowledge herself.

'Yes,' she said, trying not to give away the fact that she was barely holding it together now. 'So, see you next week.'

'Text me your flight details and we'll book a transfer for you.'

Olafur's employer, Iceland Adventures, ran transfers to and from the airport, usually combining it with a visit to the Blue Lagoon. 'Thanks. I'll skip the Blue Lagoon though.'

Gudrun laughed. 'Love you, As.'

'Love you.'

Astrid hung up and gazed out of the window at the twinkling lights over the water. Leaving Tromsø was hard because she wasn't leaving on her terms. And all the harder because she hadn't let herself think about it. Gudrun was right, she hadn't come to terms with it. Calling her sister was always going to be the point at which she'd be forced to admit to herself that Tromsø was over. That the AMMC wouldn't change its mind at the eleventh hour and tell her there had been a mistake and that she could stay after all. It was ridiculous to think that was ever going to happen. She had to get her head around the fact that she was going back to Iceland.

3

Astrid arrived at Keflavik airport, waited for her two enormous suitcases, which held all her worldly possessions, and then headed out to the arrivals hall to find the Iceland Adventures transfer. When she saw the big sign that declared "Exit to Iceland", her heart leapt. She was home.

She scanned the crowd of people, reading the signs some of them were holding until her eyes settled on the one she was looking for. The person holding it was her sister's partner, Olafur. He broke into a grin when he spotted her, and she did the same. It had been a couple of years since she'd been back, and it was good to see him.

'Astrid! Good to see you,' he said, enveloping her in a bear hug.

'You too. I didn't think it would be you.'

He shrugged. 'It's not every day your almost sister-in-law comes to visit. But it was my shift anyway.'

'You're making me feel so special.'

Olafur grinned. 'Gudrun is working today, but she made me promise I would send you straight to the shop. She should be almost finished by the time you get there.'

'Okay, that's fine.'

'We're waiting for a group of six, then we can be off.'

It was only a few minutes before the group of Americans presented themselves, then they all followed Olafur outside to the minibus.

'Oh, my goodness,' one woman in the group exclaimed as they stepped outside of the terminal building. 'The wind is biting!'

They all began pulling up their hoods and zipping their coats while Astrid and Olafur waited.

'It is chilly today,' Olafur agreed. 'The forecast for the next few days is better, but you never know. It can be very changeable.'

'Sunshine one minute, snowing the next,' Astrid said.

'You're from here? Of course you are. You look like you're better prepared than any of us.'

'I've been living in Norway for four years, which is not that different weather-wise. Where are you from?'

'We're from Texas. It gets cold, but not for very long.'

'Layers are the key,' Astrid said as they gave their bags to Olafur to pack into the bus.

'Thank you. Any other tips?'

Astrid enjoyed the brief journey to Reykjavik, chatting with the group and finding out what their plans were. She felt a little out of touch when they asked for recommendations of places to eat, but Olafur chipped in with some suggestions.

As they drove into Reykjavik, Astrid felt the comfort of the familiar wrap around her. Yes, some places looked a little different, but mostly everything looked the same. And she loved that. After the upheaval of the past few weeks, the sadness she'd felt at having to leave Tromsø, somewhere she'd grown to love, realising she loved it here just as much was soothing. It was the longest she'd ever been away for, and until now, she hadn't realised how much she'd missed it.

Olafur pulled up outside the hotel where the Americans were staying. Astrid climbed out with them and said goodbye, wishing them a great holiday and hugging the woman she'd been talking to for most of the journey.

'Want me to drop you at the shop? I can take your luggage home.'

'Okay,' Astrid agreed. It might be better for Gudrun to be at the house when she first got there. She felt a little awkward about staying there, having not seen Gudrun and Olafur for so long. 'Thank you.'

'No problem,' Olafur said with a grin. 'Gudrun would be cross if I took you home without her being there to make sure I am welcoming you correctly.'

Astrid laughed. 'Nothing changes.' On the surface, Gudrun came across as carefree, but she was meticulous about how things ought to be done. And it was her way or no way. The great thing was, she was like this while still being a person you could love. You couldn't hold it against her because she was such a cheerful person and everyone wanted to please her.

Olafur drove the minibus along Laugavegur, slowly because those were the rules at this time of day. It was one of the busiest streets in Reykjavik. Astrid hopped out when he stopped outside the Snug store, standing on the opposite side of the road while she waited for Olafur to move away so she could cross.

When the window came into view, she immediately wanted to go inside. It was so welcoming, the things in the window so tempting, she almost walked in and took Gudrun up on her original offer of a job. She didn't remember it looking like this the last time she'd been here. But then, it had been in the summer months when everything looked brighter. Now, in February, they were nearing the end of an Icelandic winter, but the hours of daylight were short. The way the shop looked today made Astrid want to go inside and snuggle up in the corner of the huge velvet sofa she could see through the window. That and the soft lighting that beckoned her in with its relaxing, cosy vibes.

She opened the door and went inside. It smelt amazing thanks to the scented candles that were right next to the door. Her fingers reached out to pick one up before she remembered why she was here. First things first. As she walked further into the shop, she could hear her sister speaking in English, serving someone at the counter. Astrid caught her eye and waved, then went back to browsing while Gudrun finished serving her customer.

Once Gudrun had said goodbye to the woman, who left with a bulging bag of goodies, she came running over to Astrid and threw her arms around her.

'I can't believe you're here!' she said, stepping back, her eyes sparkling.

'It's great to be back,' Astrid said, smiling but never quite able to match Gudrun's enthusiasm for everything.

'Did Olafur tell you about the job they might have for you?'

She shook her head. 'No.' She didn't want a pity job or a job taking endless tours of the Golden Circle while trying to sound enthusiastic, even after the hundredth time in eight weeks. 'Maybe he was giving me a minute to settle in.'

'Probably,' said Gudrun, breaking off to greet a new customer. 'I finish in an hour. Do you fancy getting coffee for us and hanging out here?'

'Sure. Is Te & Kaffi still your go-to place?'

'Yes. A cappuccino for me, please,' Gudrun said before turning to answer a customer who had a question about some pottery.

Astrid listened to her sister embark on a conversation about how the potter used a special clay that contained lava, which was how they produced such interesting colours from the glaze. If she worked here, she'd never in a million years get to the point of being able to have conversations like that. It wasn't in her nature, and sometimes it surprised her how different she and Gudrun were, given that they had the same parents.

It had started snowing, making the coffee shop look cosy and enticing from the outside. Inside was just as she'd remembered. Gazing at the tempting array of cakes made her stomach rumble, and she realised the last time she'd eaten had been at breakfast. So she ordered two cappuccinos and two cinnamon buns to take away. It would be a while before they ate this evening.

Gudrun's customer was just leaving, again, carrying a large Snug bag, and now there was no one else in the shop but the two of them.

'Come on, let's sit over here,' Gudrun said, pulling out two stools from under a kitchen island that was displaying various glassware. She moved a few things to make space for Astrid to put the coffee down.

'I bought cinnamon buns. I couldn't resist,' Astrid said, handing the bag to Gudrun.

'Oooh, it's ages since I've had one of these. I have to be strict with myself with it being so close. I could easily pop in there every day for breakfast. But since you've bought it for me, I can't say no, can I?'

'Think of it as a welcome home celebration for me,' Astrid said.

'Yes. I think I can use that excuse for the next few days.'

Once Gudrun had closed the shop, they walked along Laugavegur and up the side streets to Gudrun and Olafur's small house. It was just as Astrid remembered. Blue with a grey roof, now dusted with snowflakes, and Olafur must have beaten them home because the small windows were glowing in the most inviting way.

'You still have the fairy lights on,' said Astrid. It was

traditional for Icelanders to decorate outside with lights through the winter months to stave off the darkness of the long nights, but now spring was almost here, it was less common.

'We have them all year round, except in midsummer,' said Gudrun. 'They're just pretty.' She shrugged and went up the steps to the front door. 'Welcome!' she said as they stepped inside. The front door opened straight into the sitting room, where Olafur already had a fire blazing in the wood-burning stove.

'*Hæ*! We're home!' Gudrun called.

He appeared at the door from the hallway opposite and slung his arm around Gudrun's shoulders, planting a kiss on the side of her head.

'Astrid. I have put your cases in the spare room.'

'It's not the spare room, it's the guest room,' said Gudrun. 'Come on.'

She led the way into the small hallway, which led to the kitchen, two bedrooms and the bathroom.

'It's been decorated since you last stayed here.'

The room had previously been fairly bland. Olafur's friends stayed the odd night here and there, and they had never cared what it looked like. Aside from their friends Anna and Ned, Gudrun and Olafur lived closest to the centre of town out of everyone in their friendship group, so it was a handy place for people to crash if they didn't want to make a longer journey home. It was particularly well used in the winter months when the weather was unpredictable and one needed shelter from a snowstorm.

Now, the room was just as cosy and welcoming as the window of the Snug store. It was painted a dusky pink and had a metal bedstead, which had been painted in a deep teal shade. All the accessories, of which there were many, were in heathery shades of pink, purple, green and blue and even to

Astrid, who didn't have the first clue about anything to do with decorating, they looked stunning against the walls.

'It's gorgeous,' she said to Gudrun. 'It has such a warm and cosy feel.'

'I'm so pleased you like it,' Gudrun said. 'You're the first person to stay in here since it's been finished. I banned the men from staying over once I knew you were coming.'

'Thank you,' Astrid was genuinely touched.

'I think it's important that you have somewhere you can feel at home. And you know you can stay here as long as you want.'

'Oh, Gudrun. That's so kind, but I'll try to get my own place as soon as I sort out some work.'

'If you won't take a job at Snug, you have to take the room for as long as you need to.'

'But Olafur might not want a long-term house guest.'

'You're not a house guest, you're family. And Olafur loves having you. He's pleased I'll have someone to talk endlessly to that's not him.'

Astrid hugged her sister.

'Come through when you're ready,' Gudrun said. 'Olafur's making pizza.'

Olafur had already brought Astrid's cases into the bedroom. She'd been fairly organised, and put everything she'd need for the next few days in one case. Opening it up, she unpacked it, putting her clothes in the small wardrobe and laying her few toiletries and other bits and pieces on the dresser. She went to the small window, pausing to watch the snow fall on the tiny garden before she pulled the curtains across.Then she changed into a pair of joggers and her favourite sweatshirt, pulled on a pair of woolly socks and padded through to the kitchen where Olafur was loading one of the pizzas with thin slices of meat. He paused when he saw her.

'Are you happy with meat on the pizza?'

'Yes. It looks delicious already,' Astrid said, her mouth watering.

'Beer or wine?' Gudrun asked, opening the fridge and waving a bottle of rosé.

'I'm guessing the right answer is wine.' She didn't mind.

'Beer for me, please,' Olafur said.

He put the pizzas in the oven, took the beer from Gudrun and the three of them went into the lounge.

'*Skál*! Welcome home, Astrid.'

'*Skál*,' Astrid said, clinking her glass against Gudrun's and with Olafur's bottle of beer. She sat back, snuggled into the sofa, thinking tonight was a pretty good start to whatever she did next.

4

With *Brimfaxi* at the boat builders for the next few weeks, Leifur found himself at a loose end. Living in Hafnarfjörður had suited him while he'd been a fisherman. It was a quieter harbour than the more industrialised one in Reykjavik, and he'd always enjoyed the short voyage home after he'd landed his catch. It felt as if he were leaving work behind for the day.

But now, faced with not having a boat, and with friends who had once worked for him having had to go elsewhere for work, he was lonely. Staying in the house made him stir-crazy. After years of wishing he had more time to do this, that and the other, now that he had the time he was at a loss to remember what any of those things were. He had no hobbies and wasn't inclined to start one now, knowing that he'd be back at work again in a few weeks. It was precious time, he knew that, but knowing it just added to the pressure of feeling he should fill his days with fun while he could.

'It is no good sitting here with me day after day,' his mother, Peta, said eventually, after a week of Leifur spending his days with her for lack of anything else to do. 'I have things I want to do. I know you think old people like me sit and watch the television all day, but I am out of the house more than I am here.'

It was a surprise and a shock to him that his mother seemed to have a better social life than he did. One he hadn't been aware of until now. When he'd been fishing, it was rare to have a day off, and if he did, he had to spend the time catching up on admin, so to his shame he didn't see her very often.

'I don't think you're old,' he said weakly.

'Leifur. I know it has been hard for you, losing the business,' she said, putting her hand on top of his.

He cringed. It sounded awful. Losing the business. But that's what it was. 'It's a chance for a new start,' he said, without feeling it was true. He was saying what he thought she wanted to hear. Worrying her with how he actually felt wasn't fair, although he had an inkling she might have more of an insight into that than he did.

'It has to be the right new start. You must not make decisions based on the past. It's important that you see this as an opportunity to do something different for yourself if that's what you want.'

'This is different, Mamma. It may not seem so, but it means I can keep *Brimfaxi*. And I won't be out in all weathers like I was before.'

They looked at each other. Coming from a long line of fishermen, they both knew and lived with the risks that came with that profession. It was an unspoken, accepted part of the job. And had affected their family in the very worst way when his father had been lost at sea in bad weather.

'That's good,' his mother said, smiling. 'But if you're going to be working the same kind of hours as normal people, it's time you started socialising with normal people. See your friends, Leifur.' She stood up and chucked his cheek exactly as she had for his whole life. 'And speaking of socialising, I'm late for my mahjong game. Would you like to join me?'

'No, thank you.' He stood up too, and kissed her cheek. 'I

will see you tomorrow.'

'*Nei, nei, nei*. Please find something else to do. I love you, Leifur, but this is too much.'

He laughed. 'Okay, Mamma.'

On the stroll back to his own house, he thought about what she'd said. Because of the unsociable hours he used to work, it had been impossible to keep up friendships with anyone who wasn't also doing the same thing. How did you get new friends? He could go to the bar in town, but that was more likely to be full of people his mother's age. All the people his age would rather go to Reykjavik for a night out, but there was no way he was brave enough to do that by himself. And worst of all would be if he ran into his brother or his friends from the boat. He wasn't ready for that; to hear the inevitable fishing stories. He knew it would make him feel like an outsider, as if they had moved on and left him behind. And he'd feel like he was missing something amazing, even though the reality had been very different towards the end. Either way, neither finding new friends nor seeing his old ones were appealing options right now. Perhaps it was something that would come in time as he eased himself into a different rhythm.

As he was letting himself into his house, his phone rang. It was Jonas from Iceland Adventures.

'*Hæ*, Jonas.'

'*Hæ*, Leifur. So, the work on the boat is underway?'

'Yes. They already have the fish holds out and the equipment off the deck.' It had been hard to watch the changes, so Leifur had decided it was better to keep his distance for now. He trusted his friend at the boatyard, so there was no need to keep checking in. The few weeks it would take to complete the work would hopefully give him time to come to terms with the changes to *Brimfaxi*.

The fishing equipment was being sold, and Jonas had

insisted that Leifur keep the profits. He said it was only fair, even though it would have helped pay the loan off, and Leifur wasn't in any position to argue. He'd been living off his savings for the past few months, and there wasn't much left.

'That's good news. I was calling to see if you have time to come into the office this week. I thought it might be good to get started on some of the planning while we wait for *Brimfaxi*.'

It did Leifur's heart good to hear Jonas refer to the boat by her name. It told him that Jonas understood how much *Brimfaxi* meant to him.

'How about tomorrow?'

'Tomorrow's great. Shall we say eleven?'

'Should I bring anything with me?'

'Bring the business plan, but no, nothing else.'

Another kindness for Jonas to refer to the sheaf of paper he'd presented a couple of weeks ago as a business plan.

The prospect of having something to do tomorrow spurred him into action. He'd spent long enough lying around feeling sorry for himself. He was a ball of nervous, excited energy at the prospect of the planning meeting, and he wanted to turn up with something that showed he was all in.

For starters, there was no way he was presenting the same sheaf of paper he'd shown Jonas on *Brimfaxi* as the business plan. He'd also thought it might be useful to have some idea of what their closest competitors were doing in terms of timings and what they were offering. He rummaged amongst the cluttered mess on top of the sideboard and found the laptop he rarely used now that he didn't have to keep on top of weather forecasts and fishing quotas. Unsurprisingly, the battery was dead, and it look another few minutes to track down the power supply. But then, he absorbed himself in typing up his notes into a decent plan for the first season, or a starting point at least, adding in information from some of the tour companies who offered sea-based tours.

By the time he'd finished, he was peckish, although it was only mid-afternoon. He stood in the small kitchen and looked around him. His house was messy, dusty and, now that he took a proper look, disgusting. When he was fishing, he spent more time on the boat than he did in the small cottage he owned that overlooked the sea. He either wasn't there enough to make the place dirty, and now that he was, he was having quite an impact, or it had always been like this and he'd never noticed it before.

After eating a hastily-made sandwich, he opened all the windows, letting the gusty wind fill the house with fresh air. Then he tidied up before starting a seriously deep clean. It took the rest of the afternoon, but by the time he finished, it felt as if he'd wiped the slate clean. He was starting a new life, and now he was ready. And absolutely starving.

There were a couple of meals in the freezer that his mother had made for him. Not being organised enough to write on them what they were at the time, he had to guess. He chose one, hoping that it would be the meaty casserole that it looked like, and tipped it into a lidded cast-iron pot, which he put in the oven along with a large potato. Then he pulled a beer out of the fridge, popped the cap, grabbed a square of tarpaulin that he kept by the door and went outside to sit by the water's edge.

The bank that sloped towards the sea from his house was soft and mossy, and still had patches of lying snow that hadn't quite melted yet. The moss had covered the lava from an old eruption, so the ground was uneven and impossible to set a chair on. Leifur laid the tarpaulin out, careful not to let go of it until he was sitting down in case the wind caught it, and leant back on the bank to enjoy his beer, feeling for the first time in a long time that he'd done a good day's work.

He stared out at the sea. If he were still fishing, he'd be in the midst of the prime fishing season now, and he couldn't deny he was missing it. But he'd not allowed himself to look at the statistics. If he found out that the capelin had been good this season, it would mean he'd made the wrong choice, yet he didn't want to delight in other people's misery if the hauls had been bad, even if that validated his decision. It was better not to know.

Something caught his eye. A small wooden boat with a motor was rounding the head of the sheltered bay where Leifur's cottage sat with a few others. It was a lovely spot, but not somewhere anyone came past in a boat by themselves, unless they lived there. He raised a hand to his brow to shade his eyes from the rapidly setting sun and to get a better look. There was a woman on the boat, sitting at the back with one hand on the tiller, her eyes focused on something. From what he could see, she was wearing very practical outdoor wear and a life vest. Smart woman. She obviously knew what she was doing. He saw her turn to face him and raised an arm to wave. She paused before she waved back, a grin that he could see from here lighting up her face. He laughed and waved again. Still smiling, she turned the boat and headed back out into the fjord.

Leifur sat there, wishing that she'd ventured closer to the shore. He'd love to ask her what she was doing out there. Ridiculously, seeing her out there alone, he felt as if she might be a kindred spirit. Someone else who had an affinity for the sea like him, and he felt sorry that he would never see her again. He laughed softly to himself, shaking his head. What was wrong with him?

Relationships of that kind had been difficult to navigate with his old job. Partly because of the unsocial hours but partly because once he'd seen how his father's death had devastated his family, and how terrified his mother had been to see her sons continue to risk their lives every day, it wasn't something he felt able to ask someone to do for him.

He stayed outside until the sun had set, feeling the cold seep into him, his layers finally giving in against the chill of the night. He picked up his tarpaulin and empty beer bottle and headed towards the welcoming glow of his cottage, feeling ready for the beginning of his new life.

5

After a couple of days left to her own devices, Astrid began to feel more settled. While Gudrun and Olafur had been out at work, she'd started off by feeling a low-level anxiety that there was something she ought to be doing. Eventually, she switched doom-scrolling on Gudrun's sofa for walking down by the sea. It helped. She felt connected again, and she even hired a small motorboat for half a day to sail around the peninsula towards Hafnarfjörður. She knew she was unlikely to see any whales and dolphins so close to the land, but the feeling of the wind in her face, and the water underneath her was so uplifting, she didn't mind. It was wonderful anyway.

What was also wonderful was that a man who was sitting on the shore of a small bay around the headland from Hafnarfjörður, waved at her. He was big, she could see that from here. She reminded him of a Viking, not unlike Sofie's boyfriend, Aksel, but this man had a friendlier face. She could tell he was smiling even though his beard hid his mouth. Aside from Gudrun and Olafur, he was the first person she'd interacted with since she got back, and it gave her hope that she would eventually feel as if she belonged here again. She could feel his eyes on her as she continued around the headland, and it gave her a thrill. She rarely gave men a second thought, but this man was exactly the kind of guy she'd go for.

She laughed and shook her head as she carried on further out of the fjord towards the sea. As if she could tell anything from a quick wave from a stranger. For goodness' sake.

Gudrun had the following day off, and she had decreed that she and Astrid would spend the day together, catching up with everything. While Astrid had been in Norway, they had kept in touch mainly through the family WhatsApp group rather than directly with each other, and their mother kept each of them supplied with information about the other.

Astrid was lying in bed, thinking about getting up when there was a gentle knock at the door and Gudrun peeped her head around. 'Morning, brought you a coffee.'

Gudrun was holding two big mugs. She handed one to Astrid and then walked around the side of the bed and climbed in.

'It's a long time since we've done this,' Astrid said, laughing and shifting across to make more room for her sister.

'Olafur is always up and out. I like lazing in bed and waking up slowly.'

'Me too.'

'You are such a liar,' Gudrun said with feeling. 'You have always been a morning person. I can't believe you've changed.'

'Okay, so most of the time I am still a morning person, but I'm on holiday so I'm happy to have a slow start to the day. What's the plan?'

'I think we should go somewhere for breakfast. There's a new place that Iris told me about. Then shall we go to the pool?'

'Definitely,' said Astrid. She loved the pool, and if she and Gudrun were going to spend the day talking, there was no better place than in a hot pot. 'I've missed that so much. In Norway we went for saunas, but then you have to plunge into the cold water, and when it is cold outside anyway, I would much rather be getting into warm water.'

'See? You are still an Icelander at heart. Even if you did love Tromsø.'

'Is Olafur working today?'

Gudrun nodded. 'He's on the Golden Circle tours this week. I said we would meet everyone at the bar for dinner. Is that okay?'

'Of course.' Astrid knew that where Olafur went, his friends went most of the time too. Over the years she'd come to know their group of friends a little, mainly from listening to Gudrun talk about them. From what she said, they all had partners now, so there could be quite a group at the bar later.

'I think you'll especially like Iris. She and Siggi are together,' said Gudrun. 'He almost died when the lava tubes erupted near Grindavik and they realised how much they loved each other.'

'Oh, Gudrun. I'd forgotten what an old romantic you are.'

'I think I have magical powers because ever since I came back from Norway, every single one of Olafur's friends, apart from Anders, has fallen in love.'

Of course, it had nothing to do with the fact that they had all reached that age when they'd naturally feel drawn to settling down rather than continue behaving like teenagers, hanging out in bars and taking crazy risks with their adventures. They were all in their thirties now and had almost certainly realised that there was more to life than beer and adrenaline rushes.

'Well, that's quite some claim you're making. Maybe there's just something in the water,' Astrid teased.

'I thought you'd come back here with a Viking in tow, As.'

Astrid laughed. 'Oh my god, no.'

'What is so funny about that?'

'My career is just getting started. I can't tie myself down when I could be disappearing to the Arctic Circle on a research boat for weeks at a time.'

'If he or she,' Gudrun said, looking pointedly at Astrid, 'is the right person, they won't mind that.'

'It's a distraction though, isn't it?'

'I think it can work. You should meet Iris. She's a volcanologist, and although she works here most of the time, she travels a lot to visit places that have volcanic activity.'

'Isn't Siggi the one who travelled half the year and then came back and worked for Jonas?'

Gudrun looked sheepish. 'Okay, so maybe he goes with her most of the time, but he would wait for her if he had to.'

'Okay. Enough talk about men. Mind if I have the first shower?'

After a breakfast of waffles and coffee, then a longer-than-usual session in the hot pots at the local pool, Astrid felt more relaxed than she had in a long time. Being back in Iceland, in places familiar and comforting, helped her not to yearn after Norway too badly. It was so lovely to spend time with her sister. They'd spent the day reminiscing about all sorts of things, and that had reminded her she had belonged here once. Four years wasn't that long, and although she wished she could have carried on life in Tromsø, she had to embrace the change. She'd also managed to avoid the topic of men successfully since the conversation they'd had that morning. Romance had never been at the top of her list of things to do. She'd had the odd fling, even relationships that perhaps would have endured if she hadn't waved goodbye and left on a boat for weeks or months at a time. It had never felt like the right time to pursue anything, to make a commitment she wasn't sure she could see through. And she'd never felt strongly enough about anyone to have any sense that she was missing out on something.

They caught the bus back from the pool and after popping back to the house to freshen up and change, they set off for Islenski Barinn which had long been the favourite hangout of Olafur and his friends and still the place they gravitated to on a Friday night.

Astrid had never socialised with her sister except for the odd drink on a fleeting visit home. The four years between them had seemed like a bigger gulf when they were younger. When she'd left for university, opting to study in Sweden since at the time there were no marine biology courses offered in Iceland, Gudrun had been fifteen. Then, when she moved back to Iceland to study for her master's degree, she was in the north in Akureyri. This was going to be the longest she had lived in Reykjavik since she was nineteen.

Gudrun led the way up the steps and into the bar. It was busy, but then it was Friday night. Astrid doubted they'd be lucky enough to get a table. Then she spotted Olafur waving at them from a big table at the far end of the room underneath a piece of art with the name of the bar written in huge letters.

'Do you want a beer?' Gudrun asked.

'That'd be great,' said Astrid, pulling out her phone to pay.

'This one's on me. Go and sit with the others.'

Not wanting to go over to the table alone, but without a good reason to object, other than that she was nervous, which would sound ridiculous, Astrid headed over to where Olafur was.

'*Hæ*,' she said.

Olafur stood up to let her scoot along on the bench next to him. 'Everyone, this is Astrid.'

'*Hæ*, Astrid,' Jonas said, smiling. 'I think we met a couple of years ago at Christmas. It's good to see you. This is my wife, Rachel.' He said the last part in English. 'Rachel is getting the hang of Icelandic. Finally,' he said, earning a shove and a grin from his wife. 'But we speak English a lot of the time to give her a break.'

'And I'm Fliss. Also English. Nice to meet you,' she said with a smile. 'And I am terrible at speaking Icelandic.'

'Great to meet you,' Astrid said, laughing and feeling less nervous with every introduction.

'And this is Brun, Siggi and Iris,' Olafur said, gesturing to the last three people who were sitting opposite.

'Also English,' said Iris with a small wave. 'So you were living in Norway?'

Astrid nodded. 'For the past four years.'

'I love Norway,' Iris said. 'Siggi and I went there for a week in the autumn. The scenery is incredible.'

'Where did you go?'

'We stayed in Ålesund and did lots of hiking around there.'

'Yes, it's beautiful. I bet the views were amazing.'

'Amazing,' said Siggi, putting his arm around Iris and gazing at her adoringly.

'They are quite besotted. It is still new,' Olafur explained in a low voice.

Astrid nodded, bemused. She was sure Siggi was the one who used to be away, travelling, more than he was here. Gudrun told tales of him leaving broken hearts behind him every time he left town. But this man was in love. Perhaps Gudrun was onto something when she said she had magical powers.

'Here,' Gudrun said, sliding Astrid's beer across to her and squeezing herself onto the end of the bench on the other side of Olafur. Olafur put his arm around her waist and pulled her into him, and Astrid tried not to think about the fact that she was the only single person at the table.

After they'd eaten, and another round of beers had been collected from the bar, Jonas pulled up an empty chair from a table behind them.

'Hey, Astrid, come and sit over here,' he said.

She climbed over the bench, pressing herself against the wall behind to avoid having to make either Olafur and Gudrun or Brun move out of the way. Now that she'd had a couple of drinks, and spent the past hour or so dipping in and out of conversations on either side of her, she felt more at ease.

'I have a business proposition for you,' Jonas said in Icelandic.

'You can't talk about that tonight,' Rachel said to him. 'I know what you said.'

'She doesn't know,' he said to Astrid. 'She's just guessing because she knows how excited I am about this.'

'It's okay,' said Astrid. 'I'm keen to hear it now.'

Rachel smiled and rolled her eyes. 'It is exciting,' she said. 'I'll leave you to it.' She patted Jonas's shoulder as she stood up, taking a seat at the end of the bench next to Brun and chatting to Fliss.

'We're starting a new venture with Iceland Adventures,' Jonas began. 'We're going to start running boat tours. I've started a partnership with a friend who has a boat, but I need someone else to run it with him.'

'Whale-watching trips?' Astrid asked.

Jonas bobbed his head from side to side, seemingly reluctant to answer. 'There's a lot of competition if we go down that route. We need to offer something unique, and that's where I think you could really help us out. The guy I'm working with comes from a fishing background. He knows these waters inside out, and he has some knowledge of where to find whales. But with your expertise, could we go further? Could we focus on other marine species that are just as wonderful?'

'There are dolphins and seals as well, but they're not as

impressive as whales and can be harder to find. In Faxaflói Bay you're most likely to see humpbacks and minkes. I don't have any special insight into anything else you could reliably look for.'

Jonas looked dejected. 'I hope I haven't sunk a lot of money into this only to do the same as everyone else.'

'What made you decide to do it in the first place?'

'The guy who owns the boat, Leifur, came to me with a business proposition. His fishing business is basically bankrupt, and all he has left is his boat. A lot of fishermen are switching into tourism, but he can't afford to set up on his own. I like the idea of a new income stream, and he's a good guy. I want to help him out.'

'Let me do some research for you. See what I can find out.' She wasn't sure what she could do, but she had access to some useful data.

'That'd be amazing,' Jonas said, his face lighting up. 'Once we're up and running, there's a job for you on the boat if you want it? We'll need someone with knowledge to share with the guests about what they're seeing.'

'Thank you for the offer, but I'm hoping to find a new research position. I don't want to say yes and then let you down if I need to leave.'

'Well, how about we agree on something temporary? Any time you can give us will be valuable, and we can get someone else onto the boat with you that you could train.'

'Can I think about it?'

'Of course. Thank you, Astrid.'

She smiled and noticed Gudrun watching them with a raised eyebrow. She was desperate to know what they'd been talking about. Astrid grinned at her sister and tapped her nose.

Olafur roared with laughter. 'Oh, Astrid, it is going to be fun having you around,' he said while Gudrun tried to look furious with him but ended up laughing too.

6

After the last meeting he'd had with Jonas, Leifur was getting used to the idea of having a partnership with Iceland Adventures. Being his own boss for so long meant he was a bit of a control freak. Even if his mother didn't tell him that all the time, he was self-aware enough to know, so he'd been careful not to be too dictatorial about how the boat trips were going to look. Besides, he had to bow to the greater knowledge Jonas had of the tourist industry in general. Fishing had nothing to do with this, and that was the only expertise Leifur had.

'I love the idea of a sunset tour,' said Jonas. 'We could vary the times of that throughout the year so we always hit the right time for the sunset. Is it safe to be out in the boat after dark?'

Leifur had to remember that Jonas wasn't a fisherman, so this wasn't a stupid question. 'We are out day and night. We're not navigating using the daylight.'

'Ah, good point. Although we'll have to make sure the sunset is at the end of the trip, otherwise no one will see anything.'

'And the rest of the timings can be planned now depending on how much daylight we have. In the winter, we might only manage the sunset tour because the days are so short. But coming into the summer, we could have three tours a day.' Leifur knew he was signing up for some long hours, but if that's what it took to get his life back on track, he was willing to. It still didn't sit well with him that he had to borrow money from Jonas to finance the changes to *Brimfaxi*. He needed to pay that back as soon as possible for his own peace of mind before he could think about taking his foot off the pedal.

'Let's decide on timings for the summer say to the end of August, so we can put them up on the website. Then we'll see how things are going then. Does that sound okay?'

He nodded. 'Sure.'

'And which day do you think we ought to choose as a down day? It makes sense to choose a day when it's likely to be quieter. Do we have any idea of that from the research?'

'Obviously, the weekdays are quieter. Perhaps Monday makes sense after a busy weekend?'

'That's fine with me,' said Jonas.

They carried on working until they had a timetable ready to put on the website.

'I think I might have found someone to help you out on the boat, at least in the short-term,' said Jonas. 'She's a marine biologist in between jobs, so we might not have her for long but I think she'll be valuable in helping us with the set-up.'

Leifur felt his blood pressure rising. 'I thought we just needed someone to look after the guests?'

'Well, yes. She knows that would be part of the job. I think her knowledge of whales could be a huge selling point though.'

I know about whales, Leifur wanted to say. But he knew he'd come across as unhelpful and petty. It wasn't his place to tell Jonas how to run a tour. If he wanted to waste money on a marine biologist, that was up to him.

'Okay,' he said. 'Does she have experience of working on boats?'

'I think so. I can check.' Jonas was looking puzzled.

'I'm sorry,' he said with difficulty, realising he was being defensive. 'It's hard for me to let go.'

'I understand. And I'm sorry if I'm making the wrong assumptions. I thought we'd agreed you'd need help and even if you were the world expert on whales, you'll be in the wheelhouse most of the time,' Jonas said reasonably.

When he got home, Leifur grabbed a beer and the tarpaulin and headed down to the water. He couldn't afford to mess this up with Jonas. Once he'd decided to leave fishing behind, he thought the worst part was behind him. He now realised he still needed to learn to let go.

It was windy, and he sat watching the clouds scud across the sky, wishing he was out on *Brimfaxi*. She was almost finished. In just another ten days she'd be ready to sail again. Maybe then he'd have more perspective. Once he was back on board, what did it matter whether he was catching fish or finding whales? He'd be on the sea again, where he belonged. That was the most important thing.

Scanning the horizon as he tipped his beer bottle to take a sip, something caught his eye coming around the headland from the direction of Reykjavik. It looked as if it were the same woman he'd seen a week ago. Where was she going? He stood up and waved, but she hadn't seen him. He carried on waving, all the time hoping none of his neighbours were watching because he must look like a lunatic. Finally, after what seemed like minutes but was more likely seconds, she turned her head and noticed him. He could see her laugh, her head thrown back, although the wind was carrying any sound she made away from him. She waved back. He stuffed his hands in his pockets and stood watching her, a big grin on his face. Then she started throwing her arm away, gesturing something. She was shouting too, but he couldn't hear her. Was she telling him to head around the end of the bay? He pointed to his left, making the gesture bigger, more like hers.

She took her hand off the tiller briefly and gave him a double thumbs up. Putting a nearby rock on top of his tarpaulin to keep it from blowing away, he set off, beer in hand, to the far end of the bay. His heart was racing. What was he doing? What was he going to say? He looked to his right and saw that he was keeping pace with the little boat, and the woman was looking at him. He stopped walking. This was ridiculous. He was going to go around the headland, and then what? She would bring the boat closer to the shore and…

He couldn't imagine what might happen after that. But she was the one who had started it, so let her be the one who had to worry about what to say first.

She was out of sight now, so he picked up his pace again and carried on. Maybe she would have thought better of it and carried on through the fjord, to wherever she was heading. He climbed the headland at the end of the bay, and when he got to the top, where he could see around the edge, he saw she had brought the boat into the shallow water between two rocky outcrops. She was standing in the boat, hands on her hips, presumably waiting for him.

As he made his way down to the shore, every time he looked up, she was watching him. She was probably around his age, wearing a knitted hat, which hid her hair. Her cheeks were rosy from the wind, and her blue eyes were bright and smiling.

'*Hæ*!' she called as he clambered across the rocks to reach her.

'*Hæ*!' This was so weird.

'You live in the bay back there?'

'Yes.'

'It's a beautiful spot. I was wondering whether you ever see any whales in the fjord?'

Ah. Not so weird after all.

'Not very often. We have the odd seal and sometimes porpoises, but I don't remember seeing a whale. Unless they appear when I am not looking.'

She laughed. 'I've only taken this boat out twice, and both times you've been there.'

'That's just a coincidence,' he said, beginning to enjoy the back and forth.

'So you're not sitting out here twenty-four seven watching the sea?'

'I wish I could be, but no. Where are you heading?' It crossed his mind not to ask, but he wanted to prolong the conversation.

'Nowhere in particular.' She shrugged. 'I just miss the sea and thought I'd see what kind of wildlife is around.'

'You miss the sea?'

'I used to live in Tromsø, and I spent quite a lot of time on boats. I know Reykjavik is by the sea, but I don't feel connected to it here in the same way. That probably makes no sense.' She shook her head as if she'd said too much.

'No, I understand completely,' Leifur said, wanting to reassure her. Because he really did understand. He was standing here, right next to the sea, but he was missing being on the sea. 'I'm a fisherman, but my boat is at the boat builder's. I miss her.' Did he really just admit that to this woman?

She nodded. An understanding passed between them.

'Do you want to come along for the ride?' she asked.

He grinned and held up his beer. 'Maybe another time. I'm not prepared for a seafaring adventure.'

She smiled and pulled the cord to start the motor back up, reversing easily away from the shore while Leifur watched, sorry that their encounter was at an end. Should he have invited her ashore?

'It was nice to meet you!' she called just before she turned the tiller to head away.

'I'm Leifur! What's your name?'

He could see her respond, but her name was lost to the wind now that she was further away. But he felt sure he would see her again.

Watching her, he returned her last wave just before she disappeared from view, then headed back to the bay by his cottage. He was smiling to himself. His day turned around because of a chance encounter with a like-minded person. If he saw her again, perhaps he'd see if she'd like to join him on *Brimfaxi*. It would be good practice for the whale-watching trips. He wondered why she didn't book herself on a trip if she was keen to find whales. She'd be more likely to see them that way than she would puttering up and down the fjord, but perhaps she liked the solitude. That might explain why she was out alone. She certainly looked as if she knew what she was doing.

He walked back to the house, feeling better than he had when he'd left. A beer had taken the edge off, but the encounter with the woman in the boat had left him in a better state of mind. The tendency he had, especially lately, to be stuck in his own head, wasn't something he liked about himself. The meeting with Jonas could have gone better. His attempt to explain to Jonas why he was finding it difficult to fall in with the plans hadn't been enough. *Brimfaxi* might be his boat, but that was only the case now because Jonas had been kind enough to allow Leifur to join his business. Now that he looked back at the meeting today, he was on the road to sabotaging the opportunity for himself. Were it not for Jonas's patience, that might already have happened.

Back at the house, he sat at his laptop and tapped out a

quick email to Jonas apologising again for being overly defensive about the idea of having a marine biologist on the boat. It wasn't a bad idea. And perhaps that was something that would set them apart from the other tour companies to begin with. He hoped he had wiped the slate clean and vowed that this was the beginning of his embracing whatever came his way instead of fighting everything. The days of fighting were over. He'd fought for *Brimfaxi* and won. There was no going back now; she would never be a fishing boat again, and there were no more fights he needed to have now. Jonas was on his side, and it was about time he showed Jonas that it went both ways. He'd go into the office tomorrow and help with whatever the next part of the plan was.

And he'd hope that the next time he went down to the shore, the woman in the boat might be passing to remind him that there was more to life than bitterness and loss. That brightness could come when you least expected it, from a passing encounter with a stranger, and turn your day around.

7

Astrid had spent the past few days mulling over Jonas's offer. While she wasn't working, it was at least a way to be doing something related, and she longed to be back on the sea. Her job search had yielded nothing aside from a research opportunity in Costa Rica, which although she was more than qualified for, she wasn't likely to get since her area of expertise was with North Atlantic mammals. She applied for it anyway, just to see if she could get it, but overall the whole situation was less than ideal and left her feeling despondent.

Again, she hired the boat. It was a blowy day, and the gusting wind in her face helped her feel as if the disappointment was being blown off her bit by bit. Perhaps taking Jonas's job was the answer for now. Maybe she needed to re-establish her place here in Iceland. Spend some time here before the next adventure so that if she came back again, it would feel more like home than it did right now. It didn't help that her parents had moved out of town, out of their family home, and however welcoming Gudrun and Olafur were, there was nowhere to come back to that felt like home. If she took the job, she might be able to afford somewhere small by herself, and then staying longer would be easier.

All of this was running through her head as she headed

along the fjord, her eyes scanning the surface of the sea for any sign of life. It was habit, borne of many trips on research vessels where the instruments could tell you what was going on under the surface, but there was nothing like seeing it with your own eyes. She could still remember the thrill the first time she'd seen a blue whale. They had tracked it for years, and it followed a fairly reliable migratory route. The tracking instruments had picked it up, so they'd cut the boat's engines and all gone on deck to watch and wait. Sure enough, within a few minutes the whale surfaced, its enormous tail the last part of it to disappear under the water, giving them the most spectacular of sightings.

She rounded the headland and something caught her eye, but it wasn't in the water; it was on the shore. The guy she'd seen the other day was there again. Standing on the rocks, waving. This time, she felt less like he was a stranger and as if, bizarrely, there was something between them. How could that be after only a friendly wave?

Astrid waved back and grinned when she saw his face light up with a smile. For her to have seen him both times she had taken the boat down the fjord, he must spend a lot of time watching the water. He'd be able to tell her what the chances of a sighting would be. The shore in front of him was too rocky to pull in any closer, but she remembered that around the end of the bay, there were some shallower spots between the rocks and it would be easier to get the boat closer. She flung her arm away from her, hoping he would understand the universal gesture for "over there!". Even from here, she could see the surprise on his face and then, after a few seconds, he responded with a similar gesture. She gave him a thumbs-up. Both thumbs to avoid any doubt, cringing at herself because she felt like an idiot. But it worked. He started making his way to the headland. There was no backing out now, and even though she only wanted to ask him about whale sightings, she had butterflies in her stomach at the thought of speaking to him. Since they'd waved at each other last week, she had thought about him. It was a beautiful spot. Isolated but beautiful and she wondered what drove him to spend so much time gazing out at the water? Because if she'd been past twice and he'd been there both times, that indicated how often he was there.

As she rounded the headland, she lost sight of him, the boat outpacing his steps, and she almost decided against pulling in. She could open the throttle and be around the next headland before he made it and avoid this impulsive plan altogether. But curiosity got the better of her, and she pulled the tiller, turning the boat towards the shore, between two rocky outcrops where she could see shingle on the bottom. She killed the engine and waited.

The brief conversation they had filled her heart with warmth. She learned he was a fisherman. Perhaps no wonder then that he had a melancholy air about him. Astrid was well aware of the difficulties facing the Icelandic fishermen. And that explained why he had an affinity with the sea, something she was thrilled to find they had in common. Why she was so pleased about this was a mystery to her, particularly as their short conversation ended with her having discovered that she was unlikely to see any whales in this fjord. But she felt as if she knew him a little better, and that she wanted to know him even better than that. She found out that his name was Leifur before she was too far away from the shore to hear him, and she shouted her name to him, sure that she would see him again. Probably the next time she took the boat out.

Later that day, Astrid called into the Iceland Adventures office in the centre of town. Brun was in there, busy making phone calls to cancel the northern lights excursion for that evening. The scudding clouds had built up, and there wasn't much blue sky to be seen. It was nearing the end of the season anyway, Olafur had said, so the bookings were tailing off. Part of the reason Jonas was keen to get the boat trips going.

'*Hæ*, Brun. Is Jonas around?'

Brun nodded. 'He's gone to park the minibus. He'll be back. Are you taking the job?'

'Yes. I think so.'

Brun laughed. 'Don't sound so happy about it, Astrid. You may end up enjoying it more than you think.'

'I know. It's just not what I planned.'

'Sometimes the best adventures happen when the plan goes wrong.'

She doubted that, but she didn't want to disagree out loud. 'I'm looking forward to being out on a boat again. I'm just not used to dealing with people. Customers.'

'You'll be fine,' he said. 'It's like anything you're interested in. Once you start talking about it to other people, your enthusiasm rubs off on them. Then they'll get excited about it, and it's like a circle of good energy.'

Jonas came in then, which was good timing since Brun was making her rethink the whole thing. It sounded a lot deeper than just talking about marine mammals.

'Astrid,' Jonas said warmly. 'I hope you've come to accept the job.'

'She has,' said Brun, giving her no chance to backtrack. Not that she wanted to now.

'If you're sure you're happy with it being a short-term thing,' she said.

'Absolutely. Whatever works. I think we're lucky to have you for as long as you're available.' He made it sound as if she was doing him a favour. 'Come on, let's discuss it.'

By the time Astrid left the office to head home, Jonas had fixed up for her to meet the captain of the tour boat and had suggested the two of them book onto a rival whale-watching excursion so they could see what was involved. His name was Leifur too, the same as her Viking.

She was nervous about the prospect of the two of them basically being in charge of guests when it didn't sound as if Leifur had experience in that area either. Hopefully, going on the excursion would put her fears to rest, and it'd be a chance for them to get to know each other.

The excursion was booked for the following morning. Astrid was a little early. She'd been worried about missing the boat and had factored in too much time to walk from Gudrun's house to the harbour. Jonas had suggested she and Leifur meet by the Harpa, the concert hall down by the harbour, to make it easy for them to find each other. She paced up and down the front of the building to ease her nerves while she waited.

'Astrid?' a voice said from behind her.

As she said, 'Leifur,' she turned and saw that Leifur was "her" Leifur after all. 'It's you!'

'Astrid. I couldn't hear yesterday when you said your name.'

'You're not a fisherman.'

'I used to be. I guess it's habit to say that when someone asks. It's not been very long since that was true.'

'So you haven't done this before?'

He shook his head. 'I've seen more than my fair share of whales over the years, but I've never gone out of my way to find them before.'

They stood awkwardly for a moment before Astrid said, 'Shall we grab a coffee while we're waiting?'

The friendly guy from the beach seemed to have disappeared. Leifur seemed a little offhand with her, and there was no sign of the back-and-forth banter they'd had yesterday. When she'd turned around and seen that it was him, she'd been thrilled. And for some reason, he wasn't.

There was a cafe in the Harpa building, so they got takeout coffee and strolled towards the harbour. Astrid was at a loss as to how to find the vibe they'd had yesterday. She'd thought there might be something between them, and now he was behaving like a moody stranger.

'Jonas said you're a marine biologist?' He said almost accusingly.

'Yes, I'm between jobs. The last contract I had was fixed for four years.'

'That's tough.'

'It was, but it goes with the territory when you're a research scientist. You have to be really lucky to keep the same job for your entire career.'

He didn't say anything, and another gulf of silence spread between them.

'Is this a new career for you, or are you doing it in your spare time?'

He laughed. 'A fisherman doesn't have any spare time.'

'But you're not a fisherman.' Astrid heard the belligerence in her tone. But she was annoyed with his manner and wanted to let him know he was being an arse.

'No, I'm not a fisherman anymore. But I'd rather be doing that than this.'

Astrid didn't know what to say. Was it because it was with her? Or because he didn't want to spy on the competition. Perhaps that's what the problem was. Maybe he felt bad about the espionage they were about to undertake.

'You know we can just try to have a good time and forget that we're on an information-gathering mission.'

'I don't know the first thing about how to run a boat tour, do you?'

Astrid was so taken aback that for a split second she thought she might burst into tears.

'No. That's the whole point of this, isn't it?' When he said nothing but avoided her gaze, she decided she'd had enough of his nonsense. 'I don't know what's happened between yesterday and today, but whatever it is, I'm pretty sure it's nothing I've done.' Satisfied that her words made him squirm a little, she finished by saying, 'I'm looking forward to seeing the whales, but if you prefer, we don't have to do that together.' She stopped walking, his not saying anything emboldening her. 'So what do you want to do? It's best that we sort this out before we get on the boat.'

'Let's go our separate ways,' he said, to her surprise. His eyes were flashing. Was he angry?

'Fine. Enjoy it.'

Astrid marched ahead to the harbourside where the boat tour left from. She could hardly believe that this had happened. How had this happened? Had she overreacted? No, he'd been lovely yesterday, and today he was worse than indifferent. She'd been right to call him out on it, and she wasn't sure whether she'd be able to see through the commitment she'd made to Jonas. If Leifur wasn't even willing to spend a morning with her, how were they going to spend six days a week with each other?

8

Leifur stood on the quay and watched Astrid check herself onto the boat tour. She accepted the waterproof overalls they offered her, and he watched while she pulled them on and then went to sit on the starboard side, looking out to sea.

He sighed. He already felt bad about upsetting her. Why hadn't he just explained that he was struggling with the whole idea of the boat tours and he didn't see why he needed to go through this charade of checking out one of their competitors? He knew how to drive a boat. He knew about the responsibilities he had for the safety of everyone on board, and he knew how to follow a sonar signal to help with finding a whale. Hell, he knew where the whales were without it. He'd spent enough time on these waters to know more than the captain of this boat knew.

But none of that was Astrid's fault. It also wasn't her fault that he didn't particularly want anyone on his boat, despite knowing that it was necessary according to Jonas.

Against his better judgement, he checked himself in for the tour and managed not to bite the head off the tour guide who gave him safety instructions. He needed to make things right with Astrid. Keep hold of the feeling he'd had yesterday, before he knew who she was.

'*Hæ*,' he said, standing next to her but holding back from taking a seat on the bench beside her until he knew he was welcome.

'*Hæ*.'

At least she was still speaking to him.

'I'm sorry,' he said.

She gave a small nod. Was that an acceptance?

'Really. I'm sorry. I don't know whether Jonas told you much about my situation?'

She shook her head. He had to hand it to Jonas. He'd been very discreet about the whole thing. There weren't many people who would keep quiet about doing such a big favour for someone.

'I didn't want to stop fishing. I had to. I lost the family business, and the only thing I have left is my fishing boat. Jonas agreed to go into business with me. It means I can keep the boat, but it's hard to hand over control to someone else. And hard to let other people call the shots about what happens on my boat.'

Astrid shifted around so that she was facing him. 'Thank you for apologising,' she said with a small smile.

She was unsure of him, and it made him a little sad to know that it was down to him she was guarded. It might take some time to get back to the easy conversation they'd had yesterday.

'I thought we got on okay yesterday,' she said, echoing his thoughts. 'And then today it was like your grumpy identical twin had turned up.'

'I'm sorry,' Leifur said again. 'I wasn't expecting you to be Astrid. I guess I was already in a bad mood.'

'Because?'

He sighed. 'Because I've always been captain of my boat. And it doesn't feel as if that's the case anymore.'

'Jonas is a good guy. He's not going to do anything to

undermine your being the captain of the boat. It's not his style.'

'I know.' He took a deep breath. 'I think I'm scared that *Brimfaxi* won't feel like she's mine anymore.' And she was all he had left of the legacy his father had left him.

'*Brimfaxi* is your boat?'

He nodded. 'And was my father's before me. I don't know if I have made the right choice.'

'Look,' said Astrid, her expression softening. 'I have a feeling that after we've been on this tour, you'll feel much better about everything. It's the unknown that's sometimes the scariest part of anything new.' She shifted across the bench, gesturing for him to sit next to her. Then she leant towards him and said in a lower voice, 'And we don't have to do it like this. We might think of better ways. But let's be in it together.'

Her face was so hopeful when she looked at him, her eyes shining, making him feel better in a way he didn't deserve after the way he'd treated her earlier.

'I'd like that,' he said. 'If you're sure it's alright.'

'Of course it's alright,' she said, catching her hair in her hand as it blew across her face. They were underway, and the wind had picked up. 'Let's just have a good time. I understand that you will have concerns about how things are going to operate, but I think I know Jonas well enough to know that anything is up for discussion. He's very fair.'

That made Leifur feel even worse. He was so grateful to Jonas, yet that wouldn't be apparent to Astrid by the way he'd behaved.

'I know I'm coming off as ungrateful and like I want to call the shots instead of Jonas, but that's not it. God, I'd love to start this morning over again.'

She laughed. 'Everyone has a bad day once in a while, Leifur. You're allowed.'

'Thank you.' He paused, the silence between them easy. 'So, do you think we will see some whales?'

'I've got a good feeling about this,' Astrid said, grinning at him as she pulled a hand-knitted beanie hat out of her pocket and pulled it on, stuffing her hair inside.

Over the course of the next three hours, they were lucky enough to see a handful of humpback whales and some minkes. Each time they spotted something, Astrid was so excited, she grabbed his arm, and every time, he found himself on edge, waiting for the next time because it felt so... It was wonderful, that's what it was. This woman was smart, forgiving, enthusiastic, and he was already sorry that he'd have to say goodbye to her after the trip. Her enthusiasm was infectious, and he had to hand it to Jonas for recognising that she would be an enormous asset on a trip like this. As well as being upbeat, despite the rocky start to their day, she was a mine of information about the whales, whispering snippets of information into his ear periodically. They were doing their best to blend in and be part of the tour and Astrid had said to him she was worried the other customers would wonder why she was on the tour when she knew so much about the whales already, when he'd asked her why she was whispering.

'You must have seen a lot of whales,' she said as the boat headed back to the harbour.

Leifur nodded. 'I have. And it's hard to say without some equipment to check, but I think we would have seen more on the other side of the bay.'

Astrid tipped her head from side to side. 'It is hard to know. They must have tried and tested areas. I guess they've been doing it for years.'

'But what if they're happy to see those couple of humpback whales? They might know they're a sure thing and not be putting much effort into actually looking.'

'That is quite a conspiracy theory,' Astrid whispered, her eyes wide.

'Could it be true? How territorial are humpbacks? When I was fishing, I used to see them in the same area for a few weeks at a time, but I don't know if that was a coincidence.'

Astrid smiled and shook her head. 'No, at this time of the year they are starting to migrate from warmer to colder water. It is possible that they have a preferred feeding area. They will be here over the summer months and then will head south to breed.'

'If they're feeding here, they are probably competing with the fishermen, huh?'

'Probably. Sardines, anchovies, herrings, that's what they're after. What did you fish?'

'Capelin. Not last year though,' he said.

'Really? Why?'

Leifur shrugged. 'I don't think anyone knows for sure, but they didn't return to Icelandic waters like they usually would.'

'What did you do? Can you catch something else instead?'

'By the time we missed out on the capelin, it was too late. We fish on a quota basis, and all the other quotas were allocated, so it's hard to do anything if you're unlucky like we were last year.'

'So that's how you lost the business? Could you have pitched for a different quota this year?'

'I could have,' Leifur said. 'But the fishing industry in Iceland is changing. It's getting harder and harder to compete with the industrial fishing companies. They are taking over small businesses like mine and taking the quotas. They are operating on a huge scale and can drive prices down because they're relying on quantity. It makes it hard to make a living with one boat. It was time.'

He gazed out to sea, wondering for the umpteenth time

whether he'd made the right decision. He felt Astrid move closer to him and then felt her hand slip into his, giving it a squeeze. The past few months had been the loneliest of his life, and her hand in his felt like a huge stride towards not feeling like that anymore. He squeezed back and turned to her and smiled.

'Thanks,' he said, hoping that somehow she would realise how much it had helped.

'You know, we're not that different,' Astrid said, looking out to sea with a thoughtful look on her face. 'It's not exactly my dream to be a tour guide on a sightseeing boat. It wasn't part of the plan, but it's the best I have at the moment. It's that or work for my sister.'

'And that would be worse than working with me?'

She shot him a smile, and his heart did something that took him by surprise.

'Yes, I think it would be. I can't get into a situation where she'd be paid to boss me around. That'd be much worse than working for you, even if you're as grumpy as you were this morning.'

He laughed. 'That is saying something about your sister. My brother used to work for me, and he didn't seem to mind my bossing him around.'

'He's younger?'

Leifur nodded.

'That's the natural order of things, then,' said Astrid. 'Gudrun is younger, so I think it would go to her head if she was finally the one in charge.'

'Are you bossy to her?'

Astrid laughed and shook her head. 'I don't think so. Although maybe you would have to ask her. I'm making fun of her, but she is very good at her job and she loves it. I couldn't stand being inside all the time.'

'What does she do?'

'She's the manager of Snug. The homeware store on Laugavegur.'

Leifur shook his head. He wasn't into shopping or homeware.

'It's a very cool shop if you ever need a pillow or a scented candle.'

'I can't think why I haven't been there.'

'Are you telling me you have more than enough pillows and candles already?'

'Something like that,' he said, thinking about his functional but cosy cottage that was devoid of both pillows — except in the bed, which was surely the only place a pillow was needed — and candles.

'So you live in Hafnarfjörður? Where I saw you yesterday?'

'Yes. That is my garden, I guess.'

'Wow. Amazing to live so close to the water like that.'

'It's beautiful,' he agreed. 'But quiet. That's perhaps not always good,' he added, thinking she might assume he was some kind of hermit, being thirty-six and not living in the city.

'Well, if I lived there, I'd be spending all my free time gazing out to sea too,' she said softly. 'The city is on the water, but it's not the same. It's hard to find the quiet here.'

It was on the tip of his tongue to invite her round to his house. Maybe suggest they take a blanket down to the shore and contemplate the horizon together. But that would be weird. Unprofessional, maybe...

'When are you getting your boat back?' Astrid asked, stealing the chance away from him.

'Ah, in a day or two. They are almost finished.'

'I can't wait to see her,' she said.

Leifur's heart swelled. She sounded as if she really meant it. Almost everything Astrid said brought her a step closer to bridging the gap that he'd created this morning. He felt as if they were as close as two almost-strangers could be after spending a morning together. Admittedly, the fact that she had been so forgiving was the only reason it had happened, and he was still silently berating himself for behaving so badly earlier. Still, he felt the need to show her he could be redeemed.

'Would you like to come out on *Brimfaxi* with me? I'll take a test run to see that she's running okay after being dry for a few weeks.'

'I'd love to,' Astrid said. 'Thank you for asking me.' Her eyes caught his, and the sincerity in her gaze did something to his insides. She understood what all of this meant to him even though they barely knew each other. Whether it was their shared love of the sea or whether it was because both of them were at a point in their lives where it wasn't certain what the future looked like, Leifur didn't know. But he felt that something special might be within touching distance.

9

After disembarking the tour boat, Leifur and Astrid strolled back into the centre of town. She was heading to Snug to meet her sister, and he was heading to the Iceland Adventures office to debrief Jonas before he forgot any of the details.

'I had a great time,' Astrid said. 'In the end.'

Leifur laughed and shook his head. 'I am sorry. Thank you for being so understanding.'

'About your situation in general or about you being an arse this morning?'

'Both.' Thank goodness she was grinning too. And thank goodness she was generous enough to see the funny side of it. He would take her teasing him every day of the week over the idea that he could have missed out on working with her altogether if she'd decided he really was an arse.

'Bye, Leifur.'

Should he kiss her on the cheek? Hug her as a goodbye? While he was debating with himself, she gave a small wave and went inside the store.

He watched her pause and pick up a candle to sniff, then her sister came over and offered her a different candle to sniff. It wasn't until the sister caught his eye and then said something to Astrid, who then turned and smiled at him, that he realised he'd been staring. He gave an awkward wave and left quickly before he could do anything else to embarrass himself, ducking into the coffee shop next door to get coffees to take to the office. In the coffee shop, he exhaled in relief as if someone had been chasing him. What was wrong with him?

Armed with four coffees, in case Jonas wasn't the only one working today, he headed to the office, surprised to find himself feeling a lot more positive about the report he was about to give than he'd expected.

Siggi was in the office too and was more than pleased to accept a coffee.

'Ah, this is the kind of new team member we like,' he said, holding out his hand to shake Leifur's since it was the first time they'd met. 'Good to meet you.'

'This is Siggi,' Jonas said. 'So how did it go this morning? You met up with Astrid?'

Leifur wondered whether to level with Jonas and explain that perhaps things hadn't got off to a great start. It sounded as if Astrid's sister was good friends with Jonas, so it might get back to him anyway. In the end, he decided against it. He felt as if he'd made up enough ground with Astrid that the start of the day wouldn't be what she came away remembering.

'Yes, she's incredibly knowledgeable.'

'Do you think you can work together?' Jonas asked.

Leifur nodded. 'I think we can. She knows her way around a boat, which will be helpful as well.'

'Shall we carry this conversation on at the bar?' Siggi asked, even though none of them had finished their coffees.

'We'll catch you up,' Jonas said. 'If you want to come, Leifur?'

'Sure, that'd be great.' He answered quickly, not giving

himself a chance to think too hard about it being out of his comfort zone. None of this was in his comfort zone, so he might as well embrace it.

Siggi swigged the last of his coffee and left.

'We don't always knock off this early,' said Jonas. 'The forecast for tonight is awful, so there's no northern lights tour. It gives us chance to get together, which doesn't happen that often once the summer comes and we're taking advantage of the longer days.'

'That was the same with the fishing. We used to socialise more in the winter months, knowing we'd be busy once the season started.'

'And what did you make of the tour you went on? Any tips you picked up?'

'They ran a slick operation, but I think they have been doing it a long time. They're going to tried and tested sites where they know they will see a couple of humpbacks. Everyone was happy with that, but I think we could offer something better.'

'A couple of humpbacks is better than nothing though,' Jonas said with a frown. 'If you know you're onto a sure thing, isn't that good enough?'

'But if you could pay to see a couple of humpbacks for sure or you could pay to have a small chance of seeing a more unusual whale, what would you pick?'

'I might like the humpbacks,' said Jonas with a grin.

Leifur grinned back, seeing that Jonas was challenging him. 'You might like the thrill of the hunt. Feeling like you're part of tracking down something hardly anyone else gets to see. And with a marine biologist on hand and an experienced Icelandic fisherman, anything is possible.'

'I might pay good money to be part of that,' Jonas conceded. 'But there are people who like a sure thing. If I knew we could get a glimpse of the northern lights from a particular place every day of the week, I'd take that over the hunt we have to do sometimes. And so would our clients.'

Leifur shrugged. 'Can we do a little of each?'

'We can. And if we're going to do that, we should do it while we have Astrid because we don't know how long that will be for.'

Having spent less than a day with Astrid, Leifur already knew that he was going to miss her when that time came. As well as feeling that they'd found a connection, despite his blundering start to the day, he knew what it was like working on a boat with someone. They became like family. Closer than family, because sometimes you spent more time with them than with anyone else in your life. You got to know people in the hours spent searching and waiting for the right time to fish. And a fishing boat could be a treacherous environment, and you needed to know you had each other's backs.

'So we should start planning where we're going to go,' said Leifur. Spending time with Astrid, planning out, as far as they could, where they'd operate their excursion, was something he was already looking forward to. Her perspective on marine life was so different from his; hers informed by science and a desire to study what was in the sea rather than take from the sea with perhaps not enough regard for the consequences.

'Come on,' Jonas said, standing up and taking his coat from a hook on the wall at the back of the office. 'Let's head to the bar.'

'The boat will be ready to collect on Friday.' He watched while Jonas locked the door.

'That's great news. Have you seen her at all during the work?'

Leifur shook his head. 'I went there to begin with, but I decided it was better to let her transform and come back to me new.' Rather than mourn what was being lost. He couldn't say that, even to Jonas. It felt too raw to admit how hard it had been to see the fishing rigs being removed from the deck. She might still be *Brimfaxi*, but he was frightened that she'd be so unrecognisable she wouldn't feel like home anymore.

'Good decision,' Jonas said, clapping him on the back. 'You ever come here?' They had reached the corner of the street and were standing outside a bar called Islenski Barinn.

'Not for a long time.'

'I doubt it will have changed.' Jonas made his way up the steps and held the door open at the top for Leifur to go in ahead of him.

The bar was not all that busy, but then it was relatively early on a Wednesday. Leifur spotted Siggi at a table next to a window that overlooked the street. There were another two men with him who Leifur hadn't met before.

'What would you like?' Leifur asked Jonas.

'No, this one's on me.'

Leifur opened his mouth to object, and Jonas held a hand up.

'Really. Call it team building. Everyone's drinks are on the business today. Beer?'

With their beers in hand, they went to join the others.

'This is Olafur,' Jonas said, 'and Brun.'

'Good to have you in the team,' said Olafur. 'I hear the boat tour was fun this morning.'

Leifur didn't know Olafur well enough to know whether he'd somehow heard the truth about how things had started off between him and Astrid and was being sarcastic, or not. He decided that assuming Olafur was being genuine was probably the best course of action.

'It was. Saw a couple of humpbacks.'

'A couple of humpbacks must be a normal day at the office for a fisherman,' Brun said.

Leifur smiled. 'I've seen my fair share. Goes with the territory when we're both after the same thing.'

'Are we going to have a staff boat tour as a dry run?' Siggi asked.

'That's not a bad idea,' Jonas said. 'Before we let Leifur and Astrid loose with tourists, we can give them a proper test.'

Olafur laughed. 'I am not one for boats, I have to admit. I will stay behind to keep the berth free for when you return. Make sure none of our competitors steal our spot.'

'An important job,' said Siggi, rolling his eyes. 'I wouldn't mind being your first mate, Leifur. I love being on the water.'

'Astrid is his first mate,' said Olafur.

'Until she finds something better,' said Siggi. 'Then you will need someone else to step in.'

Jonas shook his head. 'Sadly, you are too valuable to be out on a boat all day. Besides, you're more likely to end up telling the guests where they can catch some good waves and forget all about the whales.'

They were such a good-natured bunch. It felt to Leifur that they had the same kind of bond he'd had with his crew.

'How long have you guys worked together?'

'We've all known each other since school. Then Jonas started the business, and we came to work for him one by one as the business grew,' said Olafur. 'I remember you from school. Were you a couple of years older than us?'

'Around four years older, I think.' Leifur couldn't place any of the others, but it had been a while.

He was starting to relax. The beer was helping, as well as the fact that they were so welcoming. He felt like there was a chance he could be part of something again. He had his back to the door, but he saw Olafur's face light up as someone came in.

'*Hæ*!'

Leifur turned around and saw Astrid and her sister. Olafur

got up and went to the bar to get them a drink while the women took their coats off and then sat down at the end of the table. Astrid chose the seat next to Leifur, which he couldn't help but see as a good sign. Hopefully, he was well and truly forgiven.

'*Hæ*,' she said, smiling.

'Have you been shopping for candles this whole time?'

She laughed. 'No. Would you believe I don't own a scented candle?'

'Yet,' her sister said. 'I'm Gudrun, the younger and friendlier sister.'

'Leifur. Nice to meet you.'

'Astrid tells me you're not a morning person, which is odd for a fisherman,' Gudrun said.

Astrid put her hands over her face and let out a small wail. 'This is why I don't live in Reykjavik. You have no boundaries, Gudrun.'

Olafur, busy handing the beers around the table, roared with laughter.

'I'm sorry,' Astrid said to Leifur. 'I only told her you had been a little bit grumpy first thing.' She glared at her sister, who laughed it off and took a swig of her beer.

'I'm just teasing, As.'

'You should only tease people you know. You met him less than a minute ago,' Astrid said to her sister. Then she turned to Leifur. 'I'm sorry I mentioned it to her. You should know I also told her we had a great time.'

'I can vouch for that,' Olafur said.

Leifur felt Astrid's hand tap him briefly on the thigh, in a reassuring way.

'Gudrun is going to be the first person on our list of people not allowed on the boat. Right Leifur?'

'That seems a little harsh —'

There was a more insistent tap on his thigh.

'But what Astrid says goes. She's first mate.'

Gudrun laughed and rolled her eyes at them both. 'Oh, I see where this is going.'

'What do you mean? I am the first mate. What else would I be when there are only two of us?'

'To the Captain and the First Mate of *Brimfaxi*. *Skál*!' Jonas said to defuse the conversation.

'*Skál*!'

10

Later that evening, after Leifur had left, Astrid and Gudrun were sitting with Iris and Rachel at one end of the table they'd all been sharing. Brun, perhaps missing his partner, Fliss, who was in England visiting some university open days with her daughter, had started an impromptu singalong with his guitar at the other side of the bar, which everyone was enjoying.

'I feel bad that we haven't gone over there,' said Iris, looking over to the small stage where Brun and the other men were gathered.

'It's fine,' Rachel said with a wave of her hand. 'We don't want to lose the table.'

'Good point,' said Gudrun.

'I still can't believe you said that to Leifur,' Astrid said.

'What did she say?' Iris asked.

'She told him I said he'd been grumpy this morning when we met up for the boat trip.'

'You did say that.'

'I thought you'd realise it was between us.'

Gudrun shrugged. 'Maybe I've forgotten how to be a sister. It's been a while.'

It had been a while. Too long. And perhaps she'd taken it

for granted that she could come and go from Gudrun's life as she pleased, expecting things to be exactly as she'd left them when she came back.

'I'm sorry. He was grumpy this morning but I feel awkward that he knows I told you that because he did turn it around. I told you that too.'

'Oh, this is like the time when Gudrun got cross with me because my ex-boyfriend turned up when Jonas and I had just got together,' said Rachel.

'I wasn't cross!'

'You were. But I know you were being protective of Jonas,' Rachel said. 'And as soon as you knew I wanted to be with him and not Adam, it was fine. She's just worried Leifur's going to break your heart.'

Gudrun smiled at Rachel, and Astrid felt a rush of love for her sister.

'You don't need to worry, Gudrun. We're not in heart-breaking territory at all.'

'Really?' Iris said. 'You're not into him?'

'No, I'm not going to be here that long. It's a stopgap before I start the next job,' Astrid said.

'Astrid, that's different from not being into him,' Rachel said, raising an eyebrow.

She couldn't deny that there was something between her and Leifur. They had bonded over the fact that they were both about to run whale-watching tours — something neither of them had expected to be doing. It was so clichéd to fall for someone you're working with, but when she'd met him on the shore by his house, she hadn't known who he was and there had been something. A spark of attraction, at least.

'But he's gorgeous,' Iris said, her eyes widening. 'And he might be your soulmate or something. Perhaps you should give it a chance.'

'You sound more like Gudrun than Gudrun,' Rachel said,

laughing.

'Since Iris realised I was right about her and Siggi,' Gudrun said with a grin. 'If you like Leifur, you shouldn't worry about what I think.'

'It seems pointless even to think about anything like that with him when I could be leaving soon.'

'Have you applied for any jobs yet?' Gudrun asked.

Astrid glared at her sister. She knew she hadn't applied for anything other than the Costa Rica job she had no chance of getting.

'I'm just saying, you could be here for longer than you think.'

'I didn't think I was going to stay,' Iris said.

'Neither did I,' said Rachel.

Astrid groaned. 'Fine. I like Leifur, but I don't know if he likes me. He didn't seem that pleased to see me this morning, even though when we saw each other yesterday, it was… nice.'

'When did you see him yesterday? I thought you two met for the first time today?' Gudrun said.

'I took the boat out to Hafnarfjörður and he was on the shore. We spoke to each other.'

'About what?'

'Whales and stuff.'

Rachel laughed. 'Astrid. I know you haven't known us for very long, but we're going to need more information.'

'About what?'

'All of this with you and Leifur.'

'There's nothing between me and Leifur,' Astrid said, thinking that she might have to leave rather than be interrogated about someone she'd waved to once, spoken to for a minute and spent half a day with for work. She didn't have much to go on, and she wasn't about to dissect all of those encounters with Gudrun, Rachel and Iris. She liked them, but she didn't know them well enough yet.

'Fair enough,' Iris said. 'I mean, you need to get to know him. Working on the boat together will help.'

'Jonas likes him but says he's had a tough few months,' said Rachel. 'Maybe that's why he wasn't in the best mood this morning. I expect it's hard for him changing career when it wasn't something he really wanted.'

'That's it exactly,' said Astrid. 'Which is why he's probably not looking for romance either.'

'So it went okay with Leifur yesterday?' Jonas asked the next morning. Astrid had dropped into the office to discuss the details of her temporary job.

'Yes. We had a good time.'

'He said the same.' Jonas smiled. 'That's a good start. He also said that your knowledge is incredible. With that in mind, I wondered if I could make you an offer to tempt you to stay for the whole summer.'

'The whole summer?'

'I know it wasn't your plan, but if we could have you for the first season, it gives us a solid start. It would help us build a great reputation, and it gives us more time to find someone else who can step in when you leave.'

Jonas jotted a figure down on a piece of paper and pushed it over to Astrid. It was an extraordinary amount.

'This is an annual salary?'

'No, this would be for four months' work. Now until the end of August.'

Astrid tried to be cool, but it was difficult when, even if that had been an annual salary, it was more than she had earned in Norway in a year. Probably more than she could hope to earn at this point in her career, even if she got a new job.

'It's generous. More than the going rate for a marine

biologist.'

'You're not just a marine biologist. You're also local, you have experience on boats and you get on with Leifur.'

'Leifur would be fine with anyone.'

Jonas shook his head. 'Not true. When we first spoke, he was against having anyone else on the boat.'

At least that explained his reaction yesterday. 'He can't manage a tour alone. They had a couple of people besides the captain on the tour yesterday.'

'We couldn't allow it purely for safety reasons, but I didn't think that would wash with Leifur, so I went with the idea that he needed someone to entertain the guests while he's driving the boat. You did that yesterday. I'll be honest, Astrid. We need to be up and running in the next few weeks to make the investment pay off, and I'm not sure I'm going to find anyone else before then who Leifur's going to accept. Unless you know another local marine biologist with some boat experience?'

Astrid smiled. It felt good to be valued. Not only financially, although that felt good too, but knowing that Leifur enjoyed their trip and hadn't objected to her monologue about the whales, that he'd gone from not wanting anyone else on his boat to accepting her as a colleague, touched her. She knew the boat meant a lot to him, and she was looking forward to seeing it with him tomorrow. She could imagine it was a huge step for him to invite someone onto his boat.

'I don't. And I'd love to accept the job.' What were four months in the grand scheme of things? It wasn't as if it was a complete pivot; it was using her expertise for something different, but using it nevertheless. Keeping her hand in.

'That's great news,' said Jonas, shaking her hand and then pulling her towards him to give her a brief hug. 'Can I tell Leifur?'

'Can I? He's taking me out on the boat tomorrow.'

'He is?' Jonas leant against the desk and crossed his arms, a smile on his face. 'Of course. You tell him.'

'It's not anything like that.' Why did everyone jump to the same conclusion?

'Okay. I'm just pleased that you're getting on well enough that he's taking you out on the boat.'

'He knows I like being out on the water, and I'm interested to see what his boat's like.' Astrid heard the defensive tone in her voice and immediately regretted it since Jonas had been so generous. 'My sister is giving me a hard time about Leifur, that's all. Sorry.'

Jonas shrugged. 'It is no one's business but yours. But for what it's worth, your sister and her friends only want to see you happy.'

'I am happy,' Astrid said, plastering a smile on her face. 'Thanks, Jonas. I'll probably see you at the bar tomorrow night?'

'I expect so. Happy to have you on board.'

She laughed.

Jonas grinned. 'The pun was unintentional.'

'It was funny,' she shrugged.

Astrid left the office, and she was happy. Not because of Leifur and not because of the job, but because at least now she had a reason to be here. She belonged here, even if it was just for the summer.

She headed for Te & Kaffi and treated herself to a flat white and a sticky cinnamon bun. The coffee was delicious, and as she sipped it, she had a look at what rentals were available. It hardly seemed worth moving into somewhere for a few months, and Gudrun's was more than comfortable, but it'd be nice to come and go as she pleased, especially once she started working. There were a couple of possibilities, so she emailed the agents and asked for viewings. Astrid had never chosen anywhere to live herself. It was an exciting, if temporary, prospect.

Almost immediately, she had a phone call from an agent who had just shown one apartment she liked to someone else, but they had passed on it, and was Astrid available to view it now? The agent explained that it was in a great area and would be snapped up, so it was a great opportunity. Astrid finished the bun in three bites, gulped the rest of her coffee down and headed for Miðstræti, which was less than a five-minute walk away.

The apartment was in a three-storey building and took up the whole of the middle floor. It was a traditional wooden building, with ornate details on the edges of the roof and wooden balconies that ran up one side, overhanging each other.

The agent came to the front door and let Astrid in. 'It's upstairs,' she said. 'I believe there is a young couple who live downstairs and a single woman in the roof apartment. The owner is moving overseas for six months, so it is a fixed six-month let.'

'Six months is perfect for me,' Astrid said, a sense of deep contentment settling over her as she stepped into the apartment and was enveloped within its calming walls. The whole place was white, but all the walls were lined with wooden cladding, which gave the white some texture and warmth. With dark wooden floors, it was very chic, and Astrid could imagine herself padding around there, cooking in the state-of-the-art kitchen or relaxing in the pristine white bathroom that had a beautiful deep bathtub. The high ceilings and large windows were unusual in more modern buildings, but Astrid loved the period feel of the place.

'Do you want to take it?'

She'd never made such an impulsive decision in her life, but it was what she wanted, and she wasn't going to let it pass her by. After all, in six months she could find herself working somewhere where she'd never be able to live in a beautiful place like this.

'Yes, I'll take it,' she said, a rush of adrenaline making her feel as if she had just won a hundred million krona instead of forking out thousands of krona on rent. 'How soon can I move in?'

11

Why did he offer to take Astrid out today of all days? He was on his way to collect *Brimfaxi* from the boatyard, and he was nervous. If the boat didn't feel like his boat anymore, he knew he'd be devastated, and he was worried that he might not shake off a mood like that before he picked Astrid up as arranged at Reykjavik harbour in a couple of hours. He trusted the process; he'd signed off on everything after all, but it was one thing seeing plans and drawings. They would never be able to tell him how the boat would feel after the work was done.

He parked his truck in the car park and took a deep breath. This was it. The huge door to the warehouse-looking building that housed the dry dock was open, and Leifur went in.

'*Hæ*, Leifur!'

He waved in greeting to his friend Carl, who had led the refit.

Carl came over, and they shook hands. 'Come, she's outside.'

They walked through to the door on the other side. *Brimfaxi* was waiting. Back in the water and moored on the quay.

There she was. For the most part, she looked the same.

Beautiful, with shiny new paintwork in the same royal blue shade that she'd always been, with bright white for the wheelhouse and deck.

'What do you think?'

Leifur was overcome and only managed a brief nod.

'Come on, let me show you around.'

They climbed aboard. The deck seemed huge now that the rigs had been removed. Freshly-stained planks of teak now covered it and were flawless, elevating the boat from a utilitarian fishing boat to a vessel ready to accept guests. The benches were well-fitted, and the new railings that ran around the deck matched the old ones so well, that no one but Leifur would know where the old ones ended and the new ones began.

'She's incredible,' said Leifur.

Carl smiled and headed down the new steps into the bowels of the boat. Before he followed, Leifur took a moment and stepped into the wheelhouse. It was exactly as it had been, apart from the fresh paint. He grinned, running his hands over the wheel. She still felt like his boat, and it was a tremendous relief.

'Leifur?'

'Coming!'

He could hardly take in the space below deck. It was so different from what it had been like before. Most of the space had been taken up by the ice machine and fish holds, but now, it was open, with new windows on each side and comfortable chairs. The old galley had been refreshed and now had a door that closed on the bottom to create a serving hatch.

'I don't know how to thank you.'

'All part of the service. I'm glad you're pleased, Leifur.'

Leifur set off for Reykjavik to meet Astrid with a big grin on his face as he stood in the wheelhouse, the familiar rumble of the boat, just as it had always been, beneath his feet. It was a chilly spring day but not too windy, meaning the sea was relatively calm for the time of year. He hoped Astrid was well prepared with plenty of layers of clothing on to help keep the cold out.

He spotted her waiting on the quayside as he approached. She was holding two coffees, and once she saw him, she kept pace with him as he headed to the new allotted berth that Jonas had organised for *Brimfaxi*. She was to be moored in Reykjavik harbour permanently now, so he was going to have to commute in his truck rather than come back and forth from Hafnarfjörður every day on the boat. Jonas had pointed out that it was crazy to pay for berths in both places, and Leifur had reluctantly agreed. Especially since Jonas was footing the bill.

'Permission to come aboard?' Astrid said.

Leifur jumped off the boat to secure the lines, then took the coffee she offered him.

'After you.' He held out his arm, gesturing for her to climb aboard. 'Here, I can hold your coffee.'

'Thanks.' Astrid jumped from the edge of the boat down to the deck. Without the gangplank, it was around half a metre but made Leifur realise that they'd have to use it all the time. He was so used to doing that jump on and off himself, never having to consider that anyone other than physically-fit fishermen would embark and disembark.

'She's a lovely boat,' Astrid said, taking her coffee from him and moving aside so that he could join her on deck. 'Everything looks so shiny and new. Tell me what she was like before?'

Leifur gave her the tour that Carl had given him, painting a picture for Astrid of how it used to be, especially down below where he could still hardly believe it was so big.

'What an amazing transformation. Are you pleased?'

'Yes. And relieved. She looks a little different, but she feels the same. She's still my boat.'

'Of course she is. She's beautiful.'

Leifur saw the genuine appreciation in Astrid's eyes. And that did something to him. For a moment, he considered pulling Astrid into his arms.

'Where are you taking me, then?' She headed into the wheelhouse, breaking the spell, which perhaps only he had been under.

'I thought we might head south. Take a look at something other than marine mammals. I think we're going to be over whales quite quickly.'

'Speak for yourself,' she said, feigning shock. 'Whales are my life.'

'Whales are not my life.' He was about to say that fish were his life, but that wasn't true anymore, and it still felt odd every time he realised that.

'What's your thing then?'

'I don't know. The boat, maybe?'

'As long as you're sure.'

He gave her a side-eye, and she grinned then bumped herself against him gently.

'Come on, let's go,' she said. 'Show me something better than a whale.'

He started the engine again and took the wheel, heading out of the harbour. Astrid left the wheelhouse and stood at the bow, the wind in her hair making him wish for the second time in half an hour that he could wrap his arms around her.

'Hey, get yourself inside and put a lifejacket on!' he called out. He'd been remiss in setting off without remembering the new rules of the boat, but it was the first time.

'Where are they? I'll get you one.'

'I've only got two so far,' he said, pulling two pristine,

modern lifejackets out of his bag. 'We need to sort out the equipment. I think Jonas is making a list.'

Astrid took her position back on the bow once again. It was exactly the stance she'd had when he'd seen her in the small boat near his house. Her eyes were on the water, watching. He guessed it was habit after being on research boats for her old job.

It took around half an hour for them to skirt around the coast, heading north from Reykjavik, and Leifur estimated it would be another hour until they got to their destination, the island of Andriðsey off the west coast.

'Can I get you a drink? Do we have anything?'

'There should be some instant coffee in the galley and maybe some powdered milk. Or I have a couple of bottles of water in my bag.'

'Coffee's good,' she said, and disappeared down to the galley.

Leifur liked that she felt at home on the boat. It was because she was used to boats, he told himself, not because she felt particularly at home on his boat. But whatever the reason, she fitted in here.

When the island was in sight, he let Astrid in on the surprise.

'Look in my bag. There are some binoculars,' he said, keeping his hands on the wheel. It would be time to drop the anchor in a few minutes, but they needed to get a little closer first.

She looked at him suspiciously. 'You want me to take the wheel while you look?'

'Sure,' he said, surprising himself since he'd hardly ever allowed that when he'd been fishing.

He rummaged in his bag and pulled out the pair of binoculars he'd packed along with a small picnic.

'Here,' he said, handing them to her. 'And we're not

looking at the water. You need to aim higher.'

She frowned, and then a smile lit up her face. 'Puffins?'

He nodded, enjoying seeing the reaction he'd been hoping for.

'I'm never here at the right time to see them!'

He smiled, lost in watching her looking for the first glimpse of a puffin. Once they were closer, he dropped the anchor.

'Come on, let's go to the bow,' he said.

Now that the boat had stopped, the wind seemed fiercer. Leifur pulled a woollen beanie hat from his pocket and pulled it down so that his ears were covered, then shoved his hands deep into his pockets and settled in to wait for his turn with the binoculars. It might be a while, but he didn't care. He'd seen the puffins many times, and anyway, he had come to show Astrid and was thrilled she was enjoying them.

'It's incredible seeing them dive into the water,' she said. 'I've seen a few with fish in their beaks.'

The cliffs were a mass of puffins, their white breasts clear to see even from this distance. It was the start of the breeding season, and this island was a temporary home to a large proportion of the world population of Atlantic puffins.

'Here,' Astrid said, handing the binoculars to Leifur. She glanced at his hat and reached into a pocket for her own, taking her hood down briefly and then pulling it up again over the hat.

'Cold?'

'No, not yet.'

Leifur could feel Astrid's eyes on him while he had a look through the binoculars. Watching the puffins was endlessly entertaining. He'd seen them lots of times before when he'd been out on the boat but had never had time to stop and have a proper look.

'Look! Did you see that one? It had so many fish it was

dropping them all the way back to the nest,' Astrid said.

Leifur handed the binoculars back to her. 'They're incredible.'

'Are you sure you've seen enough?'

'You go for it. I'm going to sort some food out for us downstairs. Come down when you're ready.'

'Okay,' she said with a grin. 'Thank you, Leifur. This is amazing.'

It was around twenty minutes later when Astrid appeared in the galley, by which time Leifur had laid out the simple lunch of bread, cooked sliced lamb, cucumber sticks, tomatoes and skyr yogurt with fruit.

'It's toasty warm in here,' she said, taking her coat off and sitting down opposite him at the small wooden table.

'The heating runs off the engine, so it is pretty good.' Another thing he was relieved about: finding that the heating was still in working order.

'It's really cosy.' She picked up a cucumber stick and munched it while Leifur was slicing some bread off the end of the loaf. 'Did you ever have to sleep down here?'

'Sometimes. There's a berth in there,' he said, nodding to a door in the corner. 'We usually left very early in the morning and were back very late at night. It's not very comfortable staying on the boat, but if the weather's bad, sometimes it's safer to stay out at sea rather than try to get back to the port.' He passed her a plate with two slices of bread.

'Did you ever get stuck in scary weather?'

'There is a lot of bad weather in Iceland, you know that. It is no different at sea. Fishing is a dangerous job in good weather or bad.' He didn't want to get into the details of the long night where he'd lost his father in a terrible storm. That he'd had to make the dreadful decision to turn back to port without him. And worse, explain to his mother what had happened.

Victoria Walker

'We had a couple of terrible storms when I was on the research boat. Those were the longest nights of my life.' She looked at him meaningfully, and he wondered whether she knew, or whether she assumed as a fisherman he would have had his fair share of close shaves. 'This lamb is gorgeous.'

'My mother cooked it. She sends me home with food every time I visit as if she thinks I can't cook for myself.'

'It's a sign of love,' Astrid said.

12

When Astrid had asked him about the storms, there was something fleeting in Leifur's eyes that told her he'd lost something. Maybe lost someone, which would be even worse, but she didn't think it was the right time to encourage him to share that with her. No doubt whatever it was held bad memories, and today was supposed to be a celebration of him getting *Brimfaxi* back and starting a new chapter.

'I was so carried away with the puffins, I forgot to ask you how you found the boat on the way here. Does she feel the same?'

'Exactly the same.' He grinned, and his face lit up in the way she loved but already realised she would rarely see. It had only happened the second time she'd seen him on the beach near his house and not at all on the boat trip or at the bar.

'That's great. So it was the right decision.'

'It makes me more certain of the decision now that I have *Brimfaxi* back and intact, but I'm still not sure that running a tour boat is something I am cut out to do.' He picked up his sandwich and took a big bite. For the first time, Astrid noticed that the end of one of his fingers was missing, just below where the nail would be.

'Why do you say that? Your knowledge of these waters must be amazing.' Astrid had finished her sandwich and moved on to the skyr.

'I've spent years with three other men on this boat day in and day out. We were like family, but I'm out of practice mixing with new people.'

'I hadn't noticed.'

'Thank you. That's very kind of you, especially when you've been on the receiving end.'

She waved her spoon. 'It's fine. I'm not that great at stuff like that either. My sister has always found it so easy to talk to people and next to her, I feel as if everything I say is idiotic.'

'It isn't.'

'Anyway, I only feel like that here. When I'm with Gudrun, I go back to being the older sister who everyone thinks is boring compared to her. She's always the life and soul of the party.' She had no animosity towards her sister at all. It was just a fact; it always had been, and she was glad that Gudrun had surrounded herself with people who loved her for it and that her open, welcoming personality had helped her land her dream job.

'Maybe it's always like that with family. In my family, I'm also the older boring one. My younger brother is working on a fishing boat for a big fishing company and has no worries that they are the kind of people putting traditional fishermen out of business.'

'Leaving you to worry about the future of the family business?'

Leifur shrugged. 'That is eldest child territory for sure. He doesn't take any responsibility for anything.'

'Gudrun is very responsible. In a lot of ways, I envy her because she's so carefree with it.'

'The day I saw you on the boat from my shore, you looked

carefree then.'

Astrid smiled, remembering what she'd thought about Leifur then. How he'd been standing there, looking like the vision of a solid Viking. And now she knew him, she knew he was a lot less solid on the inside.

'I have no reason not to be, especially now.'

'Why now?'

'Jonas has offered me a job with you for the whole summer.' She waited for his reaction, already knowing he wasn't good at presenting an expression that said anything different from what he was really thinking. If he wasn't happy about her getting the job for a lot longer than she'd first thought, she'd know in the next couple of seconds.

'That's wonderful news,' he said, smiling so that his eyes crinkled, telling her he meant it. 'We'll have a great summer, and it saves me having to get to know anyone else for a while.'

Astrid tried not to dwell on that being the overriding reason for him being pleased, preferring to think that he was glad it was her in particular.

'Who'd have thought we'd end up working together when I saw you from my boat that first time,' she said.

'I know. It's funny how things like that happen. I heard Siggi saying that he and Iris were in Hawaii at the same time last year and they think they were going to the same beach.'

'My sister would think that was fate.'

'You don't believe in that?'

'I don't know. I've never seen any evidence of it myself.'

'Perhaps because you're a scientific person, you don't read anything into coincidences and things like that,' he said.

'Perhaps you have to believe in the idea of there being a person who you're meant to be with as well.' She held his gaze as she said it, which somehow gave more meaning to what she was saying. She felt brave, speaking like this to

Leifur. Thoughts of it not being ideal to date someone you work with had fallen away since he'd brought her on this puffin trip and even thought as far as bringing lunch. It was almost like a date.

'It seems unlikely that someone like me would find their soulmate by staying in the town where they grew up. You probably have to travel a little further to be in with a chance.'

'Probably. Although my sister found hers in Reykjavik.'

'I don't know your sister very well, but maybe being more receptive to the idea of a soulmate makes them easier to find?'

'I suppose that makes sense.'

'Shall we take a last look at the puffins before we head back?'

They tidied the galley in companionable silence and then got their coats and hats on and headed up to the deck. It was drizzling, and the wind had picked up, making the odd larger drop of rain feel like a sting on their faces as it hit. The puffins were being buffeted by the gusts but carried on with their fishing regardless.

'I think we should head back in case this weather gets any worse,' said Leifur.

'That's fine. It's not as much fun now anyway.' Astrid tucked the binoculars back in the case and followed Leifur into the wheelhouse. It was snug in there with two people, more so when he closed the door against the elements, and it didn't take long for the heater to warm them through again.

The drizzle had reduced the visibility, and the sea was greyer and choppier than it had been on the way.

'I'm sorry, I did check the forecast but you know how changeable it can be,' Leifur said, looking worried.

'It's fine.' She put a hand on his arm to steady herself. 'I've been at sea in worse than this.'

He manoeuvred the boat around so that they were heading

back the way they'd come. Astrid grabbed onto him again as the boat tipped forcefully from side to side while he made the turn, figuring that he was the sturdiest thing in the small wheelhouse to hang onto. His feet were in a wide stance that seemed to root him to the floor of the boat so that he was at one with it. It probably helped that he was steering and had a feel for what to expect, but Astrid was struck by how reassuring it was to hold onto him.

'Sorry,' she said, banging into his side when a particularly fierce wave tipped them.

'No worries.' He looked down and smiled at her, then took her hand that was gripping his forearm and tucked it around the crook of his elbow.

'This would be awful weather to be out whale watching,' she said, trying not to think about the fact that she had her arm linked with his and how nice that felt.

'We probably should have turned back earlier. If we were on a tour, we wouldn't both be down in the galley then we'd have seen what was going on.'

'It's not so bad.' She wouldn't have wanted to miss their galley picnic. It was the first time they'd had a chance to sit down together and chat, just the two of them. It was going to take quite a few chats before she really found out what it was to know Leifur. She had a feeling that there were some depths to be discovered and that she had barely scratched the surface.

Once they were on a straight heading, she relaxed a little and started to overthink the fact that she still had her hand tucked into Leifur's elbow. Feeling his muscles tense as he adjusted the wheel to keep the boat from drifting off course was… well, it was making her feel things for Leifur that were making her blush. She slipped her hand out. He glanced briefly at her and she looked out of the window, not wanting him to see any sign of what she'd been thinking on her face.

'When do you think we'll start the tours?'

'Jonas wants to start in a couple of weeks. We'll need to do a dry run before then, perhaps with friends and family as guinea pigs. I think they've already started selling tickets on the website.'

'Really? That's scary.'

Leifur laughed. 'You're scared! I am terrified.'

'At least we're in it together.'

He nodded, his gaze fixed firmly on the horizon. 'I am grateful for that. For you.'

'It must be strange doing this on your own when you've always worked with your family.' Astrid had worked out that he must have worked with his father and his brother at some point.

'Yes, but there's no choice. I told Jonas I could do this alone and he was right when he said I couldn't. But I never thought he'd find someone like you. You don't feel like a stranger, Astrid. You fit on this boat as if you've always been here with me.'

He didn't look at her at all when he said this, yet it was the most heartfelt thing anyone had ever said to her. She put her hand on top of his hand that was closest to her as he gripped the wheel, his knuckles white, betraying the emotion he was battling to keep inside. His grip relaxed under her touch, and he removed his hand and placed it on top of hers, linking his fingers between hers and guiding their hands back onto the wheel. Then, a moment later, he released his hold and gently brought her in front of him so that she had her back to his chest and his arms were on either side of her, his hands still on the wheel.

Astrid gulped. She was so aware of him standing behind her. She thought she could feel his heat radiating into her back, even though that was impossible since they both had all their layers on. At first, she tried to stand close enough to the wheel so that she wasn't touching him, but gradually she leaned into him, enveloped in his embrace, all thoughts of whether or not it was a good idea wiped clean from her head.

'Is this okay?' he murmured into her ear.

She nodded. His breath was warm, and his beard tickled her cheek, telling her he was as close as she imagined. Her heart was pounding, and she was sure he would feel it against his chest since it felt as though her whole body was vibrating. Feeling brave, she placed her hands on the wheel, lacing her fingers between his. His skin was much more tanned than hers, and his fingers were thicker and rougher, telling of the years of manual labour they'd seen. She traced her fingers to the tips of his.

'What happened to your finger?' she asked, running her finger over the relatively smooth skin.

'It got caught in the net when we were hauling in. I was young and cocky. I should have had gloves on so it was my own fault.'

'How young?'

'Sixteen.'

'You've been a fisherman for a long time.' No wonder it was part of him. Part of his soul.

'It's time to move on,' he said softly. 'And I don't think it's going to be as hard as I thought.'

13

The following day, Leifur was on his way to his mother's house for a rare family meal. He saw plenty of his mother, but the rarity was that his brother was coming too. He hadn't seen Isak for months, and they weren't great at keeping in touch with each other. But his mind was filled less with thoughts of how the evening might go, and more with thoughts of Astrid.

The urge to keep her warm and safe while they were heading back from their puffin adventure had been instinct. He put it down to the fact that Astrid was the first woman who'd ever been on *Brimfaxi*, at least as far as he knew, and far from it feeling odd, it felt as if she belonged there. Had he overstepped? Probably. What little he knew about normal working environments was that it was a bad idea to mix business and pleasure. It hadn't happened yet, but now, he wasn't sure what the situation was between him and Astrid. It wasn't so much about the physical side of what had happened, which literally boiled down to her standing in front of him, leaning into him, and their hands had touched.

It was almost nothing.

Except it was everything.

Though he'd never had a proper relationship himself, he'd

had crushes on unattainable women, he'd had a few short-lived flings, and he knew the difference between all of that and what love looked like. He was hesitant to admit that his feelings for Astrid were as strong as that, but he had feelings for her. That she had come along at exactly the time when his life was in turmoil, bringing a calm influence, seeming to understand him, on some level felt like it was meant to be.

He let himself into his mother's house with his key.

'*Hæ*, Mamma!'

'Big brother! It's been a while.' Isak came into the hallway.

'Isak. You look good.'

His brother was looking sun kissed, even his hair was lighter. That wasn't from working on a fishing boat in Iceland.

'I've been to the Caribbean, can you believe it?'

'The new place must be treating you well, then.'

'Better than the last place,' Isak said, laughing. 'Come on, Mamma's about to dish up.'

'Leifur, it's not like you to be late,' his mother said as he took his coat off and sat down at the table.

'Sorry, Mamma. I've been in the office today finalising the tour schedule. We had to work late to get it to the website person.'

'I'm pleased you're busy and not lying around on my couch all day,' she said, winking at him.

'Do you get paid for the extra time? At the new place, I get overtime if we're back after the scheduled shift.'

Leifur glared at his brother but bit his tongue. 'I'm a partner in the business, so it is a profit share, not an hourly rate.'

'How is *Brimfaxi*, Leifur? Are you happy with the work?' his mother asked as she dished up the delicious-smelling roast lamb stew.

'She's perfect,' he said, smiling as he thought about the day before. 'I took a run out to Andriðsey Island to see the puffins.'

'Aren't you supposed to be looking for whales?' Isak said, smirking.

'Would you like to come for the trial run next week?'

'I'm working every day next week,' said Isak.

'That's a shame,' Leifur said with relief. He'd only meant to invite his mother, Peta, and he'd already had enough of his brother's jibes.

'I would love to come,' said Peta. She patted his hand. 'I'm very proud of you.'

'For ruining the family business and massacring Pabbi's boat?'

'Isak!'

'Mamma, I'm sorry, but he has taken everything this family had left, and what do we have to show for it?'

'People like you, working for the big fishing companies are killing the family fishermen!' Leifur felt the rage bubbling within him and, in the moment, he thought he'd explode if he didn't say something to hurt his brother the same way he'd been hurt. But he regretted it immediately because it wasn't Isak's fault. He had to leave the business because the capelin were no longer reliable. He hadn't left of his own accord, and Leifur braced himself for Isak's retaliation.

'Leifur! Enough!' Peta slammed her hands on the table and stood up. 'We are family. There is no blame for either of you to take or place. Isak, your brother saved this family after your father died, and he deserves your respect for that.'

'Sorry, Mamma,' said Isak.

'And Leifur. Your brother must earn a living. As the eldest son, you have *Brimfaxi*. He has nothing. You must respect his choice to continue fishing.'

'Sorry, Mamma. And I'm sorry, Isak. It was unfair of me to say that.' It hurt that they were both forgetting that he hadn't decided to close the business alone. Isak had been the one to suggest that he might work on another boat even before Leifur had realised that the absence of the capelin might spell the end for them. And Leifur had supported the idea, knowing that his brother had to earn money somehow. Isak wasn't a saver like Leifur, who kept a buffer in case of leaner times, so he couldn't afford to go out day after day only to return disappointed when there were no fish to sell. But he never expected his brother to go onto a boat run by one of the conglomerates.

'No problem,' Isak said with a shrug, but not going so far as to apologise in return.

Their mother sat back down. 'How was your holiday, Isak?'

Isak chatted for a while about his first holiday abroad. He was earning more money than he'd ever done before, and Leifur envied him. Not because of the money as much as that yes, he'd lost his job on *Brimfaxi*, but he'd been able to move on without a backward glance. He'd been unconcerned about what Leifur would do next, and there had been no suggestion that they might do something together, even though Leifur would have been open to that at the time. Not any more; the guilt he'd felt at letting his brother down had totally worn off after tonight.

'Right, I have to meet someone,' Isak announced almost as soon as they'd finished eating. He stood up and grabbed his coat before Peta had chance to put her cutlery down.

'I have *Grjónagrautur*,' she said, thinking that the creamy rice pudding type dessert might tempt him to stay longer.

'Sorry, Mamma. It's work.'

Leifur highly doubted it had anything to do with work, but it stopped Peta from suggesting he didn't need to leave. If Isak had admitted he was meeting a woman, which is what Leifur suspected, she would be upset with him for leaving early.

Peta busied herself packing up some leftovers for Isak to take with him, as well as a huge portion of the pudding.

'Good to see you, Leifur,' Isak said, shaking his hand. He sounded like he meant it, despite what they'd said to each other across the dinner table.

'You too.' He would have loved to ask Isak if he'd been at the same family meal as him, but he didn't want to upset Peta again. So he stood at the door with his mother and saw his brother out.

'He works so hard,' Peta said with a sigh as they went back to the table to tuck into the Grjónagrautur.

'He needs to if he's going to the Caribbean.'

'You ought to have a holiday, Leifur. The past few months have been hard on you too.'

'It'll have to wait until the end of the season.' As well as not having enough time before they started the tours, he barely had enough money to take a bus to the next town, let alone a holiday.

'I'm looking forward to seeing the boat. Do you have your crew organised?'

'It's just me and Astrid.'

'Astrid. She is a tour guide?'

'She's a marine biologist, but she's between jobs, so Jonas has signed her up for the summer. Her knowledge is incredible. She'll be an enormous asset.'

'It sounds as if you are quite taken with her,' Peta said, smiling.

'We get on well together. I thought it would be difficult working with a stranger on the boat, but she's…' He almost said perfect, but that would have sent his mother's imagination into overdrive and he could do without that. 'She's got a lot of experience working on research vessels.'

'I expect that will come in handy. So is it just the two of

you?'

'Yes.'

'Very cosy.'

'Mamma…'

'Leifur. I have not said anything.' Peta had a twinkle in her eye, and she didn't need to say what she was thinking for Leifur to know.

'And how are you?'

Thankfully, Peta let it go and happily chatted about the latest goings on at her book club and how there had been a newcomer at the mahjong group who had suggested they ought to play bridge.

'Who wants to get into a game that takes years to master at our age?'

'I think you've got time to master bridge.'

'I like mahjong, and at my age, knowing what you like and sticking it to the new man who wants to play bridge is one of life's pleasures.'

Leifur laughed. 'I think I'm already like that.'

Peta laughed too. 'Oh, my love. You have always been so solid and reliable. Now that you're starting this new adventure, try and let yourself have some fun. The responsibility is not yours alone anymore. Let yourself enjoy that.'

After he had several parcels of leftover food forced upon him, Leifur left his mother's house and headed home. Despite the bad feeling between him and his brother, he felt lighter. It was good to know that Isak was doing well and managing to hold down a job successfully. Working for family was different, and Isak had taken advantage of that. Leifur worried that the lack of a work ethic might be a problem for him, and now that it seemed not to be, he couldn't help but take his brother's attitude when he'd worked on *Brimfaxi* personally.

He sighed. Moving on from the fishing was one thing. Moving on from these deep-rooted feelings about his brother was harder. It was probably for the best that they were following different paths. Maybe in a few years their feelings about all of this might have softened, and they'd end up being closer. Friends, even. Leifur chuckled to himself. It was ridiculous. He and Isak were like chalk and cheese, and it was easier to live with if he accepted that.

His phone buzzed, and he pulled it out of his pocket and saw a message from Astrid. His stomach lurched slightly. It had been a long time since he'd had that kind of reaction to a text message.

Astrid: Do you want to meet for coffee tomorrow?
Leifur: Where and when?
Astrid: Te & Kaffi on Laugavegur 10am?
Leifur: *thumbs up emoji*

He'd thought about asking her what she wanted to meet about, but it didn't matter. He just wanted to see her. Since yesterday, when she'd ducked out of his embrace as he began manoeuvring into port, he'd been thinking about her and looking forward to the next time he'd see her. Maybe he'd go so far as to admit he missed her. Was she feeling the same way, or maybe she thought it wasn't a good idea to get involved with each other when they had to work together for the summer.

But his mother's words rang in his ears. Maybe he should try to enjoy himself more. After all, the whale watching tours were hopefully going to be a much easier way to earn a living than fishing. Finally, he could take advantage of the fact he'd be working normal hours and could have a normal social life. And Peta was right. For the first time in his life, the responsibility wasn't his. Jonas was his business partner and had more idea about the business side of things. Leifur had to remember that his role was captaining the boat and finding whales. If he couldn't sit back and enjoy that, there was something wrong with him. And if he couldn't share a coffee with a beautiful woman who could very well only be here for the summer, there was something wrong with the world.

14

When Astrid got back to Gudrun's after the puffin trip, the euphoria that she'd drifted home on disappeared when she remembered that tonight was the night she had to tell her sister she was moving out. She'd been putting it off, because they were finding their way again after not having seen much of each other over the past few years and Astrid didn't want to put an end to that. She was going to have to phrase it very carefully.

'Have you been out on the boat all day?' Gudrun asked while they made dinner together in the kitchen. They'd settled on a risotto, and Gudrun was dutifully stirring the rice, adding a ladle of stock every so often while Astrid was grating some cheese to stir through it.

'Yes. I thought we might just go out and back to see how the boat was running, but he took us to Andriðsey Island.'

'To see the puffins! Oh, that's amazing, As. I haven't done that in years.'

Most of what Astrid remembered from the trip was the last half an hour or so when she'd given in and leant against Leifur's chest while they headed back to Reykjavik harbour. It was one of the most romantic things that had ever happened to her. And so unexpected.

'It was wonderful. I could have watched them for hours.'

'And you got on okay with Leifur after the other day?'

'He's a really nice guy. It's a big change for him, and he's been worried about the boat. It was his father's boat. As soon as he realised she still felt the same as she did before all the work, he relaxed. You could almost see it.'

'Oh my god. You're in love with him!' Gudrun had stopped stirring and was staring wide-eyed at Astrid.

'No, of course I'm not.' She laughed, but she knew it wasn't convincing. And Gudrun was very shrewd at reading this kind of behaviour.

'Okay, maybe not in love with him yet, but something happened today, I can tell. Something that's made you fall for him. Tell me I'm wrong.' She pointed the wooden spoon at Astrid.

'Don't stop stirring. It'll stick.'

'See? You can't even deny it. Come on then, tell me what happened.'

Despite thinking that the episode in the wheelhouse was something she'd keep close to her heart, Astrid found herself sharing the whole story — if you could call it that — with Gudrun. As she told her how she had leant into him, she surprised herself by how dreamy she felt about the whole thing.

'I can't explain it, and I'm not in love with him, but I do like him.'

'And did he kiss you goodbye?'

Astrid shook her head. 'That would have been weird.' But she'd been disappointed that he hadn't. All that had happened was that they'd been in very close proximity to each other for a while. Except in her heart, it was more than that even though she knew he might not have the same feelings for her. He might have thought they were just cosying up in the wheelhouse since they were the only two on the boat and it was a fairly choppy sea. It was ridiculous to have expected that might lead to a goodbye kiss. They were colleagues. Friends.

'When will you see him again?'

'I don't know. I suppose when we're sorting out the boat over the next week or so?'

Gudrun scooped some risotto onto a teaspoon and held it out for Astrid to taste.

She blew on it and then tasted it. 'It's ready. Delicious.'

'Aren't you desperate to see him?'

Yes, she wanted to say. Desperate to be held by him properly. His arms wrapped around her so she could feel his whole embrace. 'No. I'm not going to force anything. It's a busy time for him, getting everything up and running. We'll just see what happens. Shall I dish some up for Olafur?'

'Yes, please. He'll be in soon.'

The two of them sat at the table. Astrid wondered whether to wait until Olafur got back from work before she announced she was moving into her own place but then thought better of it.

'So you know Jonas offered me a contract for the summer.'

'Mmm hmm,' said Gudrun through a mouthful of rice.

'Since it's more money than I thought I'd make, I can afford to rent my own place.'

'Why would you pay when you can stay here for free?'

It was a perfectly reasonable question, and it somewhat took the wind out of her sails. She hadn't expected Gudrun to be calm and reasonable, but then neither of them were teenagers anymore. She had to remember that.

'I love it here, you know that, but I've never had a place of my own here. I've never had anywhere that I've chosen. And now that Reykjavik is starting to feel like home again, I want to feel like I'm really living here. And I love staying with you, but it feels more like being on holiday.'

'That makes sense,' said Gudrun. 'I get staff discount at Snug.'

'My new place is mostly white, so I do need to break that up a bit.'

'You've already found somewhere?'

Astrid nodded sheepishly.

'Oh, As. I would have loved to house hunt with you.'

'I know, but it was the only place I looked at. I emailed the agent, and they called and asked if I could see it straight away, so I did. There wasn't any time to tell you.'

Gudrun looked glum for a minute or so, then she said, 'Can I help you choose things?'

'Of course you can. I have no idea what looks good, and I definitely want some scented candles.'

'I don't want you to move out, but I'm happy you're feeling at home here. I always felt as if you didn't want to be here when you visited before.'

Astrid had always felt like a stranger when she'd come home. It felt like so long since she'd lived here, and being away while her sister was busy growing up, becoming an adult and being in a serious relationship had always made Astrid feel as if she'd missed out on too much to catch up with. As if the distance between her and her family was increasing with each visit home.

'It wasn't that at all. Every time I came back, things had changed so much while I was away, it felt like I was being left behind.'

Gudrun got up, came behind Astrid and hugged her. 'Oh, As. I didn't know you felt like that. To me, you were so lucky to be living abroad doing your dream job, and I was stuck here, waiting to be old enough to do the same.'

'It's fine.' She rubbed her sister's arms, trying not to think about how it might have felt if Leifur had taken his hands off the wheel and embraced her like this. 'You don't need to feel bad for me.'

'I'm happy that you've got a place,' Gudrun said. 'I'll miss you, but I love that Reykjavik is feeling like home to you. Maybe you'll stay longer than the summer.'

'Don't get carried away. I haven't seen an opening for a marine biologist in Reykjavik yet.'

Later that evening, when Olafur was home, Astrid said goodnight and retreated to her room to give them some time alone. They were so welcoming, happy to share their home with her, but it was hard to relax at someone else's house the same way you would at your own. Astrid was so glad that Gudrun had understood why she wanted to move out. Now she could start looking forward to it.

She imagined inviting Leifur over to her new place. She could picture him there, lounging on the sofa while she made them a coffee, or sitting on the small balcony sharing a beer. And she liked the thought of that. Could that happen? She felt as if they were friends now, but it seemed like a big step to go from where they were to inviting him round to her flat. Something else needed to happen between those two things, and for her own sanity, she could do with seeing him sooner rather than later to get a feel for how things were since the puffin trip.

Before she could change her mind, she texted him and invited him for coffee the following morning. He replied straightaway and agreed.

Astrid arrived at Te & Kaffi a good ten minutes earlier than she'd planned to. With Gudrun at work only a couple of doors away, she'd been strategic and walked the long way round so that her sister wouldn't see her walk past the Snug window and come out to say hello. It would inevitably lead to Astrid having to admit she was meeting Leifur, so she hadn't mentioned it, knowing that Gudrun would probably have walked back and forth in front of the coffee shop to get a glimpse of them together. Better to keep it quiet until she knew where she stood.

She waited, wondering whether it was too forward to have suggested the coffee. What if he didn't feel the same way as she did? Perhaps she should have waited until the next time she saw him. It would have been fairly soon since they were going to be working on setting the boat up.

Leifur arrived right on time. She loved that he was prompt. It always meant a lot to her when the people she was meeting were on time, because it was a sign they were excited to be meeting and that they respected her time enough not to waste it by being late.

He came over to where she was sitting. She'd chosen a low table with two bucket chairs rather than a normal table, thinking it would be cosier. He took his coat off and laid it over the back of the chair.

'Can I get you a coffee?'

'I'll come up with you. I might get something to eat as well.'

She stood up. Leifur stayed where he was, then leant in and gave her an awkward kiss on the cheek before darting off to the counter. So many things shot through her mind; his beard was soft; he smelled great; that was brave; he liked her.

They made their coffee orders, and Leifur insisted on paying, then went back to their table.

'I was pleased you suggested this,' he said.

'Really? You didn't think it was weird?' Straightaway she was annoyed with herself for not playing it cooler.

'Not at all. I had a great time the other day.'

Did he mean the puffins or the trip back?

'Me too.'

'Can I be honest with you?'

She nodded, bracing herself in case it was honesty she

didn't want to hear.

'I've never worked with a woman before. Actually, I haven't worked with many people I wasn't related to.' He dropped his head into his hands and ran them over the back of his head. 'This is more awkward than the hello kiss,' he muttered.

'If it helps, I feel as awkward as you, I think I'm just better at hiding my feelings.'

He looked at her and laughed. 'Okay. That does help.' He took a sip of coffee and exhaled, seeming to relax.

'Is that the honest part, because I was expecting something more than that you're used to working with family. That's not a massively shocking revelation.'

'No, that's not it.' He grinned and shook his head. 'I like you Astrid, and I'm not smart enough to know whether that's because I'm not used to working with women. And who knows, maybe I'd react to any woman like that, or maybe it's you.'

Astrid took a deep breath. Did he admit he liked her?

'As a comparison, I've worked with quite a few men and never felt like this about them.' She watched his reaction.

'So I was right. Not just any woman.' He spoke softly but seemed more self-assured now. 'And you feel the same.'

She nodded. His eyes were focused on her, as if he could see inside her soul. It took her breath away for a moment as she realised this wasn't something she'd imagined. They had a connection. It had been there from the first moment they'd seen each other on the fjord, not that she'd tell anyone that, especially not Gudrun.

'I don't normally believe in fate or anything like that,' she said. 'But from the first time we saw each other, there was something. Even though all we did was wave. I mean, I wouldn't normally remember every stranger I wave to. But I remembered you.'

'And the morning when we met to go on the whale watching tour, I'd already made my mind up that I didn't need someone on the boat. I thought it was pointless. But then I saw it was you.'

She opened her mouth to point out that it hadn't felt like that, but he beat her to it.

'It took me a little while to do the about-turn in my head, but I was so happy to actually meet the beautiful woman I had seen on the fjord, looking for whales in a little wooden boat.'

They stared at each other for a minute. Astrid could hardly take in what he'd said. He'd said she was beautiful.

'To be clear, I didn't think I would actually see a whale that day,' she said.

Leifur threw his head back and laughed. 'An important clarification.'

'I'm a marine biologist. I just like being out on the water.'

He smiled, his eyes twinkling and full of understanding. 'So do I.'

15

On Saturday, Astrid was in her room, packing her cases ready to head over to her new apartment.

'Leifur's coming to help,' she said to Gudrun, who was handing her clothes out of the drawers.

'Is he? Are you two...'

'No.' Because they were something, but she wasn't sure what. She couldn't say he was her boyfriend, or that it was a relationship. And why did it need to be called anything? They were friends.

'You didn't know what I was going to say.'

'I have a fair idea.'

'What's he helping with? You have two cases.'

'Neither of us will manage to carry them up the stairs at the apartment, and now that Olafur's working, it seemed like the obvious solution.'

'I suppose so,' Gudrun said grudgingly. 'If he's helping with the cases, I could go to the shop and pick up the things we chose yesterday.'

The two of them had had a great time choosing cushions, throws, a few mugs and glasses and a couple of table lamps from Snug, hammering Gudrun's staff discount. They also went shopping for bed linen and towels since Astrid usually tried to travel light, so she bought cheap and left things behind.

'That'd be great. Then we can spend the evening together sorting everything out after Leifur's gone.' She didn't want to assume he would stay that long. And it was important to Gudrun to be involved, so Astrid didn't think too hard about how much she'd like to lie on her new sofa in Leifur's arms. There would be other evenings for that.

They got the cases down the tiny path from Gudrun's house and then wheeled one each through the streets of Reykjavik. It wasn't that far — less than a ten-minute walk and when they got there, Leifur was outside waiting for them. Astrid was ridiculously happy to see him. He was so much more in real life than how she held him in her head. His hair curled softly around his forehead and collar, and it looked as though he'd trimmed his beard. He was wearing a Lopi sweater, jeans and boots and had his hands in his pockets, and a lop-sided smile as if he was nervous.

'Hæ.' He kissed Astrid on the cheek. 'Hæ, Gudrun.' He took the case from her.

'Thanks,' Gudrun said with a nod.

'You have the keys?'

Astrid unlocked the door to the building, and the three of them went inside, taking the cases between them.

'Lead the way,' said Leifur, hefting one case onto his shoulder as if were filled with fresh air.

Gudrun, her eyes wide, shot an impressed look at her sister before she headed upstairs. Astrid couldn't help grinning. She'd had the same reaction. It was hot.

Astrid unlocked the door and stepped inside the apartment. It was just as she remembered, and the same feelings of it being exactly the right place came flooding back.

'It's very nice,' said Leifur, leaving the case in the hallway and heading into the lounge to look at the view from the balcony. You couldn't quite see the sea, but nevertheless it overlooked some of the residential streets in the city where the houses and roofs were colourful, so it was a delightful view.

When Astrid tried the door to the balcony, it was unlocked, and she stepped outside. There was a wooden bench against the wall and a small wooden table.

'Perfect spot for a morning coffee,' she said to Gudrun, who had appeared next to her.

'I'll go and get the other case,' Leifur called.

'What do you think?'

'I love it!' Gudrun said. 'It's so you, and even with the high ceilings, it feels cosy.'

'That's what I thought,' said Astrid, pleased to have her sister's agreement that it was a great place, as well as her blessing for moving out.

'Oh my god, As. The way he picked up that case. No wonder you've fallen for him.'

It was going to get tiring batting away Gudrun's constant assumptions that something was going on between her and Leifur. And now that there was something, even if she wasn't sure exactly what, perhaps it was time to give in.

'He's very fit,' said Astrid. 'It's probably from being a fisherman, hauling nets and ropes around.'

Gudrun raised an eyebrow but said nothing, which was just as well because Leifur came back with the other case.

'Shall I put these in the bedroom?'

'I'll help you,' Astrid said, taking one case herself and leading him into the bedroom.

'I should leave. Let you get settled in,' he said.

'Stay for a coffee?'

'Do you have any coffee?'

'No. But there's a coffeemaker.'

'I'll go and get coffee for us.'

'You don't have to do that.'

'I want to.' He took her hand in his. Astrid thought she might never take another breath.

'Oh, I love this room,' said Gudrun, ruining the moment.

Astrid dropped Leifur's hand, and he smiled and pointed to the door. She nodded and turned her attention to Gudrun.

'The great thing about white walls is that you can make the place yours without much effort at all. You need to put one of your new lamps in here. The one with the glass base would be perfect for a bedside light,' her sister said.

'Okay. Leifur's gone out for coffee. I think when he gets back, I'm going to go grocery shopping while you pick up the shopping from Snug. Then we can meet back here, set everything up and then open a bottle of wine.'

'That's perfect!'

Once the three of them had the coffees and pastries that Leifur returned with, they all trooped back down the stairs. Gudrun headed into the centre of town to collect the Snug haul, leaving Leifur and Astrid alone.

'Thanks for helping today.'

'No problem. Enjoy getting settled in. Your sister seems pretty excited about it.'

Astrid laughed. 'I know. I think she secretly wishes she could cut me out and decide on everything herself.'

'It's nice that she wants to help.'

'It is. I've been away so much, it's taken me a while to get used to her being an actual grown-up. It's the longest I've been back in years.'

'I used to work with my brother every day, and I'm still not sure I know him.' He shook his head. 'Anyway. I'll text you about tomorrow. Can I pick you up from here?'

'That'd be great, thank you.'

He leant in and kissed her cheek. 'Bye.'

'Bye.' Astrid watched him walk away. Even that was sexy,

and she ached with the need to be held by him. She could imagine the warmth of his woollen sweater softening the firmness of his chest that she knew was hiding underneath. She sighed. That was at least a day away, but if he didn't kiss her on the lips tomorrow, she'd have to take matters into her own hands.

Once she got back from the shop, she let herself in and found a pile of Snug bags in the hallway. Gudrun didn't have a key, so someone must have let her in. The door to the ground-floor apartment was open, and a woman came out just as Astrid was heading upstairs.

'*Hæ*, you must be Astrid. I'm Solveig, but everyone calls me Sol. Welcome to the building. Your sister asked me to let you know she's gone to pick up the bed linen.'

'Thanks for letting her in.'

'Oh, that's okay. I love that shop.' Sol nodded to the Snug bags. 'I'm in there all the time, so I knew she wasn't a burglar.'

Astrid laughed. 'No, she definitely likes giving people stuff more than taking it.'

'Hope the moving in goes well. Give us a knock if you need anything.'

Astrid took her groceries upstairs and then went back down for the Snug bags, by which time Gudrun was back and knocking on the door.

'I didn't think we bought as much as this,' she said, putting the bags she was carrying down in the hall, before dramatically collapsing onto the bottom of the stairs.

'Thank you. I would have helped if you'd waited. There's more there than I realised too.'

'I picked up a few more things that I thought you might need.'

In light of what she had just said to Sol, Astrid giggled. 'Thank you. That's very thoughtful. Move over so I can take this all upstairs.'

Gudrun recovered quickly, presumably so as not to miss out on Astrid rediscovering what they'd bought yesterday, grabbed the last of the bags and headed upstairs.

Once they'd put the groceries away, cleaned the bathroom — not because it didn't already look clean, but because Gudrun insisted you couldn't know it was clean unless you did it yourself — made the bed and unpacked the two cases, they opened a bottle of wine and took their glasses out on the balcony.

'Here,' Astrid said, handing Gudrun a cushion and taking one out for herself, as well as a woollen blanket she'd chosen at Snug.

'This is so nice,' Gudrun said. 'Olafur and I have chairs on our porch, but we never think to sit outside.'

'I didn't have any outside space in Tromsø, but it wasn't far from the harbour, so I used to sit down there sometimes.'

'I can't believe I never came to visit you.'

'Well, you'd only just moved back here from Norway when I started working there. You had your hands full starting a new job and getting things back on track with Olafur.' Astrid felt guilty that she'd never suggested it, but she and Gudrun had never been close back then. 'And things weren't the same between us then.'

'I suppose so. You know what, As? Even if you move away again, I don't want things to be distant between us. I've loved being around each other all the time again.'

'Me too.' Astrid shifted along until she was closer to Gudrun and pulled the blanket around both of them. 'Anyway, we have the whole summer.'

'I have a feeling you'll be splitting your time between me and someone else.'

'Don't worry about that. Any guy I'm with…'

'Any guy?' Gudrun teased.

'Needs to be lovely and easy-going like Olafur. Willing to hang out with me and my sister, like he is.'

'Based on this morning, I reckon Leifur might be like that. He's quiet, but we can bring him out of his shell.'

'Give him a chance,' Astrid said, laughing.

'Don't worry, I won't scare him off. People love me. Oh, I met your neighbour, Solveig.'

'Yes, she said. Maybe I should have a housewarming party. I could invite her, and I think she has a partner.'

'She does. And you could invite Leifur and the rest of the gang.'

A housewarming party was a great excuse to invite Leifur. And although at the back of her mind she worried about commandeering Gudrun's friends as her own, she enjoyed spending time with them.

'You think they'd come?'

'You're going to be working with half of them. Of course they'll come. Besides, it'll help you out in case the neighbours are boring. And I want to see how Leifur behaves in a social situation.'

'I don't think that's necessary.'

'It is,' Gudrun said. 'I need to make sure he's good enough for you. Today he showed his chivalrous side, and he won some extra points for carrying a suitcase in the sexiest way possible. But will he have your back in a social situation? That's the next test.'

And although Astrid laughed at Gudrun for being too serious about testing Leifur, she couldn't deny she was interested to see how it was going to go.

16

The housewarming was a welcome relief from working on *Brimfaxi* every day. Not that she wasn't enjoying it, but there were limits to what she could do without going over and over the same things. Leifur had more to do on the practical side of things, whereas she was helping with purchasing everything they needed, from weatherproof suits for the guests, to sick bags, to supplies for the galley. It was the best way to get to know the vessel though, and by the end of the week, she knew what Leifur was referring to when he said things like the "foredeck port-side cleat" and was pleased that her limited experience of working on research vessels had stood her in good stead.

When she'd left the apartment this morning, she'd met the woman from upstairs. She was in her fifties, Astrid guessed.

She introduced herself. 'I've taken on the apartment in the middle for six months.'

'Nice to meet you. I'm Ingibjörg. Are you from Reykjavik?'

'Yes, although I've only been back a few weeks. I've been living in Norway for the past few years. I'm having a get-together tonight at my place, if you'd like to come? Sol from downstairs and her partner are coming, and my sister and some friends from work.'

'That sounds great. What sort of time?'

'Around seven.'

Astrid was pleased that she'd run with Gudrun's idea of having a party. It was nice to know her neighbours, and it was a good excuse to invite Leifur over.

She called Gudrun and asked her to extend the invitation to everyone.

'Brilliant. I'm pretty sure Jonas, Rachel, Siggi and Iris will be up for it. The others aren't around at the moment.'

Jonas was her boss, and Leifur's, so it was good he and Rachel could come, and after meeting Iris briefly at the bar, they had enough in common for Astrid to feel like she could easily be a friend if they had the time to get to know one another.

'Looking forward to the party?' Leifur asked her as they sat on deck eating their lunch together. It wasn't warm, but it wasn't raining, and they'd taken to sitting outside rather than in the galley whenever they could since so much of the time they were working below deck.

'Yes. I only met my upstairs neighbour this morning for the first time, but she's coming, and Sol and Thor from downstairs. I think it'll be good.'

'You don't have any friends from school here?'

'No. I lost touch with most people when I went to university, and my best friend lives in Australia now, so we keep in touch but hardly ever see each other. How about you?'

'I grew up in Hafnarfjörður, and it was much smaller than it is now. As soon as anyone was old enough, they came to live in Reykjavik because it was livelier. I'd always helped out on the boat, even when I was still at school, so it felt like I was the only one left.'

'You must have been close to your brother then because of that?'

'Not really.'

'Me and Gudrun weren't close growing up because of the age difference. It felt like she was a little kid when I left for university. We had nothing in common then.'

'But it's different now?'

'Yes. It's taken me a while to catch up with the fact that the age difference has disappeared. In fact, most of the time she's so bossy you'd think she was the oldest.'

She and Leifur finished working on the boat around four o'clock.

'I'll head home and be back later for the party,' he said.

'Okay. Don't be late. I don't want to be on my own.' She knew it was ridiculous, but she was worried about a person she didn't know very well arriving first and then having nothing to say to them.

'I'll come early then,' he said, grinning. 'I wouldn't want you to have to deal with your friends alone.'

'That makes me sound like a crazy person. They're not my friends yet. That's the problem.'

'Have a glass of wine before anyone gets there to take the edge off. You'll be fine.'

Astrid decided that was good advice, so by the time Leifur arrived — first, she was halfway into her first drink.

'Here,' he said, handing her a bottle of wine and kissing her on the cheek at the same time. 'Am I first?'

'Yes. And thank you for that.'

'The place looks great,' he said, walking into the lounge with his hands in his pockets.

He was wearing a dark grey sweater and jeans with brown boots. Overall, it was a great look on him and made her stomach feel strange, in a good way. His hair was combed to one side rather than being tousled like normal, and even his beard looked... tidier.

'It's kind of the same, but I got carried away in Snug with

Gudrun's staff discount.'

'It feels like your place,' he said, turning to face her.

'Can I get you a drink?' She felt slightly flustered at the way he was looking at her, and the fact that he looked so polished compared to normal made her feel less at ease with him.

'Do you have beer?'

She opened the fridge and handed him a beer and then rummaged in the drawer for a bottle opener.

'Have you sat out on the balcony much?'

'Only on the first night. It's not warm enough in the evenings yet.'

'True.'

Why had she asked him to be here first? This was excruciating. How could it be so different from every day on the boat?

Thankfully, there was a knock at the door, and Sol and Thor joined them. Astrid busied herself with sorting drinks out for them while Leifur chatted to them and then everyone else arrived.

'So you're staying for the summer?' Iris asked her.

'Yes. It's a relief to have something solid for a few months.'

'You don't think you'll stay here long term?'

'Honestly, I don't know what I'm going to do. At least the tour boat work is linked to my career. Why did you decide to stay? Was it because of Siggi?'

'Kind of. I was working for a geology lab in the UK, but my boss and I didn't see eye to eye. I thought I'd be hard pressed to find another position that allowed me the freedom I had to pursue my research, but when I came here to study the latest eruption, a spot opened up at the Icelandic Met Office. By then, Siggi and I were together, but I can't honestly say whether I'd have chosen him over my career.' She looked over her shoulder to see where Siggi was, then laughed. 'He knows, but I don't like to remind him too often.'

'After so many years, I can't imagine what I'd do if I couldn't find another research post. I don't feel like I've finished yet.' There was more to discover and more to research, and in her heart of hearts she knew that wasn't going to be possible if she stayed in Iceland, however much it had started to feel like home.

'I completely understand,' said Iris. 'Keep looking. You never know what will come up. And in the meantime, enjoy the summer with that lovely boat captain.' She nodded to Leifur, who was chatting to Jonas and Olafur.

'There's nothing going on,' Astrid said. It was hard to see how there could be when things had been so awkward earlier. Perhaps that's what it would always be like if they weren't on the boat.

'Maybe not, but I don't think that'll be the case for much longer. Have you seen the way he looks at you?'

Two glasses of wine had softened Astrid's inhibitions. 'He smells amazing,' she said to Iris in a low voice.

'How do you know that?'

Astrid told Iris about the puffin trip.

'I can't believe you two haven't got it together yet.'

'I'm not into a quick fling, and I don't think he is either. And I might only be here for the summer.'

'He'll take the summer, I'd bet good money on that. Be upfront with him and be honest with each other about how you feel and no one will get hurt.'

It was good advice. Perhaps she'd speak to Leifur after the tours had launched, once they were into a normal routine and the worst of the work was behind them. After their meeting in the coffee shop, she knew the feelings she had for him were mutual but she also knew that they were both out of practice when it came to relationships. And how did the fact that they like each other translate into something more than that?

'Why don't you tell him you like him?' Gudrun said, coming from nowhere. 'He must already know if you look at him like that all the time.'

'He knows,' Astrid said

'What are you waiting for, then? Life's too short to be wasting time with stolen glances across the room like you're both teenagers in unrequited love.'

'It's not the right time, that's all. I'll wait until we start the tours properly when he's under less pressure.'

'It might help with the pressure,' Gudrun said.

At around ten-thirty, people drifted off, with most of them having work in the morning. When Gudrun and Olafur left, Astrid thought that was everyone, and then Leifur came out of the bathroom.

'Oh!'

'Sorry, I didn't mean to scare you,' he said, laughing as she stood there with her hand on her chest.

'I thought everyone had gone,' she said, laughing herself.

'Well, I was just about to.'

'You're not driving home, are you?'

'No, I'll stay on *Brimfaxi*. I'll have the coffee brewed by the time you get there in the morning.'

'Do you want a coffee before you go?'

'That'd be great. Maybe a decaf?'

Astrid made coffee and took it over to the sofa where Leifur was sitting, lounging in the corner, his ankle resting on his opposite knee.

'I enjoyed that more than I thought I would,' she said.

'Me too. I'm not great at small talk normally, but those guys are easy to get along with. Did you know Thor owns a bar down by the harbour? It's where Ned Nokes tried out his stuff when he went solo.'

'I didn't know that. So Jonas and Olafur must know Thor already?'

'Yes. Small world, huh?'

'Tiny,' Astrid agreed. 'Did you ever think of leaving?'

'I considered it when we lost the business. I could have gone overseas and fished somewhere else, but I think I'm too old to start again somewhere else.'

'You're not,' Astrid said.

'You've done it plenty of times, I'm guessing?' She nodded. 'It's different when it's something you're used to. I've never done it. I never even left to go to university. I'll never leave Iceland.'

Astrid was surprised he could be so certain about that. She couldn't imagine knowing or planning to stay in the same place for the rest of her life when there was so much to see everywhere else.

'You don't want to see the world?'

'When you're brought up with expectations about your future, you tend not to think about what you might be missing. I knew I was going to be a fisherman from, well, forever. I knew I'd make no more money than I needed to house and look after myself, certainly not enough for holidays overseas, and I was okay with that because it was the only option open to me. To be where you are, you would have been brought up to know that the world was yours for the taking, that you could do whatever you wanted.'

'That's true.' She felt bad that she'd assumed that was the case for everyone.

'I don't mind. It's all my parents knew because they were both from a fishing community, and that's how it is. I mean, not always now, but I have a strong sense of loyalty to my father and the legacy he and his father and grandfather left behind. That's what drives me.'

'It's very special to have such a strong connection to your family.'

'It is. It's different now because of what happened to the

family business. I've had to come to terms with it being lost on my watch. But the fact that I don't have kids makes it easier. I'd feel like I'd taken their future away if I did.'

'But you didn't want a bigger change for yourself when you had the chance?'

He shook his head. 'I don't think there is anywhere more beautiful than Iceland. And this way I still get to be on the sea every day and close to my mother. That's all that matters.'

17

Almost two weeks later, Leifur and Astrid were on *Brimfaxi* early in the morning preparing for the first whale watching tour. It was for friends and family only, so they could check they were ready for anything before they started for real in two days.

'Lifejackets.'

'Check,' said Astrid.

'Weatherproof suits.'

'Check.'

Leifur appreciated her patience with him. She was going along with it even though they'd done exactly the same checks yesterday and no one had touched anything since. But she knew he was anxious, and it helped him feel as if he was in control of something by checking the things that could be checked. A lot.

'First-aid kit.'

'Check. Weather forecast?'

His head snapped up from the list he was reading before he realised she was trying to move things along. 'Sorry.'

'It's okay. Remember today is going to flag up anything we haven't thought of. But we do know we have everything on that list.'

The days they'd spent equipping the boat had been a crash course in getting to know each other, and it had gone pretty well. The biggest lesson Leifur had learned was that he was used to being in control and had a hard time letting go of anything to do with the boat.

He sat on the nearest bench and felt his shoulders drop. 'The weather looks okay. We're expecting winds of ten knots, which will give us reasonably calm seas. We might run into some rain in about an hour.'

'That's good. It'll give the new gear a good test.' They had racks of all-in-one waterproofs for guests to borrow.

'And if there's anything wrong with it, it's too late to do anything about it before we start for real in two days.'

'They're the best ones you can buy. The same as the ones we wore when we went on the tour with the other company. And it's still better to find out today than in two or three days' time.' Astrid sat next to him and rubbed his thigh soothingly.

Leifur would never have said he was an anxious person, but these past few weeks had been stressful. There was so much more riding on this than whether tourists saw a whale while they were in Iceland. This was his life. If he couldn't make a success of this, what was he going to do?

'Hey,' Astrid said softly. 'Let's take a break and get a coffee from Rust.'

'We have coffee here.' The galley was fully stocked, ready to serve guests with hot drinks and snacks.

'No, we're getting off the boat before you make me count the lifejackets again.' She pulled his hand until he stood up. 'Come on, it'll do you good to have a break so you're fresh when everyone gets here.'

'Okay, you win,' he said, thinking that over the past two weeks he'd also learned that he'd do almost anything for Astrid. She was easy company and, aside from today when his anxiety levels were so high that nothing could touch them, a very soothing presence.

They walked to Rust, one of the restaurants that sat along the harbour side, ordered coffees and sat on a bench overlooking the sea.

'Feel better?'

'I'll feel better when today is over.'

'Oh, come on.' She leant into him. 'Aren't you excited to show off the boat to everyone?'

'I'm worried about what my mother will think of the changes.' He had his mother's blessing, but it still mattered that she thought he'd done justice to *Brimfaxi* and his father's legacy. But talking about it wasn't helping. 'Are you looking forward to seeing your parents?'

'Yes,' she said emphatically. 'I haven't seen them since I've been back, and it's the first time I've been home since they moved out of the city. It's strange not having them around. They're staying with Gudrun and Olafur tonight. I was going to ask, would you like to come out to dinner with us?'

'You don't want to wait and see how today goes? You might be glad to see the back of me.'

'What do you think is going to happen today, Leifur?' She sounded impatient. 'It sounds like you're expecting a disaster of some sort.'

He shrugged. It felt like impending doom, but he wasn't sure why.

'Look.' Astrid pulled on his arm and he swivelled slightly. 'All we have to do today is take some people who already like us on a boat ride. You just have to drive your boat out there.' She jabbed her finger at the sea. 'And if we don't find a whale, no one will mind.'

'They will when we start for real.'

'Let's concentrate on today. It's not about the whales today, okay? It's about seeing if we can entertain people on the boat without killing them.'

He couldn't help but laugh. 'I think we can manage that.'

'Of course we can.'

'Thank you.' He reached for her hand and squeezed it. 'And thank you for the dinner invitation, but perhaps another time. I'll have to drop my mother home afterwards, anyway.' He already knew that even if things went well today, he wouldn't be in the mood to charm Astrid's parents. He'd be tired and would need to be alone to overthink every aspect of the day in peace.

'Okay. Another time. Come on then, we'd better get back. I want to get the boiler going so I can make hot drinks to welcome everyone on board.'

They were both on deck ready to greet their guests just as Gudrun and Olafur arrived with Astrid and Gudrun's parents.

'Hæ, Mamma, Pabbi!' Astrid called, waving at them with a huge grin on her face.

'Astrid, you look wonderful,' said her mother. 'Look at the colour in your cheeks.'

'Oh, Mamma,' Astrid said, hugging her parents. 'This is Leifur, captain of the *Brimfaxi*.'

'And Astrid's boyfriend,' Gudrun chipped in.

'Gudrun!'

'Oh, don't mind your sister,' her mother said. 'It's nice to meet you Leifur.'

'Welcome on board. It's a pleasure to meet you both.' He shook their hands and stood aside while Astrid instructed them on what to do next.

'Well, this is exciting,' said Jonas, who was the next to arrive with Rachel. Leifur shook hands with Jonas as they both climbed on board.

'Welcome. Astrid will show you what to do to get ready.'

'It all looks amazing, Leifur. Congratulations.'

The praise from Jonas was heartfelt and a salve to Leifur's nerves. 'Thank you.'

A few more people arrived who Leifur didn't know but who were friends or business acquaintances of Jonas. He relaxed as everyone greeted him with wide smiles, their excitement building into a palpable buzz. Then he spotted his mother walking along the quay. She waved a hand once she saw he'd seen her.

'Oh, Leifur.' She had tears in her eyes, and for a moment his heart clenched in horror until she smiled and put a hand on his cheek. '*Brimfaxi* looks wonderful. Her fresh paint makes it look as if she's left the hard work and had a makeover ready for a new adventure. The start of her new life. Just like you.'

Leifur pulled Peta into his arms and buried his face in her shoulder, feeling as if he were five years old again. '*Takk*, Mamma.'

'Now,' she said, swiping under her eyes with her forefingers, 'are you going to find me some whales?'

'I hope so.'

With Peta on board, Jonas gave the nod that everyone he was expecting to show up was here, and Leifur went to find Astrid, who was helping people with their suits.

'We're ready to go. Help me with the ropes, and then you can start the safety briefing.'

'Okay.' She picked up a suit and held it out for his mother. 'I think this one will be a good fit for you.'

'Thank you. You're one of Leifur's colleagues?'

'Mamma, this is Astrid,' said Leifur. 'We'll see you soon. We have to get started.'

'Nice to meet you,' Astrid said, following Leifur.

'Call me Peta!'

'Your mother is lovely.'

'Thank you. Here is the headset. Come on, you take the

ropes off and throw them onto the dock like we practised.' He could hear himself being curt, but there was no time to have a cosy chat about how nice his mother was. They had work to do.

He climbed into the wheelhouse and started the engines. He turned to see Astrid waiting for his signal, as they had planned. He raised his hand, and she unhooked the two ropes that were left, the one at the bow first, followed by the stern. With just two of them on the boat, the other lines had already been taken off by Leifur once everyone was on board.

As Leifur manoeuvred *Brimfaxi* towards the harbour entrance, Astrid stood on the bow and started her safety briefing. The headset that she wore transmitted wirelessly to speakers all over the boat so that wherever a guest was, they could hear her. He listened, the combination of being on their way, and the soothing sound of Astrid explaining to the guests what to do in the event of someone falling overboard, relaxed him so that when they passed through the yellow buoys that marked the entrance to the harbour, he actually started to enjoy himself.

The plan was to head out into Faxaflói Bay. Astrid would spend the first part of the trip making refreshments for guests before going onto the deck to look for signs of whale activity. The hope was that the guests would join her on deck, but if they preferred to stay inside, the view from the new windows was good enough that they wouldn't miss out if there was something to see.

From his years as a fisherman, Leifur knew the classic signs to look out. One of them was birds. Seabirds that were gathering together in a particular area were a sign that whales were around. The whales made circles of bubbles that pushed fish up to the surface so that they could eat them, and the birds could benefit from that too. Also, the telltale vapour releasing from a whale's blowhole could be seen from quite a distance.

Leifur had his eyes on the horizon, scanning as he always did, but this time trying to pay attention to spotting blows. He was surprised when Astrid came in with a coffee for him.

'Thanks,' he said. 'How's it going down there?'

'Good. Everyone's kitted up and heading outside. I've left the galley as a help-yourself. Do you think that's okay?'

'Sure. It's only coffee and cake.'

'That's what I thought. Any sign of anything yet?'

She leant in front of him to peer out of the window, and he resisted the urge to touch her hair. It was glossy and fell from her shoulder, brushing past him so he caught the scent of something sweet.

'Nothing yet.' Though he'd not been concentrating since she came up here.

'Okay. I'm going to start.'

'Good luck.'

She grinned at him and pushed the headset on, then took her hair and pulled it into a bun with a twist of her hands. 'Thanks.' Then she leant in and kissed his cheek, turning and leaving before he could say anything.

He took a deep breath and then settled in to listen to her commentary. She began by explaining the signs to look out for, the four Bs: birds and blows, which he already knew about, and bubbles and boats. The bubbles signalled that a whale was surfacing, and boats because where there were tour boats, you hoped there were whales.

The guests were gathering around the edge of the deck.

'I can see a blow at two o'clock,' said Astrid. 'I will use the clock numbers to direct you, with twelve being the front of the boat and six the back.'

Leifur was impressed by how well Astrid was coming across. She sounded as if she'd done this countless times before. He watched at the spot she'd said and saw the next blow for himself, changing the heading of the boat starboard to head in that direction.

'There are minkes approaching from five o'clock,' said Astrid, although he wasn't sure how she could tell. 'We have two individuals at twelve o'clock.'

Some of the guests headed up to the bow, phones in their hands, while most of them stayed on the main deck.

'Minkes are fast. These won't be with us for long,' Astrid said. 'I can see a blow at nine o'clock, about five hundred metres from us.'

Leifur turned the boat slightly in that direction. He hadn't realised that Astrid's scouting and relaying what she could see to the guests would help him out too. He thought he'd have to rely on looking for fish on the sonar as a starting point.

'The whale we have at twelve o'clock is a humpback. Each humpback whale has distinctive markings on the underside of its tail, and they're individual, like fingerprints. There's a library of known individuals kept by the Marine and Freshwater Research Institute, so if you get a good photo of a tail today, they could tell you information about that whale if it's already known to them.'

The humpback appeared ahead of them, and as Astrid carried on with her commentary, Leifur received a radio message on an open channel from another tour boat letting him know the location of a group of four humpback whales about two kilometres from their position. He wasn't sure what to make of that.

'How's it going?' Jonas appeared at the door of the wheelhouse. 'You guys are doing a great job so far.'

'And we have whales already,' said Leifur.

'And a boat of happy guests. Was that a radio message from another tour boat saying they'd found whales at another location?'

'Yes, we have to keep in radio contact with other vessels as part of the code of conduct, but I wasn't expecting them to share information like that.'

'I wondered if that might happen. On northern lights tours, we often share information on where the best sightings are, especially if it's cloudy and hard to find a clear spot. I wasn't sure they'd do the same on the whale watching. That's great.'

'It is,' Leifur agreed. 'I thought it'd be more competitive than that.'

'We all want the same thing. By the time the customers are on the boat, they've spent their money with us, and we have to meet their expectations.'

'And I guess one day we might find the whales and another day someone else might,' Leifur said.

'Exactly. It's bigger than us. If every visitor to Iceland leaves having seen what they came to see, we're all doing a great job.'

18

When they'd been out at sea for over an hour and seen countless whales, Astrid announced to the guests that they were heading back to Reykjavik and it was the last chance to look at the whales. She was exhilarated but exhausted. It had taken a lot of energy this morning to help ease Leifur's anxieties while feeling just as anxious herself. But knowing that there was more at stake for him helped her to push her own feelings aside, and concentrating on keeping him calm had taken her mind off her own worries. Being responsible for the commentary had felt daunting, but she'd loved it. As soon as she spotted the first blow, she felt right at home. She could just as easily have been on a research vessel, and the details she knew about the whales came flowing out naturally. A couple of guests came over to her and asked questions, which she took as a good sign that she was keeping them interested in the search.

'Great job, Astrid,' said Jonas, coming over as she took her headset off. 'You and Leifur have an excellent system set up here. Letting him know where to head and telling us where to look, it's very clever.'

'Thanks.' They hadn't planned that at all, but she had noticed Leifur steering in the direction she was spotting whale activity, and he got as close as he safely could to give everyone some magnificent views. 'I think it was a pretty good first attempt.'

'I think so too. I think you need another pair of hands, though. If there's an emergency while you're at sea, pulling you away from the other guests, it's not ideal. I'll find someone who can man the galley while you're at sea and help with the kitting out so you and Leifur can concentrate on the safety side of things and the whales,' said Jonas.

'That'd be great, thank you.' Astrid wondered what Leifur would think about that idea given that he was less than enthusiastic about her being on board to begin with. But it made sense. With Leifur in the wheelhouse while she was looking for whales, they could do with another person to monitor things.

'Astrid, that was wonderful,' said her mother, giving her a hug.

'Incredible,' said her father, who was a man of few words perhaps because he struggled to get a word in when Gudrun was around, but he was beaming with pride at her and it felt amazing to share what she loved with her family.

Once the guests had taken their weatherproof suits off, they were almost back in the harbour. Astrid got ready to throw the ropes around the mooring posts. It was the most nerve-wracking part of the entire tour because the guests were all on deck ready to disembark. She'd practised over and over for the past few days, throwing the loops of rope over the mooring posts at the bow and stern until Leifur stopped the engines and could help secure the lines himself. Now, as she waited for him to pull alongside the dock, she was sure she was going to miss. Of course it had happened plenty of times, and Leifur had assured her it didn't matter too much. There was time for a couple more attempts before *Brimfaxi* would drift past the point of no return, and he would have to switch the engines to reverse to compensate. She would die if that happened today. In the event, she looped the stern rope over the mooring post on the first attempt, and everyone on deck cheered, which may have been why she needed two attempts for the bow rope.

Leifur jumped from the boat onto the dock and tied off the rest of the lines, then he joined Astrid to say goodbye to their guests as they disembarked.

'That was wonderful, thank you,' Astrid's mother said to Leifur. Her eyes were sparkling, and she gave her daughter a knowing look as she turned to her. 'We'll see you back at Gudrun's.'

'Very impressive,' her father said, shaking Leifur's hand before he briefly hugged Astrid. 'Very proud,' he whispered in her ear.

It brought a tear to her eye. She'd never done anything before that had made her parents say they were proud of her. Of course, she'd known it when they were at various key moments, like when she got her degree, but this felt different. Maybe it meant more to them because they'd been part of today. They'd been able to see her in action in a way they never had before.

'Awesome, As,' said Gudrun, hugging her.

'You'll be giving the rest of the team a run for their money,' said Olafur, grinning at Leifur. 'Great job.'

The other guests left, saying how much they'd enjoyed it. Astrid and Leifur were grinning at each other from either side of the gangway, neither one of them able to believe that it had gone so well.

'Have you ever had a day that has turned around quite so dramatically?' Astrid said to him. She enjoyed seeing him happy. The anxiety had lifted off him, and he looked like a different man. She was sorry now that she had to leave to have dinner with her family because all she wanted to do was dissect the day with him and revel in the success they'd made of it.

'I can't believe it went as well as it did,' he said. 'Your directions were spot on. I knew exactly where to head.'

'I knew you realised you could do that! I can't believe we never thought of that before.'

'And the other tour companies shared the locations of where they had sightings over the radio.'

'Did they? Did you share ours?'

'Yes, once I realised what was going on. Jonas said it's common practice with the northern lights excursions.'

'Amazing!'

'I wish we could go and celebrate,' he said softly. 'I couldn't have got to where we are now without you.'

'We did it together.' She wished more than anything that it was just the two of them on the boat, but she saw Leifur's mother waiting on the bench around the edge of the deck. 'What do we need to do before we leave?'

'You don't need to stay. Go for dinner with your family. It won't take me long to tidy up.'

'No, your mother's waiting. We'll do it together.'

'I'll be ten minutes, Mamma,' he called.

She raised a hand, waving him away with a smile. 'I can wait,' she called back.

All they needed to do was tidy the suits, empty the bins and clean the galley. Astrid headed up to the deck with a bag of rubbish while Leifur checked everything was off. His mother got up and headed over to Astrid.

'I haven't seen Leifur happy like this for a long time,' she said. 'You two have done something wonderful with this old boat. Given her a new lease of life.'

'I'm just along for the ride. Leifur's done all the hard work to get her ready.'

'The hardest part for him was deciding not to be a

fisherman anymore. Thinking he was letting his father down. I wasn't sure he'd find his way.'

Peta was sharing more with her than Leifur had, and that made Astrid feel uncomfortable, but she liked Peta and didn't want her to think she'd said anything wrong.

'It was a big decision to change the boat, but I think he's pleased with how she turned out.'

'She's certainly very smart,' said Peta, scanning the deck appreciatively. 'And I think the two of you will have a great success on your hands.'

'I'm only here for the summer,' said Astrid.

'You might love it and decide to stay,' Peta said, laughing.

'I loved today,' Astrid admitted. 'It didn't feel like work at all.'

'That is the best kind of work. And my boy needs more of that in his life. He's had more than his fair share of tough days.'

'Mamma, are you telling Astrid all of my secrets?' Leifur was trying to frown at his mother, but since he was still smiling, he was doing a poor job of pretending to be cross with her.

'Of course not. I was saying how happy you look, and how wonderful today has been. I can hardly believe it was your first run. It was incredible. You're very knowledgeable, Astrid.'

'Thank you.'

'Mamma, here are the keys to my truck. I will only be a minute behind you.'

Peta took the keys. 'It's been a pleasure to meet you, Astrid. I hope we cross paths again soon.'

'Me too.'

Leifur waited until Peta was out of earshot. 'So we can't talk endlessly about how amazing we are tonight. Can we tomorrow?'

Astrid nodded. All she wanted to do was stay here, with Leifur. Today had changed things between them. She knew she wanted to be with him, and it was going to be difficult to wait until tomorrow to see him again, when maybe the high from today had worn off.

'Meet here? At eleven?'

'Perfect,' she said.

Dinner with her parents was great, and she wouldn't have missed it for the world, it happened so rarely these days. But Leifur was at the forefront of her mind the whole evening. His expression when they'd been seeing everyone off the boat, hearing what everyone thought about the tour, it melted her heart. She wanted that for him every day of the week. She was realising that she wanted him every day of the week too. And now that the first tour was out of the way, the pressure was off and the time they spent together could be about something other than setting the boat up.

'Hey, As. What are you daydreaming about?' Gudrun was sitting next to her and shoved her arm gently as if she were twelve years old again.

'Nothing. Just thinking about today.'

'Astrid, can we come to see your new flat tomorrow?' their mother asked. 'Gudrun said it's beautiful.'

'I have to work in the morning.' Meeting Leifur was work related, but if she said that's what she was doing, everyone would read too much into it. 'Why don't you come for dinner?'

'We'd love to.'

'So would we,' said Gudrun.

'I don't think we'll all fit around my tiny table. You two can come another day.'

'Fair enough,' said Gudrun. 'Did you invite Leifur tonight?'

'Yes. He had to take his mother home.' Thank goodness,

because who knows what kind of inquisition he'd be facing now? Astrid hadn't realised quite how forthright her sister was. Perhaps she'd not noticed before, when she wasn't the object of her interest.

'Is there more to things with Leifur than being work colleagues?' Ah, perhaps Gudrun got it from their mother.

'Maybe,' Astrid said honestly. 'I like him.'

Gudrun scoffed. 'I saw you both mooning at each other when we got off the boat. It's more than that, and he feels the same way.'

'We were on a high from how well things had gone, that's all. Nothing's happened between us at all.' She almost said "yet" at the end of that sentence. Because she was certain that something would. These past two weeks, they'd both been too focused on the job in hand to let anything derail them from getting the tours up and running. Then today, when the tour was over, Astrid had an overwhelming urge to throw herself into Leifur's arms, and she probably would have done if his mother hadn't been there. It was as if they both knew that today marked the end of one thing and the beginning of something else. Gudrun was right about one thing, because Astrid had seen Leifur's face and thought the same. Yes, they were both elated because the day had been a success, but that had just set a fire under what was already beginning to smoulder between them. Hopefully, in the morning she'd find that Leifur was feeling exactly the same.

19

Leifur called into Bakarameistarinn on his way into Reykjavik to meet Astrid. They were a small chain of bakeries that had only recently opened in Hafnarfjörður, and he was glad of the excuse to buy some of their sugar buns. With the pastries secure on the front seat of his truck, he headed to the Old Harbour to meet Astrid.

On the way to his mother's house yesterday, he'd got the impression that she was gently persuading him to pursue Astrid. Peta had mentioned more than once how incredible her commentary had been, and did he know whether she was planning on staying in Reykjavik for good? He didn't know, and he told Peta that, pointing out that they were work colleagues and not in the habit of having heart-to-hearts about what direction their lives might go in next. What he didn't share with his mother was that he very much wanted to know all of those things about Astrid. Now that yesterday had gone well, it was as if everything had become clear over the course of the day, and he could finally see what was what. Not that he hadn't noticed Astrid before. Of course, he had. The trip back from Andriðsey Island had stayed with him. The way she'd felt, her back gently pressed against his chest. Now, in the post-tour glow, having forgotten how stressed out he'd been for weeks, he wondered why he hadn't taken one hand off the wheel and looped it around her waist to pull her closer to him. He could have nuzzled into her neck and properly breathed in the scent that had been teasing his senses for that entire journey.

He parked the truck, interrupting his thoughts. He smiled to himself because that was probably a good thing. They were work colleagues first. He had to remember that. Picking the bag of pastries up, he set off towards *Brimfaxi*, looking forward to seeing her as much as he was Astrid. The bright sunshine glinted off the water, making it look inviting. If it weren't for the fact that there was still snow to be seen on the mountains, and it was cold enough to need a coat or at least a thick sweater, it could be a summer's day.

Astrid was already on the boat, on deck. She stood up when she saw him and waved. Her hair was down, making her look more relaxed and off-duty than he'd seen her before.

'I bought buns,' he said, holding up the bag.

'It really is a celebration,' she said. She was smiling at him, but he could see there was something else she wanted to say.

'Astrid…' He reached out a hand and took her fingers in his, hoping that the gesture could help her understand what he wanted to say but couldn't find the words to. He'd never been any good at talking about his feelings. Especially not to women.

She took a step closer, lifting their hands so that they were resting on his chest, between them. He could hardly catch his breath. Her eyes were searching his, and he knew in that instant exactly what she was trying to say because it was the same as him.

Now he knew, he bent his head and moved towards her, heading for a kiss but pausing just before he landed on her lips, in case he'd read it all wrong. But there was nothing in Astrid's eyes that told him to stop. Her eyelids fluttered closed, and she brought her lips to meet his in the most glorious moment of his life.

They both laughed shyly when they pulled apart.

'I wasn't sure you felt the same,' he said.

'I thought I'd wait until we got yesterday out of the way. I wasn't sure you were in the market for a kiss or anything before now.'

'You thought about it before now?' As if he hadn't. He just wanted to hear every detail about how she'd arrived at the same place as him.

'On the way back from the puffins. I kept thinking you were going to dip your head down and kiss my neck.'

'I thought about it.'

'You did?' She grinned at him, and he could feel himself doing the same.

'I thought it was too soon. We didn't know each other very well, and I wanted it to be more than a hookup.' It was only now he realised that's why he hadn't acted sooner.

'It would never have been that. You're not like that. I sense you're an all-in kind of man.'

'I don't know.' He felt bashful, and might have blushed.

'Well, I'm very happy to have had to wait. It's all the more special because of yesterday. It felt like we did that together.'

'We did do it together.' Leifur took the hand that was still clasped to his on his chest and moved it around to sit on his hip before letting go and taking her in his arms. Properly. She fitted into his embrace as if they'd been made for each other. As if they'd wrapped their arms around each other so many times before that they knew exactly where to hold. It was perfect. Until, in classic Icelandic style, the weather turned, and it started to rain.

'Come on,' Leifur said, handing Astrid the bag of buns so that he could unlock the door. Once they were in the galley, they both took their coats off, and Leifur made coffee.

'Do you think this is a mistake because we work together?' Astrid asked.

'No, it's no one's business. It won't affect our work. Are you worried about it?'

'It's more than... I don't know, a summer fling.'

'It is for me too.' He sat down next to her, handed her a bun from the bag and a coffee and decided that it was time to be honest with her. 'Astrid, I haven't had a girlfriend before. Obviously, I've been with women, but no one I felt anything for other than a brief physical attraction.' As he said this out loud, he half expected Astrid to pick up her coat and leave, thinking she had just kissed someone who had something fundamentally wrong with them.

'But why? You're attractive and a lovely person.'

'Thank you.' He smiled at her and squeezed her hand before taking a bite of his own bun to give him a minute to think. 'Fishing isn't a great career if you want to have a social life too, so it's hard to meet people who understand.'

He took a breath before continuing because this was the hard part. The part he'd never said out loud to anyone before, mostly because it had taken him an awfully long time to realise it himself. 'My father was lost at sea one night when we were out fishing. The weather was bad, and one moment he was next to me on deck and the next moment he was gone.'

'Leifur, I'm so sorry.' She moved closer to him and reached up and stroked his hair in a soothing way that felt more intimate than the kiss they'd shared.

'My mother was devastated. We all were. And I knew then that I couldn't fall in love with anyone and let that happen to them.'

'You wouldn't let yourself love anyone? But what if you'd already met the person for you and you let them go?'

'You're the person for me, Astrid. I have never felt like this about anyone. There was the odd woman that I liked, and I told myself it couldn't go anywhere, but I never liked them like I like you. Maybe it's because you love the sea too, I don't know. But I feel lucky to have met you now that I'm not fishing anymore because it would have been the hardest thing in the world to walk away from you.'

'I know I said this before, and it's ridiculous, but I knew there was something between us when I saw you standing on the beach in Hafnarfjörður. Then when I saw you again, it felt like fate or something.'

He patted his legs, inviting her to sit on his lap. She did, straddling his thighs and facing him, arms looped around his neck. 'So you think this is it for you too?'

She nodded, but there was a hint of reservation in her eyes. 'I only planned to be here until I got another job. I already know the summer with you isn't going to be long enough, but I don't know what will happen after that.'

'You don't want to work on *Brimfaxi* forever?' He made it sound as if he were teasing her, but deep down he meant it.

'I can't abandon my career for you, Leifur,' she whispered, nuzzling into his neck.

She was going to break his heart. She'd leave him, and he'd be heartbroken.

'I won't ask you to do that. Let's give ourselves the summer with no expectations.' It was not what he wanted to give, but he got the feeling it was all Astrid could give, so he was willing to go along with it. He'd worry about it at the end of the summer.

They began kissing again. He felt Astrid tugging at his waistband to untuck his top, and he gasped as her hands found his skin.

'Your hands are cold,' he said, pulling them out and cupping them in his own before breathing warmth onto them. Her eyes were on his as she put them back exactly where they had been and he realised it hadn't been the cold making him gasp. Her touch was like a shot of electricity, giving him the sudden certainty that this was nothing ordinary.

'God, you're beautiful,' he said, losing himself in another kiss as he began to explore her in the same way.

'Leifur…' She dropped her head back, inviting him to continue. Decisively, he picked her up, and she wrapped her legs around his waist.

'Where are we going?'

'The forward berth.'

Leifur opened the door at the back of the galley and ducked through it, still carrying Astrid, who felt as light as a feather to him. Abandoning the buns and coffee, they spent an hour or so cementing their new relationship and, as far as Leifur knew, christened the forward berth.

'Would you like to come to dinner tonight at mine?' Astrid asked afterwards, lying in bed and nibbling on a bun that Leifur had fetched in from the galley. 'My parents are coming. That's not a warning,' she added, with a grin.

'Are you sure?'

'I'd really like you to come.'

'In that case, I'd love to. Shall I bring something?'

'Maybe a toothbrush?' Given what had just happened, he was surprised she sounded shy, but it was endearing.

Dinner at Astrid's was highly entertaining. All that Leifur knew of her was on the boat, where she was highly organised, calm and clear-headed. Domesticity was not her forte. She hadn't realised that she didn't have enough forks for all four of them, so she was eating with a spoon and a knife. The bread she'd put in the oven to warm was burnt to a crisp by the time she remembered it, at which point they were halfway through the main course anyway. Then what she thought was an easy frozen desert needed defrosting for two hours before it could be eaten. Her parents were clearly more used to seeing this side of her than he was and didn't seem surprised as one mishap led into the next over the course of the evening.

'I'm not always as disorganised as this,' she said, as they flopped onto the sofa after dinner.

Leifur noticed a smile pass between her parents.

'It's because I'm not used to entertaining.'

'It was a lovely meal,' Leifur said supportively.

'Thank you.'

'Do you live in the city too, Leifur?' Astrid's mother asked.

'I'm in Hafnarfjörður. I used to fish out of there.'

'Gudrun mentioned that,' said Astrid's father. 'Tough times in that industry.'

'It's true. It felt like the right time to start something new.'

'So this is a new start for both of you,' said Astrid's mother.

'Not for me, Mamma,' said Astrid with a small frown, as if her mother ought to know better. 'It's just the summer.'

'Of course.' Her mother looked into her wineglass, but Leifur could see the hint of a smile. If it weren't for the talk earlier in the day, he'd feel bruised by Astrid's comment. As it was, he wished she didn't feel like that, but he was content to accept her terms. He'd agreed to them after all.

'And how has it been moving out of the city?' Leifur asked Astrid's parents.

'I don't miss it as much as I thought I would,' said Astrid's mother. 'The pace is a little slower where we are, and there are plenty of other retired people. There's never a dull moment.'

'My mother has a better social life than I do,' Leifur said.

Astrid smiled at him. 'You'll be able to improve on that now you're working a normal day.'

'That's what I'm hoping.' Without meaning to, in front of her parents, he couldn't stop looking at her. She was gazing across the small coffee table at him, and silence descended, although neither of them noticed.

'Well, it's time we were going,' Astrid's mother said, standing up. Astrid's father hurriedly finished half a glass of wine before standing up too, looking surprised.

'You don't have to go, Mamma.'

'No, we don't want to be too late. Your sister will think we're having too much fun without her. Thank you for having us. I'm so happy you've got this place and can settle properly while you're here.'

Leifur stood up, feeling a little awkward that he was seeing her parents out. It really spelled out that he was staying the night. But then he reminded himself that he was a thirty-six-year-old man and didn't need to worry about what her parents thought.

'Lovely to see you both again,' he said, standing at Astrid's side.

'You too, Leifur. I hope we'll see you again soon.'

Astrid's father said nothing, but shook Leifur's hand strongly, as if there was some meaning behind it. Leifur met his eyes and nodded. For some reason, it felt like the right thing to do.

'They really like you,' Astrid said, leaning against the back of the door after her parents had gone.

'I liked them. But I like you more.'

'Good.' She wrapped her arms around his neck and he lifted her so that he could carry her through to the bedroom, marvelling at how much his life had changed in just one day.

20

The days leading up to the tours beginning for real settled into a routine of spending the mornings on *Brimfaxi*, early afternoons in the office answering emails from customers and then by late afternoon the rest of the day was their own. Since staying the night at her apartment for the first time, Leifur had stayed every night apart from the one when he went to his mother's for dinner.

'You're welcome to come,' he said. 'She'd love to meet you properly, and she'll be thrilled we're seeing each other.'

'Maybe next time?' She had a feeling Peta had already known that something was going on between them, and she thought it might be good for them to talk alone. Knowing how worried Peta must have been about Leifur over the past few months, she wasn't sure about Peta's reaction if Leifur told his mother that their relationship was planned to be short-lived, just for the summer.

It felt huge to Astrid to have committed to the tours for the entire summer, potentially missing out on some golden opportunity that might present itself. But now that she and Leifur were together, she was pleased that she had this time to take a breather from her real life. She couldn't contemplate staying in Reykjavik on a tour boat for the rest of her career, because although she loved working on the sea and seeing the whales, it was a tiny fragment of what else was out there to discover and that's what she didn't want to leave behind.

The following day was going to be the first full day, with three fully-booked tours. Astrid could see the tension in Leifur as they prepared the boat. Not that there was much to do because they'd checked and double-checked everything a dozen times. The only difference between the trial run and their plans for the real thing was that Jonas had introduced them to Eva, a university student from Reykjavik who was studying marine biology in Canada and was home for the summer. She was going to run the galley and be in charge of the guests when they were on board, leaving Astrid free to concentrate on the whale-watching side of things. Leifur had been reluctant to have another person on the boat, and Astrid had to remind him he'd felt like that about her and that it was important to give Eva a chance.

'She's the friendly, sunny kind of person who will be perfect for looking after the guests. And I want to help her out. This will be great experience for her if she wants to join a research trip on a boat one day.'

Leifur couldn't do anything but agree. He was a creature of habit, and he didn't like change. Astrid knew that adding Eva to their tiny crew felt monumentous to him after two weeks of it being just the two of them. It was all the years living with the structure and repetitiveness of working on a fishing boat. And although the boat tours felt like the definition of repetitive to Astrid, it was nowhere near what Leifur was used to. All the checking was him trying to feel at ease with every small part of what they were doing.

'Come on, let's go for a walk,' she suggested. The sun was shining, although it was a blustery day, and a bracing walk along the seafront to the lighthouse at Grótta might be just the thing to blow Leifur's anxiety away.

'I think we should go to the office and check in.'

'No.' She was as diligent with her work as he was, but she also recognised the importance of taking time out to decompress. 'We'll only be a couple of hours, then if you want to go to the office we still can.'

Astrid led the way. It had been years since she'd ventured along the peninsula that led to the lighthouse, but almost as soon as the harbour was behind them, she remembered the feeling it gave you of leaving the city behind. There were more houses along the coast road than there had been the last time she'd walked along. They were getting ever larger, more sprawling and a long way from the typical Icelandic houses closer to the centre of town.

'The coast here is so different from Hafnarfjörður,' said Leifur.

'No lava fields.'

'No, although I like the moss and lichen on the rocks by my house.'

'Will you take me to your house sometime?' She asked with the certainty that he would say yes. She felt as if nothing was off limits between them now.

'Of course. I would have before, but your flat is much nicer. My place is dark in comparison.'

'I bet it's cosy,' said Astrid, slipping her hand into his.

'It is,' he conceded. 'It's a great place to watch storms from. With the fire blazing and a hot drink in your hand while the waves crash on the rocks and the lightning lights up the fjord.'

'I can imagine you doing that. You looked so content watching the sea when I saw you on the rocks.'

'I still can't believe you thought you were going to see a whale.'

'Hey!' She laughed, shocked but thrilled that he felt he could tease her and she'd take it in good spirit. It felt like a milestone. 'At least I wasn't the maniac waving to a stranger.'

'That's fair.' He threw his head back and laughed, and Astrid felt warm inside that she was the one who had done this to him. At least partly. She had to give *Brimfaxi* some of the credit.

There was a set of metal steps that bridged the huge rocks stacked as sea defences that stretched along the coast and led down to a small sandy beach about halfway along.

'Shall we walk along the sand?'

He nodded. 'Sure.' Almost as soon as they set foot on the sand, he picked up a piece of seaweed. A huge bunch of kelp on a thick stem, like a cat-o'-nine-tails. 'Look at this.' A glint appeared in his eye and Astrid knew exactly what he was going to do. She yelped and started running away from him, a quick turn of her head confirming her suspicion that he was chasing her with the seaweed.

She felt like she'd outrun him and turned around. 'If that touches me, you're dead, Leifur Magnússon!' She could barely shout her threat properly for laughing.

'That would be a shame. Just when we've got to the fun part.' He threw the seaweed into the sea, where it floated on the surface, making its way back to the beach with every wave. She watched him walk towards her with a smile on her face, knowing that he would take her in his arms when he reached her. He did, and then he pretended he was going to throw her into the sea.

'No!' she screeched, clinging to him with every ounce of strength she could muster, even though she knew he would never actually do it.

'One, two, three…' He lifted her and let her fall quickly, never letting her go, but making her feel like she was falling for a split second.

'Leifur!'

Then he pulled her to him, holding her closer than she'd

ever been held before. She nuzzled into his neck, breathing him in and letting his beard scuff her cheek. It felt so good. The warmth of him, the solidness and the safety of feeling his arms around her was intoxicating. Why had she suggested a walk when they could have taken some time off by staying in the cabin?

As he put her down on the sand and they resumed their walk along the beach, she spotted something on the high tide line and pulled Leifur's hand until they reached it. There was something among the small rocks and pieces of seaweed.

'You look as if you're expecting to find something,' he said.

'Seaglass.' Astrid couldn't drag her eyes from the sand. 'Look!' Holding the emerald green nugget up to the sky, the sun glinted through it. 'I think green and clear are the most common ones.'

'Let's see if we can find something special then,' Leifur said.

It was addictive looking for the small pieces of broken glass that the sea had tumbled into jewels just waiting to be discovered. Astrid smiled at him as he bent down to pick up a piece of clear glass, thinking how nice it was to share things like this with someone else. One of her favourite things in the world was to hunt for seaglass at every beach she went to, and of all of them, this was always where she'd found the best of it in abundance.

'I've never done this before,' said Leifur.

'Perhaps it's more of a girl thing.'

'Perhaps. But it's very absorbing. I can understand the appeal. What do you do with the glass?'

'I have a glass jar. I put it in there and keep it on a windowsill. I love seeing it in the sunlight, and it's nice to have a jar of souvenirs from all the places I've been.'

'I've collected pieces of driftwood over the years. It washes up on the shore by my house.'

'What do you do with those?'

'All sorts of things. I collected a lot of small pieces and strung them together to make a decoration for my mother. I have a larger piece across my mantelpiece. It must have been out at sea for a long time because it's so smooth and bleached by the sun.'

Astrid loved these small glimpses into Leifur's life. They were like little gifts he gave her every so often.

'I'll come round to yours on Sunday night.' They'd agreed to have Monday as their day off.

'That gives me no time to prepare,' Leifur said, bending to pick up another piece of glass and putting it in his pocket.

Astrid loved that he was enjoying collecting the glass too. 'What do you need to prepare? It can't be untidy. Aren't fishermen renowned for being very organised and precise and tidy?'

'I think you're confusing me with being a sailor. A fisherman isn't at home enough to keep everything like that. But then that helped keep things tidy. Now I'm at home more… or I was,' he grinned at her. 'It's not that tidy.'

'I don't mind. You don't need to tidy up for me. I want to see it exactly as it is.'

He chuckled and shook his head. 'Well, that's not happening. I might need to retract the offer.'

She snuggled into his side, and he put his arm around her shoulders. It was the best feeling ever. She felt happier than she had ever remembered and never thought that would be because of a man. Finally, she realised what it had been like for Gudrun when she'd met Olafur. She understood the looks that passed between them even now, years later, and that scared her a little, because that was love. Was that what this was with Leifur? Love? It couldn't be. More importantly, she couldn't let it be, because it would be heartbreaking to leave him after the summer. They needed to keep things light, keep having fun without getting too serious. If she was starting to feel like she belonged in his arms, if his embrace was the one place in the world where she felt like she'd come home, it would make everything harder when she had to say goodbye.

'Why don't you stay at yours for a couple of nights?'

He frowned. 'Really? So I can tidy my house for you?'

'No. I meant it when I said you don't need to. But maybe it's a good idea since we're starting the tours. We need to focus on that. And we both need some sleep.'

'Okay,' he said, shrugging.

Her suggestion had ruined the mood between them, and she felt guilty because on some level she'd done that intentionally. It was self-preservation. She needed to be more careful, and being together every night, as if they lived together, wasn't the way to guard her heart. Moving out of Gudrun's was deliberate, so that she could be independent and enjoy living in Reykjavik on her own terms and she had lost sight of that.

'I'm sorry.'

'What for? It's a sensible suggestion.'

But Astrid felt as if she'd spoiled it before they'd even started. Being in a relationship wasn't something she was used to navigating, and clearly she wasn't very good at it.

'Hey,' she pulled his hand to stop him walking. When he looked at her, he had sad eyes, and it was like a punch to her gut. "Stay with me every night," was what she almost said, but it was too late to turn that around and anyway, now she'd decided, she knew it was the right thing to do. Both of them being tired on the first day wasn't an option. 'It's just for a couple of days. We'll be exhausted and probably not great company for each other. Let's give ourselves a break from having to talk to anyone, at least overnight.' She hoped it sounded lighthearted, and it elicited a half-smile from Leifur.

'It's okay,' he said, wrapping his arms around her. 'We don't have to spend every night with each other. That would be ridiculous.'

'It would be wonderful, but we can work up to it.' She reached up and kissed him.

'Come on, I want to make it to the lighthouse this side of midnight.'

21

Despite being secretly devastated when Astrid suggested a couple of nights apart, Leifur had been grateful for his own bed. He'd tossed and turned, worrying about anything and everything that could go wrong on the first day of the tours. Would they see any whales? Would the weather be favourable? How was it going to be with Eva on the boat when she hadn't been part of the trial run?

But mostly he was thinking about why Astrid wanted to spend a few nights apart. Perhaps she'd had a hunch he'd be like this and wanted to steer clear, wanting a good night's sleep herself. Deep down he knew that there was more to it, but they'd been so honest with each other. If she was having second thoughts, he was sure she'd tell him after they'd been open about it being just for the summer.

Except he didn't want it to end. By the end of the summer, he hoped that they'd be in too deep to think about ending it. It was unfair of him, knowing her reasons for putting an expiry date on their relationship, but spending the past two weeks with her had made him selfish. He wanted her like he'd never wanted anyone before, and it seemed stupid to put something as amazing as that in jeopardy because Astrid was hoping for a future that didn't exist yet. But then he remembered that the best things about her were her passion, drive and her impressive knowledge. Who was he to undermine her passion for her career by tempting her to stay here with him and letting all her hard work go to waste working on a tourist boat?

Something had happened yesterday to make Astrid feel she needed to pull away, and Leifur wasn't sure whether finding out what it was would make him feel better or worse. Over the course of the afternoon they'd got back to normal, assisted by the sea air and a pit stop at the Kvika foot bath, a circular pool hewn out of the rock where a weary walker could soak their feet in the hot spring water, and they'd fallen back into how it had been before Astrid had said anything. He didn't believe that she was worried about how much sleep they'd get, but maybe she'd changed her mind about it all and didn't want to say in case it made it awkward working on the boat together.

After realising at four in the morning that he wasn't going to get back to sleep, he got up, showered, dressed and ate the overnight oats he'd left in the fridge the night before while he checked the weather. It looked okay. They might have some rain, but nobody would mind that once they had their weatherproof suits on. Out of habit, he packed a bag with a spare set of clothes just as he would if he'd been going out fishing, then pulled his coat on and drove to Reykjavik.

He arrived at the harbour as dawn broke. The clouds hanging over the mountains to the north were a sure sign that they were in for some rain later on. After he'd done his usual checks, he went down to the galley to make some coffee, looking forward to having an hour to himself to unwind before Astrid and Eva arrived and he had to be in charge of everything.

'Morning.'

He turned to find Astrid standing in the doorway. She was

dressed in plenty of close-fitting layers, and her hair was plaited intricately around her head.

'Hey. Coffee?'

'Buns?' She held up a cardboard box.

'Are those from Sandholt?' The bakery on Laugavegur did the most amazing brown sugar buns and iced cinnamon buns, and he'd bet that Astrid had plumped for one or the other.

'How do you know that? The box is plain.'

'I've had enough take-outs from there over the years to know.'

Astrid sat on the bench seat and opened the box. There were three brown sugar buns nestled inside.

'Two for me, one for you?' He put the coffee on the table.

'One for Eva.'

Ah, Eva. He had nothing against her, but he'd be sad that it wasn't just him and Astrid anymore.

'That's why I thought I'd come early,' she said. 'So we could spend some time together.'

'How did you know I'd be here early?'

She rolled her eyes. 'Do I seriously need to answer that? How many hours have you been here?'

'Less than one.'

'That's something. I missed you last night.' She put her hand on top of his.

'Me too. Maybe you had a premonition I might have been restless. At least one of us slept well.'

'Tonight you'll sleep like a log, and you'll wonder what you were worrying about. What are you worrying about?'

He put his bun down, having not yet taken a bite. 'Everything. Weather. Whales. Mechanics and everything in between.'

'Try and remember how great we felt at the end of the trial tour.' She pulled her phone out of her pocket and showed him a photo of them on the boat together. They were standing side by side with big grins on their faces, and they were looking at each other. The connection between them was unmistakable. 'Gudrun took this when she got off the boat that day. Look how happy you are.'

It surprised him to see his expression. No wonder Astrid's mother and his own had realised there was something between the two of them that day.

'Can you send me that?'

'Yes, and you can look at it whenever you feel like things are going to go badly. There's no reason to expect the worst.'

It was easy to say, but since the night his father died, when he had to put into practice what he and the rest of the crew had been trained to deal with but never thought they would face, he'd always expected the worst. Having Astrid around had eased the feelings of dread somewhat, but it was hard to break the habit of half a lifetime.

'I'll look at it all the time,' he said. 'You look beautiful.'

Astrid bit her lip and stared at him as if she had never heard anyone say that before. 'Thank you.'

'Come here,' he said, taking her in his arms, filling the void that had been there since the walk on the beach the day before. He felt her nuzzle into his neck and his worries melted away, because nothing else mattered.

'I kind of liked missing you last night,' she said. 'I was so looking forward to seeing you this morning.'

He said nothing because he hadn't felt like that. He'd not allowed himself the luxury of missing her, or looking forward to seeing her because he'd been too busy dwelling on what had been wrong yesterday.

'It's okay if you don't feel the same,' she said, reading his mind. 'I know you've been too busy preparing for today.'

'It didn't stop me from wishing you were in my arms last night. My bed felt empty without you, and you've never even been in it.'

They sat for a few minutes kissing and caressing each other's faces before they heard footsteps on the stairs.

'Hello?' It was Eva.

Astrid sprung off Leifur's lap. 'Morning! You're bright and early, Eva.'

'I was so nervous. I just want to get started.'

'Take a seat,' said Leifur. 'I'll make more coffee and we can eat our buns before we start.'

When the first guests arrived, they were completely ready for them. Astrid met them on the quayside, checked them off on her list, welcomed them onto the boat and sent them downstairs to see Eva, who would help them get kitted out and make them drinks. They had a full boat of thirty that morning, and once everyone was on board, Astrid notified Leifur, he started the engines, and Eva and Astrid let off the lines. They were off.

Once they were heading out of the harbour, Astrid turned on her headset and began the safety briefing, primarily letting people know what to do if anyone fell overboard. Her voice was being broadcast throughout the boat, and as she moved on to explaining what they hoped to see today and the signs to look out for, more of the guests appeared from below to stand on deck.

'It is likely to rain during the tour, which won't matter to the whales, but if you don't already have a weatherproof suit on, you might want to grab one now. We're heading out to about fifteen kilometres from the harbour, which is a common place to find whales feeding. It'll take us around twenty minutes to get out there, then our captain, Leifur, will slow the engines. We'll be on the lookout for groups of seabirds, a sure sign that there are fish to be had and therefore whales feeding, and blows, which are the classic vapour release from the whale's blowhole. We can see those from a kilometre or two away.'

Astrid felt the boat turn and wondered whether Leifur had received some information from another tour boat. Five minutes later, scanning the horizon, she saw the first blow.

'And we have a blow at twelve o'clock. It's probably a humpback.'

Just as everyone started peering at the horizon, two minke whales swam along the starboard side of the boat. Astrid noticed before anyone else and called it out, but the minkes were gone before anyone could get a photo, although there were lots of excited comments from the guests who spotted them.

'Look! They look like dolphins!'

'They're so close!'

It was wonderful to know that they were having a great time, and with each sighting, there was renewed excitement. She also took it as a good sign that most of the guests stayed on deck. It was a relief because even after the trial run had gone so well, she'd had a niggling worry at the back of her mind that of course everyone enjoyed that tour. They were family and friends and out on a free trip. The guests today, their reaction was the validation Astrid realised she'd been waiting for.

Eva came up around halfway through. 'Is it okay for me to be up here?'

Astrid switched her mic off for a moment. 'Of course. I don't think the guests are going to want anything from the galley while this is going on,' said Astrid.

'I've never been on a boat tour. Isn't that crazy?'

'Not that crazy. I never went on one before Leifur and I went to do a recce for this.'

'Oh, look!' Eva said, pointing.

Astrid smiled, pleased that Eva was getting to experience her passion firsthand. She switched her mic back on.

'And we have two individuals, two humpbacks at nine o'clock. They're diving, I think they will come under the boat. Look at two o'clock for bubble rings and dark shadows.'

Everyone went over to the starboard side and waited. This was what made them different from the other companies; thirty people could all gather in about the same place and see whatever was going on. As it was, they'd mostly lined the bow, and there was no one who wouldn't see the humpbacks if they came up as Astrid predicted.

The stars aligned, and a minute or so later they could see the shadow of the whales under the water, with the telltale rings of bubbles expanding and reaching the surface at the same time as their creators. It was a wonderful sight, even when you'd seen it before, and Astrid knew she'd never tire of seeing it.

'Incredible,' breathed Eva next to her, eyes wide in genuine wonderment. 'I've never seen the bubble rings for real before. They're beautiful.'

Astrid felt quite overwhelmed for a moment as she took in everyone's reactions. This was more than being a tour guide. Right now, it didn't feel second best to anything else she could be doing, and that felt amazing and frightening at the same time. There had been times on research boats when they'd made a breakthrough or seen something incredible, but that was once in a blue moon in amongst all the hard work, data crunching and false leads. Today was already incredible, and it was the first tour.

'I'd better go downstairs,' said Eva. 'This is going to be the best summer ever!'

And Astrid was inclined to agree with her.

22

As they waved the last of the guests off the boat at the end of the third tour of the day, Astrid wondered whether she'd bitten off more than she could chew. She'd never had a job that was rigidly timetabled, or done anything that had a customer-facing role before. The time between each tour had seemed as if it would give them all a chance for a break, but by the time they had tidied up, restocked the galley, made sure the weatherproof suits were hanging ready for the next tour, or in the drying room if they were wet, the next guests arrived and they started all over again.

'That was amazing,' Eva said, full of the enthusiasm Astrid and Leifur had had after the practice run.

'They all seemed pleased when they left,' Leifur said wearily, although being in the wheelhouse for most of the time meant he didn't have a feel for how it had gone.

'We'll know when they start leaving reviews,' said Astrid.

'They all saw whales,' Eva said.

'That's true, although it was a shame that the last group didn't see the minkes.'

'Minkes are fly-by-nights,' said Leifur. 'They're here one minute and gone the next. The humpbacks are what people really want to see. Slapping their tails and blowing bubble rings, they know how to impress people.'

He unzipped his weatherproof suit and pulled his arms out, knotting the sleeves around his waist. Astrid was surprised by how sexy it was. With his hair tousled and a smile in his eyes now that he was relaxing, she was suddenly desperate to pull the rest of his clothes off and run her hands over him.

Eva laughed, snapping Astrid out of her daydream.

'Exactly! And at least everyone saw that, even if it wasn't as good as we saw this morning. It's nature. Everyone knows that.'

'Hmm, I'm not so sure,' said Astrid. 'One woman asked me when we were going to see the fin whale and the blue whale, as if she was on an outing to the zoo.'

'What did you say?' Leifur asked, amusement in his eyes.

'I told her we can't predict which whales will show up.'

'Ha! She probably went away thinking she still has a chance to see them in Faxaflói Bay.' Leifur chuckled to himself.

'It's too shallow, right?' Eva said.

'Yes, it's only thirty metres deep. Nowhere near deep enough for a blue whale, although I did hear that a blue whale brought her calf here to keep them away from some orcas who were further out in the ocean,' said Astrid.

'I saw that,' said Leifur.

'Really? That's incredible,' said Eva.

Astrid thought so too and waited for him to elaborate.

'It was about six years ago,' he began, settling himself down on a bench and taking a swig of the bottle of water in his hand as if it were a bottle of beer and he was a salty old sea dog of a fisherman telling stories in a dimly-lit seaman's bar.

'I heard it was ten years ago,' said Astrid, grinning.

'Who's telling this story?' Leifur said, raising an eyebrow.

It was very sexy, so Astrid sat down on the deck, leaning back on her arms and with her legs out in front of her to listen. Eva did the same.

'I was out on *Brimfaxi* on a frosty February morning. The sun was barely up, but I heard a noise I'd never heard before. It was like the sound the humpback whales make, but deeper. It felt as if it was vibrating through the boat. I cut the engines because I had a feeling it was something out of the ordinary, and I waited.' He paused for dramatic effect. 'All of us were standing on the deck and it was eerily quiet, then we heard the sound again and this time, we saw the calf breach. That calf was bigger than a humpback. Bigger than anything else I've seen in these waters. Then the mother came up beside it, and she was huge. And when she dived, her tail in the air, it was one of the most incredible things I've ever seen.'

'You never told me about that,' Astrid said.

Leifur shrugged. 'I haven't thought about it for a while.'

'Incredible,' said Eva, shaking her head.

'Eva, thank you for today. You can go. We'll see you in the morning,' said Leifur.

'Are you sure? I don't mind staying to help.'

'No, you've had a long day. We can finish up,' Astrid said, hoping that Leifur was thinking the same as her. 'Thank you, you've done a great job.'

Eva blushed with pride and headed off, waving as she walked along the quay.

'I don't know about you, but I might need a lie down before I start prepping for tomorrow,' Leifur said.

'Oh, so that's why you sent Eva home.'

'Think of it as a debrief,' he said, raising an eyebrow before taking her in his arms. She lifted the bottom of his sweater and ran her hands over the front of his chest, sighing at the release it gave her. It was hard, even for the few minutes since he'd pulled his suit down around his waist, to sit with the feeling of wanting to rip his clothes off. All the pent-up frustration came out in that sigh when she touched him.

They headed below deck and into the cabin. Astrid untied the sleeves of Leifur's suit and pushed it down his legs. He sat down on the edge of the bed and pulled her so that she was standing between his legs. Now it was his turn to run his hands over her, and in one swift movement, he pulled all of her top layers off.

'Look at you,' he murmured, his hands on her waist.

He dropped tender kisses onto her stomach, but impatiently she wanted more. She pushed him with one hand on his chest so that he was lying on the bed.

'Who's in charge here?' he said.

'*Halló?*'

They both froze.

'It's Jonas,' Leifur said, hurriedly shifting out from underneath Astrid, pulling his suit back up, which was still around his ankles. '*Hæ*, Jonas!' He headed up to the deck, leaving Astrid to pull her clothes back on and follow him.

'*Hæ*, Astrid,' Jonas said when she appeared on deck a minute behind Leifur. 'How did it go today?'

'It was great,' she said, looking to Leifur for input. The details of the day had been so fresh in her mind a few minutes ago but now seemed distant and fuzzy, being replaced with thoughts of what had been about to happen in the cabin.

'Good sailing conditions,' Leifur said.

'And good sightings?'

'For the first two tours. The third, we did see some humpbacks but nowhere near what we'd seen in the morning. Have you had any complaints?'

'No, and actually we have the first five-star review on the website. They said they saw minkes and humpbacks,' said Jonas.

'That wasn't from the woman who wanted to know when we were going to see a blue whale, then. I'm expecting a one-star review from her,' said Astrid.

Jonas laughed. 'Really? She thought she'd see a blue whale?'

He didn't seem worried at all about the prospect of a bad review.

'You're not upset?' Astrid asked.

'I've been in this business long enough to know that you can't account for people who have unrealistic expectations. If she leaves a review complaining about the lack of blue whales, other people will take it with a pinch of salt. Besides, we're very clear in our terms and conditions that we can't guarantee whale sightings.'

'Neither of us are used to dealing with customers,' said Leifur.

'None of us were when we started. Don't worry about that side of things. It comes with experience. Anyway, I'll let you get back to it.'

Astrid felt herself blush and saw Leifur do the same, although he recovered himself more quickly and shook Jonas's hand.

'Thanks for stopping by. I think it's going to be a great summer.'

'Me too. I've wanted to get into boat tours for a while, and the two of you have made it easier than I thought it would be. It hasn't been a distraction for me at all, so thank you for that.'

'No problem,' said Leifur.

They waved him off, then stood on the deck looking at each other.

'Let's finish up and go to my place,' said Astrid.

'Almost getting caught doesn't do it for you?'

'It was so embarrassing. I'm sure Jonas realised.'

Leifur shrugged and raised an eyebrow. 'It doesn't matter. I'll come to yours. Maybe we could get dinner? And then I'll head home.'

Astrid was torn. In the moments before Jonas arrived, she'd been so full of longing for Leifur, and not only was that longing burning inside her even more strongly, she didn't want it to be over at all.

'Stay tonight,' she said.

'It's okay, I don't mind going home. We can stick to the plan.'

'I don't like the plan anymore.'

His face lit up. 'New plan. I take you to bed so that I can show you what was waiting for you before Jonas turned up.' His eyes flicked downwards. 'Then we eat and sleep.'

'I love that plan.' She looped her arms around his neck and kissed him. 'But keep your suit on until we get to my place. It's sexy.'

'My waterproofs are sexy?' He pulled back and looked at her with one eyebrow raised. 'That's where I've been going wrong all these years. I've never worn them off the boat before.'

'Lucky for me that you didn't.'

He looked at her with something like gratefulness in his eyes. 'Come on. Let's lock up. I can't wait to get out of these waterproofs.'

She quirked an eyebrow at him. 'Neither can I.'

They both climbed into his truck, and he drove them the short distance to Astrid's apartment. She unlocked the door to the building, but before they could head upstairs, the door to the ground-floor apartment opened and Sol appeared.

'Astrid, I am so happy to see you,' she said. Her jeans were wet at the knees, and her sweater was damp around the cuffs even though she'd pushed them up to her elbows. 'There's something wrong with the toilet, and it's leaking. Thor is at work, and I don't have enough strength to turn the main water tap off.'

'I can take a look,' Leifur said.

'Oh, would you? I'd be so grateful. Come in. You'd better keep your boots on.'

On one hand it only made Leifur seem sexier to be saving the day for Sol, but Astrid was going to die of frustration if they didn't make it upstairs soon. Hopefully, it would be something simple.

She ushered them into the apartment, which was like Astrid's, but with lower ceilings, which gave it a cosier feel. There was a pile of towels in the bathroom doorway, making a pretty poor job of damming the water of which there was around three or four centimetres.

'The flush on the toilet is over-running, and it looks as if the overflow isn't working,' said Leifur from the hallway.

Sol gave Astrid an impressed look. 'Can you stop the water? The tap is in the kitchen.'

He headed into the kitchen, which was a separate room rather than open plan with the lounge like Astrid's. 'Under the sink?'

'Yes.'

He knelt down and reached for the tap. 'It's stiff,' he said, grunting.

The tap or you? Astrid stifled a giggle as that thought ran through her head. It wasn't the time. Her hormones were having a strange effect on her, desperate for release and in the meantime, sending her loopy.

He stood up and brushed his hands against each other a few times. 'It's off. Let's have a look at the toilet.'

With his waterproofs and boots on, Leifur stepped over the threshold into the bathroom and lifted the top off the toilet cistern. He rolled his sleeve up and plunged his hand into it, trying to reach something.

'Oh no,' Sol muttered.

'What's wrong?' Astrid asked.

'Ah, this is the problem,' Leifur said, holding up a plastic bag containing a box. 'It was blocking the overflow

Sol hid her face with her hands. 'It's my fault. I put that in there.'

'What is it?'

'Pregnancy tests. I'm such an idiot,' said Sol. 'I hid them in there a while ago, and I'd forgotten.'

'Look, you don't have to worry,' Astrid said. 'It's none of our business. Let's get this cleared up.'

'You don't have to do that.'

'We're happy to.'

By the time they'd helped mop up all the water, leaving Sol grateful and apologetic, it was late. They hadn't eaten, and neither of them felt like doing anything except sleeping.

'I'll warm some soup and bread,' Astrid said.

'Do you mind if I shower?'

'Of course not.'

'Are you sure I should stay?'

'Yes. I want to fall asleep in your arms.'

'You don't think today has been the universe telling us we shouldn't be together?'

'You believe in that kind of thing?'

'I don't know. It feels like a conspiracy.'

Astrid abandoned her soup prep and came to sit on his lap. 'We might have been thwarted once or twice today, but don't be put off. I still think you're sexy as hell, even if the universe wants me to think otherwise.'

He raised an eyebrow. 'Sexy as hell?'

'Shall we have the soup in a bit?'

23

Sunday evening couldn't come soon enough for Leifur. After four days, part of him was beginning to enjoy the repetition of the days, the structure that it gave back into his life and the purpose he finally had again. But the rest of him was exhausted. It was unfortunate timing that he and Astrid couldn't keep away from each other, and she had quickly caved in on her decision to spend a couple of nights apart. They hadn't had a night apart this week, but tonight, she was holding him to his promise of having her over to his place for the evening, and then they could have a lazy start to Monday, their day off.

He and Astrid arrived on *Brimfaxi* on Sunday morning shortly before Eva — a tactical decision so that she wouldn't see them arriving together every morning. Leifur's truck hadn't moved from the parking space in the harbour car park for four days, but perhaps no one was looking out for things like that as much as Astrid thought they did.

'If my sister ever came down to this part of town, you can bet your life she'd notice that your truck was in the same place. Even if you told her you just pick the same spot every day, she'd still know whether it had been moved or not.'

'She didn't seem like the intense stalker-type,' Leifur said.

'She has a very keen sense of what's going on between people before they know themselves. I can't explain it.'

Fair enough, if Astrid wanted to keep their relationship quiet for now, he didn't mind. He knew it was nothing to do with how she felt about him, and more to do with the fact that other people would have expectations of where their relationship might go which could put undue pressure on them when they'd basically decided it was going to be a summer fling.

'The weather doesn't look too good today,' Leifur said, having checked the forecast before they left Astrid's apartment. 'The seas are going to be rough. Make sure Eva offers everyone a seasickness tablet if they haven't taken one already, and maybe you could give some tips when you do the safety briefing. We don't want to be clearing up sick later.'

'Definitely not. Our day off starts the moment we see the guests off the boat after the last tour today.'

Astrid and Eva set out small piles of sick bags, just in case, and Eva had the tablets ready in the galley and would offer them to the guests when they came downstairs to get their weatherproof suits on. When they went back on deck ready to welcome the guests, there was a steady drizzle and the cloud had dropped so low that you couldn't see much further than the harbour entrance.

'This weather is a shame,' said Eva.

'It'll be okay as long as we make sure the guests are prepared. They'll probably come on board wishing they'd chosen a different day to sail, and we need to turn that around for them,' Astrid said.

Leifur loved hearing her talk like that. It made him feel they had a connection through their shared values. Icelandic people were hardy when it came to bad weather, whereas tourists came expecting stable, seasonally-accurate weather patterns, a forecast you could count on and neither of those things were often the case. The weather in Iceland was so changeable in such a short time and as a fisherman, he'd had to go out whatever the weather, unless it was too dangerous. Astrid, on the other hand, hadn't lived in Iceland for a long time, and even in Norway, because the weather was more settled, there wasn't the same mentality that as long as you had the right clothing, it wasn't a problem.

Of the thirty guests they had booked, the number had dwindled to twenty-three where people had postponed their tour to another day because of the weather. It was their choice, but Leifur knew that there might not be a better day if their holiday wasn't very long and they could risk missing out altogether. But the guests who had braved it were all standing on deck in their weatherproof suits, hoods up and gloves on, listening to Astrid do her safety briefing as he took *Brimfaxi* out of the harbour.

Once they were out in the open water, the sea was tossing them around a fair bit. It didn't feel too bad to him, but he knew that for anyone unaccustomed to it, it would feel like the roughest sea in the world. He heard Astrid advise them not to look at the surface of the sea. It would help to focus on the horizon if anyone felt peaky. She also advised them to stay on deck because the fresh air helped. It was true, but he knew it was also so that it would hopefully stop any mess inside.

They headed out to the same place they'd been every day so far. By the time they got there, Eva had come up on deck and was gripping the rail, staring determinedly at the horizon, taking deep breaths. He opened the door of the wheelhouse.

'Hey! Eva, are you alright?'

She turned, looking pale but smiling, and gave him a thumbs up. 'Feeling better now I'm up here,' she called. 'I think it's worse below deck.'

That was almost certainly true. Not long after, they had their first sighting of a humpback, and Leifur could tell by the enthusiastic taking of photos and the excited chatter carried on the wind that the whales were probably the best cure for any hint of seasickness.

It was an exceptionally good turnout by the whales. They even saw a fin whale, which Astrid could hardly believe. Her voice rose in excitement as she told the guests how unusual it was, then he saw her turn around to catch his eye and her face was a picture. He loved that this thing they were doing together could make her feel like that, and that they could share it together. And in his heart of hearts, he wondered whether it might be enough to make her decide to stay.

'This is *Brimfaxi*. We have a fin whale sighting,' he broadcast over the radio to the other tour boats, giving their location.

'Received,' said one boat. 'Great sighting, but we're heading in. The weather is turning in the next thirty minutes.'

Leifur checked his screen and could see from the radar that the other boat was right. He was reluctant to leave too soon, but he had to think of the safety of the guests. It would take twenty minutes to get back to the harbour, so he reckoned they could stay out for another ten with no risk other than a rougher voyage back than they'd had on the way. Besides, he couldn't turn the engines on yet while they were surrounded by whales.

Fifteen minutes later, Leifur gathered from Astrid's commentary that the whales were heading away from the boat and rather than follow them, which he would do in normal circumstances, he headed back to shore. Astrid looked up to the wheelhouse, questioning him, then she switched the mic off and headed up to see him.

'We have to turn back,' he said as soon as she opened the door to the wheelhouse.

'The weather?'

'Yes, it's going to deteriorate, and we might not make it back before the worst of it hits.'

'Okay. I'll explain to everyone.'

The rain pelted down more heavily, and most of the guests retreated below deck for the ride back to Reykjavik. For Leifur, he was less concerned about the rough seas and more concerned with how bad it would be if they all got sick and left terrible reviews.

Thankfully, they made it back to the harbour just as the wind picked up, so the relatively sheltered waters gave them some respite from the waves.

Once they'd docked and Eva and Astrid had tied off the ropes, he headed down to see the guests got off the boat safely.

'It was wonderful!' One couple said to him, their own waterproofs hardly a match for the rain that was beating down on them but smiling with joy, nevertheless.

'Thank you! What a fantastic tour,' someone else said.

'Can you believe they all enjoyed it?' Leifur said to Astrid and Eva when they were sitting in the galley with cups of coffee before they had to gear up for the next tour.

'It makes it more of an adventure,' said Eva.

'You didn't look as if that's what you thought,' said Astrid. 'Are you feeling okay now?'

'I was so busy giving out the seasickness tablets that I forgot to take one myself until it was too late,' she said. 'I'll be okay for the next tour.'

'I need to call the office because I'm not sure we should go out until this weather's passed. We might be okay for the evening sailing, but the next one might be a bit dicey.' He pulled his phone out and made the call. In the end, they decided the best course of action was to cancel the rest of the day's sailings to give guests more certainty rather than waiting until the last minute.

'So that's it?' said Eva. 'We have the rest of the day off?'

'Yes,' said Leifur, looking at Astrid and knowing she was thinking the same as him; that their day off started now.

Once they'd locked up the boat, Astrid and Leifur made a run for his truck. They were wearing waterproofs, but the rain and wind were so fierce that it stung if a raindrop hit your face.

'I didn't think about this happening,' said Leifur. 'I thought I'd have to manage with one day off a week but actually we might have to cancel sailings.'

'You used to go out whatever the weather when you fished?'

He nodded. 'Probably plenty of times when it would have been safer not to, but if you don't fish, you don't get paid.'

'Can you believe we saw a fin whale? That's incredible. I know they're rare, and I never thought we'd see one at all, let alone in the first week.' Her eyes were bright, and his heart melted.

'It's amazing,' he said, squeezing her thigh with his hand, then leaving it there.

She put her hand on top of his. 'And now we get to spend the rest of the day watching a storm from the comfort of your cottage.'

'That's not all we're going to do.'

'I hope not. I feel like it's the first chance we've had to be properly together without it being to do with work, or just overnight at my house.'

'It is.' Then he remembered he hadn't had a chance to get his house ready. The last night he'd spent at home, he'd been in a fug of anxiety and had thought he'd do it the following night when he'd need to distract himself from the fact that Astrid wanted another night apart and then that didn't happen. 'My house isn't ready for visitors, Astrid. I never did get around to that.'

'I don't care. I won't notice anyway.'

He hadn't changed the sheets. Hadn't cleaned the bathroom. Had a pile of dirty washing behind his bedroom door.

'You'll have to promise to wait in the lounge for a few minutes when we get there.'

'No! Don't be silly. Leifur.'

'Astrid. I mean it. Agree to that or I'm taking you home.'

'Oh my god!' She looked at him with wide eyes, realising he wasn't joking. 'Do you need to get rid of a body or your secret wife before I can come in?'

He was going to have to guilt-trip her. It was the only way. 'I've had dinner with your parents. I've fixed your neighbour's toilet at great personal cost to myself, I should add.'

'In what way?' She burst out laughing.

'If you think about where we were heading when she asked me…'

'Okay, you win.'

He knew he would because so far, he hadn't asked her to do anything for him. He didn't need to because the only thing he wanted was for her to want him. And he wasn't sure if she saw his cottage in the state it was now, whether that would be the case. He only hoped ten minutes was enough.

24

Astrid sat in the lounge listening to Leifur moving around inside the bedroom, tidying up and changing the sheets on the bed. She loved that he was so concerned about his cottage being perfect for her first visit, so even though she'd found it funny that he wanted her to stay in the lounge, she didn't mind at all.

The first thing she noticed when she walked in was the driftwood mantelpiece. It was exquisite and perfect for the cottage. A huge squashy sofa faced the fireplace, with small tables on either side of it and a compact dining table behind. Two equally comfy-looking smaller chairs faced a tall window that reached from floor to almost the ceiling and gave a wonderful view over the fjord. The dark hardwood floors added to the cosy feel, as did the creamy-coloured walls. Leifur had lit the stove and a couple of candles as soon as they came in and the fire flickered welcomingly as the flames took hold.

'This is gorgeous,' she said. 'Exactly as I imagined it would be. It's like you in cottage form.'

'I'll take that as a compliment,' he said.

'It is. You're snuggly, safe and strong. This place is all of those things too. I love it.'

'I won't be long,' he said.

She checked her emails while she waited, excited to see she had one from Sofie. It was the first time she'd heard from her friend since she'd left Tromsø, but she decided not to read it now but wait until she had time to savour it, and there was a response from the Costa Rica research team which was almost certainly a rejection after all this time. But there was no time to check now since Leifur had finished.

'Want to see the bedroom?' Leifur said softly, but with a glint in his eye. He held out his hand.

'Thought you'd never ask.'

He led her into his bedroom, which was at the back of the cottage, also with a view over the fjord from the two small windows. It had a dark wooden floor like the rest of the cottage, and the walls were navy blue, which gave it a masculine feel. Astrid felt almost intoxicated with it, the feeling of being totally immersed in Leifur's space. It felt more intimate than anything else they'd done so far. The bed was enormous, low to the ground and with a headboard that reminded Astrid of the driftwood mantelpiece in the lounge.

'You made the bed?'

'Clean sheets and everything.'

'No, I mean, you made the bed.'

'Oh. The headboard, not the entire bed.'

'I love it. It's beautiful.'

'It feels as if I made it for you. I didn't know then, but I knew it was for someone I was going to fall in love with one day.'

Astrid felt a lump in her throat. He'd fallen in love with her?

'Leifur —'

'I'm sorry. That sounded like I've fallen in love with you already, and I didn't mean —'

'I'm falling in love with you too.'

He was still holding her hand, and now, he pulled her towards him and looped his arms around her waist. She looked up at him, at the same time noticing that his beard smelled insanely good.

'You are?'

She nodded and leant her cheek against his chest. He kissed the top of her head.

'The summer's going to be over before we're ready. It makes it harder,' he said, reading her mind.

'It'll be hard whenever we have to say goodbye now.'

'Let's make sure we have plenty to think back on then.'

He pushed her gently backwards until her calves hit the side of the bed and she sat down. Then he kept coming until he was lying on top of her, leaning on one elbow while his other hand began exploring.

As they kissed, she reached down and ran her fingers around the inside of his waistband. He'd taken some layers off, as well as his waterproofs, so there wasn't much between her and the hardness she could feel inside his trousers. He gasped into her ear as she continued, briefly taking his erection into her hand before letting go, eliciting a moan from him instead.

'Astrid…'

She moved her hand upwards, burrowing up and under his top, loving the feel of his muscles under her hands. He had an incredible body. It looked strong and capable and made her feel safe. Even feeling safe felt sexy. Here, in his bedroom, she felt the connection between them more strongly than when they'd been on the boat, or even in her apartment, which didn't feel like home enough yet. She didn't know why, but this room, this cottage, felt like home and gave what they had together some deeper meaning. Being invited here, when she knew it wasn't something he was in the habit of, felt as if he was letting her in. Leifur was a man of deep feelings but few words, but now she was here, she knew how he felt about her. It was scary, but it was too late to run away now. And for the first time since she'd arrived back in Reykjavik, she didn't want to.

As she lay in his bed, naked, thanking the weather gods for the storm that had given them the afternoon off, Astrid realised her priorities had shifted. This was what life was about. Connection, having somewhere to call home that really felt like home, and love. Because she had to be honest with herself and admit she was in love with Leifur. It hadn't been part of the plan, but then she remembered what her friend Sofie had said before she left Tromsø. The best adventures in life happen when the plan goes wrong. Perhaps that was true.

Leifur was dozing next to her, with the hint of a smile on his lips. What would it be like to wake up like this every morning? With her legs tangled in his and her arm lying across his stomach, rising on each breath he took. How would it be sharing her life with someone for good rather than the way they'd been together for the past couple of weeks, which until now, had felt temporary.

'Morning,' he said a couple of minutes later, his eyes still closed but the lazy smile growing.

'It's not morning, it's still yesterday.'

'That's the best news I've heard all day,' he said, reaching his arm around her waist and pulling her to his side. Feeling the warmth of him against her whole body was delicious.

'Shall I make us some food?'

'I can take care of that,' he said. 'I have a freezer full of food from my mother. We just need to gamble on what it is and heat it up.'

'You don't have your frozen foods immaculately organised and labelled?'

'Do you?'

'No, but I don't have home-cooked food donations to

freeze very often.'

'I can't get out of bed.'

'I need to go to the bathroom. Can I borrow a sweater?'

'Middle drawer,' he said.

She slid out of bed and chose a soft navy-blue sweatshirt from the drawer, then opened the top one and pulled out a pair of woolly socks.

After she'd been to the bathroom, she went into the kitchen and opened the freezer. There were cartons and bags of all shapes and sizes, and it was impossible to know what they held.

'I'm going to choose some freezer food and put it in the oven,' she called.

'On your head be it! Come back to bed!'

She picked up a foil carton and peeled back the lid. It was as unidentifiable as everything else. She shrugged, turned the oven on and pushed it inside before padding back to the bedroom.

'What did you pick?' Leifur asked, welcoming her back into the bed and opening his arms out so that she could lie next to him with her head on his shoulder.

'I don't know. But your mother's a good cook, right?'

'I'd say so.'

'It'll be fine then.' She reached over and grabbed her phone, setting a timer for twenty minutes. Being with Leifur was like a time warp. It felt like days since they'd been on the boat, and it was only a few hours ago. 'This is so nice.'

'Having the day off or spending it in bed with me?'

'Both, but mainly this. What will we do tomorrow?'

'I want to have a lie in and I know we'd planned to spend the night together, but I need to go and see my mother in the morning before she goes to her mahjong group. Sorry.'

'I don't mind. Can I come with you?'

'You don't have to. And you can stay here if you want to.'

'I liked your mother. It'd be great to meet her properly.'

'She's going to read more into it than there is.'

That would have been enough to make Astrid rethink her offer a week or so ago, but she wanted to visit Peta, and she liked Leifur far too much to be worried that anyone might get the wrong idea about their relationship, even his mother.

'I'm not sure she can read much more into it than there actually is,' she said, turning to look at Leifur, making sure he understood what she meant.

He grinned. 'We're there already? Even though it's only for the summer?'

Astrid propped herself up on her elbow and laid her other hand on his chest. 'Have you ever heard that the best things happen when your plans go wrong?'

'No, but I like it.'

'So do I. And I didn't have a plan anyway other than to come back to Iceland while I found a job. And now I have a job, and it's so much more than a job. I hadn't expected to love working on the tour boat, but I really do.'

'I want to make sure I'm not misunderstanding you. You're saying you might stay longer? Keep working on the tours?'

She took a deep breath. It felt as if she was about to make one of the biggest commitments of her life. But she was ready for it. 'I'm going to stay for as long as I can, if Jonas will have me.'

'Never mind about Jonas. I'll have you.'

By the time they left the bed, the food had been in the oven longer than was ideal, but neither of them cared. It felt like they'd reached a milestone in their relationship. As they gazed at each other with grins on their faces, eating food they still couldn't identify but which was surprisingly delicious despite being half charred, Astrid didn't have any regrets.

'You don't think you'll get bored with looking for whales

all the time in the same place instead of being off around the world?' Leifur asked her later, when they were back in bed and supposedly going to sleep.

'I don't think so. I've loved this week. And I know it's too early to make a proper assessment, but I like the interaction with the guests. It's so immediate. I've never worked in a job where you're with customers like that and you get to see the difference your job is making to them. I won't get tired of that.'

'I'm not looking forward to the day when we don't see a whale. Imagine the backlash.'

Astrid giggled. 'That'd be awful. But I suppose the day will come when they move away from the feeding grounds and head south to breed. Do you think that's how we'll know the season is over?'

'We can probably switch to something else in the winter. We would still see whales, but the chances would be lower. Perhaps we can run northern lights boat trips instead.' He paused and then said softly, 'Do you think you would still want to be here then?'

The northern lights didn't hold as much appeal for Astrid as the whales, but now, neither of those were what was keeping her in Iceland.

'You come out as the top reason why I would want to be here, Leifur.'

'You like me more than the whales?' He shifted, so that they were facing each other.

'Yes,' she said softly. 'Although if I saw a blue whale, that might trump you.'

He laughed and leant in to kiss her. 'That would be understandable.'

25

Even as he knocked on the door of his mother's house before he let himself in, Leifur wondered whether it was a good idea to bring Astrid with him. Although she didn't mind if Peta thought she was on the verge of gaining a daughter-in-law, he still had the feeling that he was more invested in their relationship than Astrid.

She said all the right things, and he had stopped trying to keep himself from falling in love with her because it was too late for that. He still didn't believe that she was going to stay here for him, whatever she said. It was one thing for him to be heartbroken if she left, but he wasn't sure he could cope with his mother knowing quite how hard he'd fallen for Astrid. Peta would be heartbroken for him, and it would be difficult to hold himself together in the face of her sympathy.

As it was, he'd been right to be wary because his brother was there. As soon as he saw Isak, he knew it would not be good. If his brother was here on a Monday morning, it meant he'd lost his job.

'Hey, Leifur,' said Isak. 'Who's your friend?' He got up from the table looking far too keen to meet Astrid.

'This is Astrid,' Leifur said.

'Astrid! It's lovely to see you again,' said Peta, coming over and hugging her as if they'd known each other for years. 'And you too, Leifur.'

'Hey, Mamma.' He hugged his mother. 'Astrid, this is my brother, Isak.'

'Great to meet you,' Isak said, hugging her.

Leifur clenched his fists. Peta noticed and put a calming hand on his arm, shooting him a meaningful look at the same time. The split-second glance said to him, calm down, you don't need to worry; you know what your brother's like.

'Coffee and cake for you both? I made a *Skúffukaka*,' she said.

'Ooh, lovely, thank you,' said Astrid.

He nodded to his mother. She knew he loved the rich chocolate cake.

'Day off?' Isak asked.

'Yes, our first day off since we started,' Astrid said brightly.

If only he'd known Isak would be here, he could have warned Astrid.

'Day off for you as well, is it?' Leifur asked his brother, unable to resist.

'I've been laid off,' Isak said as if it was nothing of concern.

'Oh no,' Astrid said. 'That's awful.'

'Isak was wondering whether you have any jobs going on the boat,' Peta asked.

'No, I'm sorry.' He wasn't sorry at all. The last thing he wanted was to involve his brother in his new start. It was one thing when he was running the family business, because Isak was family and that had given him some protection, but the fact was he was a shirker who never took responsibility for anything, and he wasn't about to subject his new business partner and the wider company to that. He'd seen how hard everyone worked, and Isak would let him down. 'There's only me and Astrid on the boat.'

'You run that boat with just the two of you?' Isak said.

'Well, we have Eva to help, but that's more for guest comfort,' said Astrid.

'I told Isak that it had only been the two of you on the trial run, and I thought you could probably do with another pair of hands,' Peta said, looking innocently at Leifur.

'It isn't up to me,' Leifur said. 'Jonas does all the hiring.'

'But you could put a word in for your brother,' said Peta.

Leifur sighed. Hadn't he already said they didn't need anybody? 'Okay, sure.'

Peta clapped her hands together. 'Wonderful. Come on, sit down and let's eat this cake.'

Being around Isak put Leifur in a bad mood, and his spirits didn't rise even after he and Astrid had left Peta's house and were walking back to his.

'I enjoyed that,' Astrid said. 'Your brother seems like fun.'

That was it exactly. Isak was the fun one, and whenever he and Leifur were in the same room together, Isak won everyone over, leaving Leifur looking like the boring sensible brother. Even Astrid thought Isak was fun. What else could she think without knowing what he was really like behind his happy-go-lucky exterior? And it felt too late to explain to her. Anything he said now would sound as if he were being childish.

'Hey, Leifur.' She tucked her hand into his elbow since he had his hands in his pockets.

'Sorry. Yeah, I suppose he is.'

'You two don't get along?'

'Not really.'

'So I'm guessing you're not planning to put a word in for him with Jonas?'

'No.'

'Right.'

'You think that's bad?' Because it suddenly seemed worse that Astrid might think badly of him than anything Isak could do.

'No. I mean, I don't know him, but he seemed perfectly nice, and keen to work with you.'

He sighed. 'I think it was my mother more than Isak. I'm not sure he actually asked.'

'You're right,' she said. 'I hadn't even noticed, but yes, it was your mother.'

That little chink of light, of realisation by Astrid that things hadn't played out how she thought, gave Leifur the opportunity he needed.

'That's how it is with Isak. He charms people, especially our mother, into helping him get what he wants. He makes no effort, takes no responsibility and yet somehow manages to be everyone's favourite person.'

'You're my favourite person.'

He looked down at her and smiled, although he still felt down in the dumps. 'Thanks.'

'And you don't have to do anything about helping him out if you don't want to. We genuinely don't have a job for him on the boat, so even if you wanted to say that you had spoken to Jonas for him, you can be pretty certain the answer would be no.'

He took his hand out of his pocket and reached for Astrid's hand. 'I'm sorry. He brings out the worst in me.'

'I have an idea. Let's head back to town and go out. We can have an early night out and be back at mine in time for a decent night's sleep.'

That sounded good. He needed to blow off some steam, and besides, he hadn't taken Astrid out anywhere yet, and it was as good a time as any to start now.

'Okay. Early dinner and a couple of drinks?'

'Do you have anywhere in mind?'

'I have the perfect place,' he said.

Kaffivagninn was on the far side of the harbour and was

supposedly the oldest restaurant in Reykjavik, housed in an unassuming wooden building with the name in lights across the roof and a large wooden terrace that overlooked the sea. It had been renovated during the past few months and looked more modern and perhaps more inviting than it had done before, but it still held all the nostalgia that Leifur remembered, and he loved it. He'd eaten there with his father and brother and their crew many times when they'd dropped off their catch in Reykjavik. If it had been a good day, his father would treat them all to fish and chips before they headed home.

'I always thought this place was just for fishermen,' said Astrid.

'It used to be years ago, but every time I come here there are more tourists than the time before. I guess that's why they renovated it.'

They sat at a table for two next to the windows that overlooked the sea. They each ordered a beer and fish and chips.

'*Skál*,' she said. 'To us.'

'To us. *Skál*.'

'Do you think your brother can find a job on another fishing boat?'

Leifur had been hoping that Isak could be left behind for the rest of the day, but he didn't want to be short with Astrid and refuse to talk about it. Anyway, he got the feeling that she was on his side, which made him feel less defensive.

'He could.'

'What do you think happened?'

'I expect he got too comfortable and thought he could get away without pulling his weight.'

'That's the voice of experience.'

'I wish I was closer to him, honestly. I wish we had what you and Gudrun have, something more like a friendship but I realised a long time ago it wasn't going to be like that between us. It was hard to come to terms with, and I'm not sure our mother will ever accept it, but that's how it is.'

It hurt that Isak didn't seem to place any value on the concept of being a family. He kept in touch with their mother, popped in every so often, usually when he wanted food or money, and Leifur was grateful for that for Peta's sake.

'Was it hard being his boss?'

'It was impossible.'

'Because he was angry that you had the company, and he didn't?'

'It was just as much his as it was mine. He could have been captain of *Brimfaxi*, but he didn't want to be. It wasn't anything to do with me being the oldest. I was the one who carried everything on after our father died, and Isak dropped in and out when it suited him. When he needed money. If it'd been anyone else, I would have fired them, but Mamma is very good at pleading his case, so I gave him a hundred second chances.'

'And I understand why you can't do that anymore. Aside from it being heartbreaking to give someone chance after chance when all they do is take advantage of your good nature, you worked hard to make this happen with Jonas and you don't want to jeopardise that.'

Leifur felt a lump in his throat and took a slug of his beer to clear it. He coughed and looked out of the window, willing his eyes to dry up before he had to look at Astrid again. No one had ever understood the relationship he had with Isak. But Astrid did. She'd listened to his version of how things are with his brother rather than taking Isak on face value. And it meant everything to him.

He reached across the table for Astrid's hand. How incredible was it that she had his back?

'Thank you for being on my side.'

She smiled, the warmth in her face making the lump in his throat threaten to return again.

'It's the best side, Leifur, and you don't need to wonder whether I'm there. I always will be.'

He couldn't let himself believe that she actually meant always. It was easy to say, but they weren't there yet. Talking about Isak, something he'd never done with anyone before, helped him feel confident about sticking to his guns and not helping Isak get a job at Iceland Adventures.

'I'm not going to help Isak get a job, but I could talk to some fishing friends who might have something. If I don't help, it feels as if I'm letting my mother down.'

'That's a good idea. He needs a job, and it doesn't have to be with you.'

Their fish and chips arrived, and Leifur realised how hungry he was. They hadn't eaten anything except a couple of pieces of toast and the cake at his mother's.

'Oh god, this fish is incredible,' said Astrid. 'I want to savour it but also shove it in as fast as I can, I'm so hungry.'

Leifur laughed, feeling lighter and finally able to shake the day off. 'I think we should go for ice cream after.'

'Oh, can we go to Valdis, the pink place back along the harbour?'

'Sure. I've had the odd rye bread ice cream from there. It's good.'

'Rye bread ice cream?'

'Don't knock it until you've tried it.'

'I'll have some of yours. I'm a salted caramel girl.'

After the ice cream, or half an ice cream, since Astrid liked the rye bread flavour so much she ate most of his, they wandered back into town in search of somewhere to have a beer before heading back to her apartment.

'Hey! Astrid!'

Gudrun was on the other side of the street. She crossed

over and gave Astrid a hug, smiling at Leifur over her sister's shoulder.

'I haven't seen you for ages. How're the tours going? Olafur said they've been full.'

'It's been brilliant so far,' Astrid said, taking his hand. Gudrun clocked it straight away, and shot her sister a look he couldn't quite understand the meaning of.

'Great. So, will you both come for dinner tomorrow night? We're never going to see you otherwise.'

Astrid looked at him, and he smiled, letting her know it was fine with him.

'Okay, we're on,' said Gudrun. 'See you tomorrow. Is seven too early?'

'Eight is better,' he said. 'We won't be back until seven, and we need to prep for the next day.'

'To save us having to get up too early,' Astrid explained.

'Right…' Gudrun gave them a wicked smile, and Astrid rolled her eyes and laughed.

'See you tomorrow.'

26

The following evening, after a successful day of tours with plenty of whales watched, Leifur and Astrid called into her apartment to change before they headed to Gudrun and Olafur's. On the way back out, Sol stuck her head out of her apartment.

'Astrid! I'm so glad I caught you both.' Astrid's heart sank, wondering what she might want this time.

'What can we do for you?'

'I'm so grateful to you for helping with the flood the other day, I wanted to invite you to Thor's bar on Thursday night. Drinks are on us to say thank you.'

'Oh, that sounds great. We're working every day this week, though, so I'm not sure —'

'No, you have to come,' Sol insisted. 'Thursday's the best night because it's open mic night. It's always great. You'll really enjoy it.'

'We'd love to,' Leifur said, taking Astrid by surprise.

'Fabulous! You know the place? Down by the harbour?'

'I know it,' Leifur said. 'Thank you, we'll see you on Thursday.'

'You actually want to go to the open mic night?' Astrid said once they were out of the building and walking towards

Gudrun's.

Leifur shrugged. 'It's supposed to be good. Remember, I told you Ned Nokes has played there. Isn't he friends with your sister?'

She remembered the conversation at her housewarming party. And Gudrun had mentioned an open mic night a few times, but Astrid hadn't put two and two together.

'Yes, he and Brun play together.'

'Have you met him?'

'No. Are you a secret Ned Nokes fan?'

Leifur looked sheepish. 'I like the stuff he's done since he went solo. I'm not a fan of The Rush.'

'I'd be worried if you were.'

Gudrun answered the door and ushered them into the kitchen. 'We're eating straight away since you three need to be up early.'

'What are you doing tomorrow, Olafur?' Leifur asked.

'I'm taking a group on a glacier hike. Pick-ups start at five from the hotels.'

'He doesn't mind the early starts,' Gudrun said, placing an enormous dish of lasagna in the middle of the table.

'I'll be glad when the days draw out a bit more and we're not getting up in the dark,' said Astrid.

Gudrun looked at her questioningly, and she realised she'd said "we".

'This looks delicious, Gudrun,' said Leifur.

'Thank you. How are you finding Astrid's cooking?'

He smiled at Astrid, letting her know he was okay with being questioned. 'She's pretty good. We're not thinking too much about food, though.'

Astrid almost choked on her mouthful of lasagna, such was her surprise and delight in his answer. Gudrun looked at him with admiration, which amused Astrid all the more.

'You're living together?' Gudrun said when she dragged

Astrid into the lounge on the pretence of showing her something. Olafur and Leifur were washing up.

'Sort of, although not in the sense that we decided to live together. We're just together all the time.'

'Oh my god. It's been two weeks, As. That's the speed of light, especially for you.'

'What do you mean, especially for me?'

'No offence,' said Gudrun, making Astrid feel her first reaction, to be offended, had been correct. 'But you haven't really had a serious relationship, have you, unless you kept it a secret from me?'

Astrid wished she'd made an effort to keep this one a secret.

'No, but it's been an intense few weeks. We've spent so much time together, I suppose it's progressed quicker than if we saw each other a couple of times a week.'

'That makes sense. Even so, it seems serious already. What are you going to do when you leave?'

When she left. That hadn't even been a possibility, but the email she'd had from the Costa Rica research team, that she'd forgotten about until this morning, might change that.

'I have something to tell you. I haven't told Leifur yet because I don't know what to do.'

'You've got another job,' said Gudrun.

Astrid didn't bother asking her sister how she'd jumped to that conclusion, because she was right.

'A three-month contract on a research vessel in Costa Rica.'

'When?'

'Next week.'

'Next week?'

'Shhh,' Astrid said, looking at the kitchen door. 'I know. I don't even know if Jonas will let me out of the contract, and even if he does, I'm leaving them in the lurch.' And leaving Leifur before the end of the summer.

'You know Jonas will let you out of the contract,' Gudrun said confidently. 'But is it what you want?'

'It's an amazing opportunity, but I'm not sure I want to leave now.'

'Because of Leifur?'

Astrid nodded. 'And if I tell him about it, he'll encourage me to take it even if that's not what he wants.'

'And that makes him a great guy.'

'I know. I love him.'

Gudrun sighed. 'This is a huge decision. You can't change your plans for a guy you've only known for a few weeks.'

'I know that too. At least my head knows that.'

'It's the first time you've been in love, As. How can you know he's the one if you have nothing to compare it to? You can't stay here and work on a tour boat forever instead of following your dreams.'

'I don't know what my dreams are anymore. But I do know that being with Leifur is a dream I didn't know I had. I don't know how I can tell him I'm leaving.'

'He'll understand.'

Gudrun was probably right. He would understand, even if he didn't like it, but that didn't make it any easier to tell him, or to be sure it was the right decision.

Astrid slumped onto the sofa and, after a moment, Gudrun sat next to her.

'I'm thrilled that you and Leifur are together. I really like him, and I can see he makes you happy. What I'm saying is that until now, you've loved your work and you had no plans to change course. It should be the easiest decision in the world.'

'I do love my work, and I never thought I needed a relationship to make me happy. But now, I look back and realise that I wasn't as happy as I am now. I might not have much experience of being in love to compare that against, but

I know how I feel, Gudrun. I'm happy. And on some level, I wonder whether that's all that matters?'

Gudrun hugged her. 'You're right. It's so important. I just worry that a couple of weeks is not long to base a big decision on.'

'Leifur and I have talked about this. We agreed we'd have the summer, and now I'm going back on that promise.'

'It's only three months. You could come back afterwards and pick up where you left off.'

'It's not fair. I can't ask him to wait for me.'

Astrid led the way back into the kitchen, giving Leifur a broad smile when he flashed her a concerned look. She'd have to talk to him about it later. Now that she'd told Gudrun, she realised she'd already decided to leave Reykjavik.

'Leifur was saying you're coming to the open mic night on Thursday,' Olafur said. 'Should be a good night. Ned and Anna are back this week, so I expect Ned and Brun will play a few songs.'

'Oh, that sounds great,' Astrid said.

'It's a good night out,' said Gudrun. 'Do you play anything, Leifur?'

'Only the harmonica. One of the crew on the boat had a guitar, so it was good to while away the time.'

'Perhaps you should join in on Thursday?' Gudrun said.

Leifur held his hands up and shook his head. 'Absolutely not. I'm looking forward to watching, not taking part.'

'I'm with you there,' said Olafur. 'My idea of hell, having to stand up in front of everyone and do that.'

'You kind of do that every day at work,' Astrid said. 'I actually love that part myself, and I didn't know if I would be any good at it.'

'I suppose I do,' said Olafur. 'If you love what you're talking about it's easy, right?'

'Exactly. I love working with people, guests. It's so satisfying,' said Astrid.

'Not all the time,' said Olafur, laughing.

'Maybe not.' She told him the story of the woman with the checklist.

'Ah, yes. We have had people ask us to take them to the spot where they can see the purple aurora. I guess it's important to remember that's what we're there for. To inform people. That's why they come on a tour. But you'll always get people who get cross if they don't get what they were expecting, even if what they're expecting is impossible.'

'You love the customer service stuff? I do too. I never thought you'd enjoy that,' Gudrun said.

'Neither did I. It's taken me by surprise.'

'You could have worked for me after all.'

'I'm not sure I'd do as well talking about candles and cushions. The whales have got something to do with why I like it.'

As they said goodnight, Gudrun gave Astrid a tight hug. 'Love you,' she whispered in Astrid's ear.

'Love you,' she whispered back.

'Do you think I'm winning your sister over?' Leifur asked as they walked hand in hand back to Astrid's apartment.

'Definitely.' She paused, knowing she couldn't wait any longer. 'She thinks you're the right man for me because you'll understand.'

'Understand what?'

'When I tell you I've been offered a job and will need to leave next week.'

Leifur stopped and looked at her, his face grief-stricken. 'Next week? But what about the summer?'

They sat down on someone's garden wall.

'I wanted the summer too, but this is an amazing opportunity. I applied for it when I was still in Tromsø. I didn't think I had a chance because my specialism is with North Atlantic mammals, but it turns out they're keen to include the different migratory patterns between the northern and southern hemispheres in their study. It's only for three months.' Inside, her heart was screaming, three months? How will that be possible? You can't survive without him for three months. And now she'd said it out loud, nothing would be the same again.

'Of course you should take it,' he said, with no enthusiasm or feeling.

And this was what she'd expected. He'd say it was fine because he wouldn't want to stand in her way. She knew his heart was breaking because hers was too, but he wouldn't admit it. She could already tell his heart was closing ranks to protect him. He was distancing himself even before she'd told him her decision.

'I'm having trouble seeing past the fact that I want to be with you, Leifur. I know this is a great opportunity, but things have changed for me since I came here, since I met you.' He had to know that it wasn't easy for her either. That she wasn't waltzing off to Costa Rica without a backward glance.

'You're not made to stay here forever, Astrid, we both knew that. It's easy to fall in love but not so easy to stay in love in the face of opportunities like this.'

'It doesn't mean I'm not in love with you anymore,' she said, wanting to push back against what she knew was his instinct for self-preservation.

He looked at her with such tenderness in his eyes. She knew he was battling to say what he thought was the right thing over what he felt in his heart. 'I can't be in love with you. I can't wait for you to come back because you might not come back, and that's okay. It means we're not meant to be.'

A sob came out, unintentionally, and Leifur put his arm around her shoulders and pulled her to him, comforting her even though she was the one doing all the hurting. 'I'm sorry,' she said.

'Come on. Let's go.'

They walked back to her apartment in silence, their arms wrapped around each other in comfort. She could hardly believe that this was going to lead to anything good. Nothing was worth this. She'd hurt the only man she'd ever loved. Driven him away, although he was too generous to treat her as she deserved and leave.

At the door to the apartment building, she opened it and stepped inside, but Leifur stayed outside.

'I'm going to sleep on the boat.'

'No, please…'

'I need to be alone. I'll see you in the morning.' He gave a small smile, turned and left.

Astrid gulped down a sob, closed the door and ran up the stairs two at a time until she was in her own apartment and could cry for what she'd done to him. What she'd done to herself, because what she'd said to Gudrun earlier was still true. These past few weeks had been the happiest of her life. It had taken over thirty years to make that happen, and now she'd ruined it in the space of less than an hour. What if the Costa Rica trip wasn't her dream job after all? She'd have lost everything. And how would Leifur ever trust her again even if she came back, and they picked up where they left off?

27

'Is everything alright?' Eva asked Leifur on Wednesday morning. He knew he looked awful. It was just as well he had stayed on the boat because he'd spent most of the night awake and angry with himself, and if he'd stayed with Astrid, he'd have put a brave face on and been feeling much worse for that.

'I didn't sleep very well,' he said.

'Is Astrid okay? You usually arrive together.'

He laughed because despite everything, it was funny that he and Astrid had tried to keep their relationship away from work, even timing their arrival every morning to be before Eva, and yet she knew. 'She'll be in.'

Astrid arrived just before the first guests. Unusually, she was wearing makeup, which he assumed was so that she could look halfway better than he did.

'Good morning,' he said, smiling. He felt a lot better now that he'd had all night to think about it. There was no point in hoping she'd change her mind and stay, because even if she did, she would never be here for good. He also knew that falling out of love with her was going to be the hardest thing ever, and he wasn't going to even try until she'd gone.

'Morning. Are you okay? I mean, I know you're not, but

are we going to be okay today?'

'Of course we are. Let's have a normal day and talk about it tonight.'

'*Hæ*, Astrid. Are you okay? You both look awful,' Eva said.

They both laughed, and Leifur was glad that they were on the same page and could work together whatever else was going on.

'I don't get the joke,' said Eva, shaking her head and going below deck.

'I'll tell her later,' said Astrid. 'I'm going to ask Jonas whether he'd consider letting her step up to do the commentary. What do you think?'

'It's a great idea. She's already been trained by you, and it's easier to find someone to run the galley than it is to find a marine biologist.'

Thankfully, the day went to plan, which Leifur was grateful for because although he had somewhat come to terms with the situation, he wasn't in the mood to deal with anything out of the ordinary.

'Shall we pick up some fish and chips and take them home?' Astrid suggested after they left the boat for the day.

He tried not to think too hard about how she'd said home as if that was actually the case. 'Sure. Good idea.'

While she dished the food up onto plates, he took two beers from the fridge and popped the tops. This was probably going to be tough, however much he thought he'd come to terms with it last night.

'I emailed them this morning and accepted the job,' she said.

'That's good.'

She looked at him as if he'd said something wrong, and suddenly he realised that the conversation they'd had last night was about to continue.

'Do you think this is okay, Leifur? Do you care that I'm

leaving?' She had tears in her eyes, and he wanted to ask her why she would think that on any level he would be happy about her leaving. But he didn't because it was her decision and what he wanted couldn't factor into it. She knew he loved her, and she knew he wasn't leaving Iceland. If he had to remind her of that to make her stay, then she would never be his anyway.

'I want you to be happy. If this is what you want, you have to go for it.'

'It takes away our summer.' Tears were spilling from her eyes now.

He reached over and wiped her cheek gently with his thumb. 'This summer is not our only chance. If it's meant to be, we'll have more than a summer in the end.' He wanted to believe that they were destined to be together, and that this was a blip on the road designed to test them. To give them certainty about their feelings for each other. He'd never believed in destiny before, but now the hope that even if she left now, she might come back someday was all he had. And he'd wait. He wouldn't tell her that because it was unfair to place an expectation on her. But he'd be here if she ever came back.

'Am I taking this job because it's what I should do? I want to know I'm choosing the right thing, and at the moment I can't think straight. Costa Rica should be my dream job, but it feels like I'll be leaving everything behind.'

She leant into him, and he cradled her head against his chest, willing her to know that if he thought it was fair, he'd be telling her to listen to her heart. And at the same time, he wanted to scream because did she know how it felt having to comfort her when everything she was doing was killing him?

'The only way to be sure is to take the job. If you're on the research boat in Costa Rica and desperately missing the humpback whales in Faxaflói Bay, you'll be certain that coming back to Reykjavik is the right decision.'

'You think I should do it?'

He exhaled. He had to be patient, but she'd already told him she'd taken the job. It'd be so much easier for them both if she would accept that she'd decided and move on without dwelling on it. Then at least they could try to enjoy the time they had left together. 'You know I can't tell you that.'

She pulled away from him and smiled, tears still shining in her eyes. 'Thank you. I know you're trying not to be a part of this decision. And it only makes me love you all the more.'

Leifur spent another night on *Brimfaxi*. He could have stayed with Astrid; she wanted him to, but he needed some space to lick his wounds. Again.

The first two tours on Thursday went perfectly. The weather was fine, cloudy with patches of glorious sunshine, and only the gentlest breeze. Then, as they left the harbour for the third tour of the day, something happened and the engine died.

Leifur came out of the wheelhouse and beckoned Astrid over from the bow where she'd been about to start her safety announcement.

'I'm going down to the engine room to see if it's something I can sort out myself. Otherwise, we'll have to get towed back in.'

'How long before you'll know?'

'Give me five minutes.'

He headed below deck. In his experience, there were two or three things that caused the engine to cut out, and he was confident he could fix one or more of them and have *Brimfaxi* back on her way. He checked the fuel line first, and it was fine. The spark plugs were still clean from when he'd done the scheduled maintenance a few weeks ago. The next thing he checked were the fuel filters, and there was the problem. Considering he changed them a few weeks ago, there was no way they should be clogged, but they were. That meant there was water getting into the fuel system somehow, or the fuel was contaminated. Either way, they were going to need towing back into port because he didn't have spare filters on the boat, and even if he did, it wasn't a five-minute job to change them.

'It's not anything I can fix,' he told Astrid. 'I'm going to radio the harbour master. Do you want me to explain to the guests?'

'I can do that. I never thought something like this would happen. We'll have to bump them onto tomorrow's tour, and then I suppose we bump every group onto the next day…'

'We're still catching up from last Sunday, so maybe we need to run an extra tour on Monday to catch up.'

'We had extra time off this week because of the weather, and now it's payback time,' she said with a rueful smile.

While they waited, the guests went below deck, and Astrid and Eva made drinks for them and entertained the guests as best they could until they could be on their way again.

Leifur waited in the wheelhouse. He'd reported the engine failure and requested a tow back into the harbour, but that was going to take some time. But another whale-watching company was going to send out a couple of its rigid inflatable boats to take the guests back to the quay.

'They're here to take the guests,' he said to Astrid. 'You and Eva should go too.'

'I'm not leaving you alone.'

He relented. It was basic health and safety. 'Okay, thanks. I don't know how long it'll take, though.'

'If you'd rather Eva stayed…'

'Astrid,' he said softly.

She turned and left, and he sighed. Was this going to be a repeat of last night because he wasn't sure he could listen to her going back and forth anymore about a decision she'd already made?

They gathered on deck and helped the guests transfer into the RIBs, then he and Astrid waved them off.

'Coffee?'

'That sounds good,' he said.

'I'm sorry about last night,' she began. 'I shouldn't have landed my indecision on you. It wasn't fair.'

'It's okay.'

'No, it isn't. I hurt you, and I was asking you to help me feel better about that.'

'Hey, don't be hard on yourself. I understand.'

She brought the coffee over and set it on the table, taking the seat across from him.

'You're too good,' she whispered, staring into her coffee.

'I'm not as good as you think. I was this close,' he held up his finger and thumb, 'to begging you to stay.'

'Really?'

He nodded. 'I don't want to lose you, but I also won't be the person who stands in the way of your dreams.'

She moved around the table and sat on his lap, looping her arms around his neck. 'Is this okay?'

'Of course. My feelings haven't changed. Have yours?'

'No. If anything, the thought of not being together anymore has made me realise how much I love you.'

For her to say she loved him now made it bittersweet to hear. He put a hand on the back of her neck and gently pulled her to him, kissing her tenderly, moving from her lips to her neck.

'Leifur… this will make it harder.'

'It'll be hard anyway.'

She answered him by tipping her head back and accepting the kisses that he dropped onto her neck. This wasn't going to make it harder. But if it did, he was willing to take the risk for the extra time together. More time to remind him he could be loved, even if the love wasn't strong enough to triumph.

They found each other's lips, switching from soft caresses to needy, breathy kisses.

'Come on.' She took his hand and led him into the forward berth.

He had mixed feelings about that, given it was most recently where he'd spent the night heartbroken, but perhaps this would help vanquish those memories.

'You're sure?' He had to ask. While he was ready — as ready as he could be — to accept the fate of their relationship, he wasn't sure it was going to help Astrid in the same way. 'No expectations.' He hoped that made his position clear; he wasn't holding her to anything, or reading anything into the fact that they were about to make love. He wanted this and wasn't willing to use more words that might talk her out of it.

'Goodbye sex.'

That stung, but they were just words in the heat of the moment, and he forced himself to remember that not five minutes ago she'd told him she loved him.

'I love you,' he breathed into her neck as they lay on the bed in the cabin, the slight roll of the waves adding to the rhythm they were in.

'Leifur… I love you.'

They made love more slowly than they'd done before, with the care of two people who knew it might be the last time. The playful and light-hearted love they'd shared until now had changed into something deeper, full of intention and tenderness.

'I don't want to make things harder by adding hope into the mix, but if I come back afterwards…'

'We should take the weeks we've had and hold them close, but we can't let ourselves be guided by them. It wouldn't be right.'

'It wouldn't be fair,' she whispered with a small nod. 'It's like asking you to wait for me.'

He nodded and gently pushed her hair behind her ear so that he could see her face. 'Don't look back when you go, Astrid.'

She nodded, her face crumpling into a sob before she buried it in his shoulder. He took a deep breath. He didn't need to cry anymore, but that didn't mean his heart wasn't breaking watching Astrid.

It wasn't long before the boat arrived to tow them, announcing its arrival with a blast of its horn. Astrid, who'd fallen asleep, stirred as he got up and pulled his clothes on.

'Hey, we need to go up.'

'Okay. I'm coming.'

He headed up to the deck feeling better. Loving someone for three weeks, however fiercely, would not be his undoing. Not when he'd worked so hard to build his new life. He had to keep moving on, and work through the pain. And that was something he knew how to do.

28

'I wish we could blow off tonight.' Astrid said when they had been towed back to the harbour. She was helping Leifur replace the fuel filters. Not exactly helping, but watching and passing tools when he asked for them.

'Why don't we? We're going to end up being late by the time I go home and get changed.' He was oily and probably tired.

'You don't have to go home. You could come to my place. Some of your clothes are on the chair in my bedroom.' This afternoon in the forward berth had been very cathartic, and although she was still heartbroken at leaving him, she had come to terms with her decision enough to know that he was right. It was going to be hard whatever happened, so what point was there in staying away from each other?

'So you do want to go?'

'We don't have much time left. It might be fun.'

'We don't have much time left, so you want to spend it with other people?'

'I know you were looking forward to seeing Ned Nokes. I want that for you.'

Leifur guffawed into the engine. 'You got me.'

They were both exhausted when they got back to Astrid's,

even though they hadn't been out much longer than a normal day in the end. Astrid defrosted some soup and warmed some bread in the oven.

'Sorry, I haven't got anything else in. You'll have to fill up on bread,' she said.

'It's delicious, thank you.'

They ate in comfortable silence, then Leifur said, 'I won't stay tonight.'

They hadn't discussed the fact that he hadn't stayed since she had told him about the job. Tonight felt like any other night when they'd got in from work, so she guessed that's why he'd said it, because he needed her to know that despite what had happened that afternoon, things had changed between them.

'Okay. But you know you could.'

'I know.'

Maybe this afternoon had been the last time. And if it was, that would be okay. It had been a goodbye of sorts and made her realise that her decision had been made. Of course, she had already decided. She'd be flying to New York on Tuesday for the flight to Central America, and she'd emailed Jonas yesterday to ask if she could leave, but it hadn't stopped her from ruminating on the whole thing, going over and over it. Until this afternoon. Now, she felt more peaceful about it. Perhaps because she knew Leifur loved her, and that was something she didn't have to leave behind. She could take that with her because that was hers forever, even if his heart couldn't be.

They called for Sol on their way out, as they'd arranged. Thor was already at the bar.

'He's saved us a table,' Sol said when they got there. The place was heaving, and they made their way through the people standing around the bar area, those who hadn't got a table, to the front where there were tables and chairs all facing the stage.

'Hey!' Gudrun waved from a table at the far side.

'We'll just go and say hello,' Astrid said to Sol, who was heading in Thor's direction anyway.

'I'll get the drinks,' said Sol. 'Our table is the one next to Gudrun's.'

Leifur followed Astrid over to where Gudrun and Olafur were sitting with the rest of their friends.

'That's Ned over there,' said Gudrun, nodding to the side of the stage where Brun was holding a guitar and saying something about it to Ned.

'He looks different in real life,' said Astrid.

'I think it's just that he lets himself relax here,' said Gudrun.

'I didn't know he wore glasses,' said Astrid.

'Those are for me,' said a woman over Gudrun's shoulder.

'This is Anna, Ned's partner. Anna, this is my sister Astrid and her friend Leifur.'

'Great to meet you both,' said Anna. 'Are you joining us?'

'No, but we're on the table next to you.'

'Thor and Sol live downstairs from Astrid,' Gudrun explained. 'So they've got the VIP treatment tonight.'

'How is it being back in Reykjavik?' Anna asked Astrid.

'I've loved it, but I'm leaving for a new job on Tuesday.'

'Just a flying visit, then.'

'Yes, in the end.' Although it had been so much more than that. It was life-changing in the sense that she'd fallen in love for the first time ever, taken on the challenge of working with guests and found she loved it, and connected with her sister properly.

'I love it here but mainly because I don't live here all the time,' said Anna. 'I can't cope with the winters, but I guess that's not why you're leaving since you must be used to them.'

'I don't mind the weather,' said Astrid. 'I go where the work takes me, and since I specialise in North Atlantic mammals, it's usually cold.'

'Why are you going to Costa Rica, then?' Gudrun asked, frowning.

'I'm joining a study on southern hemisphere humpback whales. They're migrating to warmer places during the southern hemisphere winter.'

'You're going to Costa Rica?' Rachel said, joining in the conversation. 'Jonas never told me that. How amazing!'

'It'll be interesting having had some close encounters with the northern hemisphere humpbacks over the past couple of weeks,' said Astrid. 'And it's the rainy season in Central America so it's probably just a warmer version of bad weather.'

'Did I hear my name?' Jonas said, appearing next to Rachel and putting his arm round her.

'You didn't tell me Astrid's going to Costa Rica.'

'Didn't I?'

Rachel rolled her eyes. 'It's typical. I'm sure half the conversations he has with me only happen in his head.'

Jonas laughed. 'I know I said it in my email, but I'm sorry to see you go,' he said to Astrid, moving between everyone to give her a hug. 'You set us off with high standards, and it'll be tough to fill your shoes.'

'Will you ask Eva to take over?'

'I'm going to see if we can find another qualified marine biologist, but Eva has agreed to take over in the short term.'

'That's great. And Jonas, thank you for offering me the job. I never imagined I'd love it as much as I do.' It was still a constant surprise to her that even with twenty-plus tours under her belt now, she never found it boring.

'I had a visit from your brother today,' Jonas said, turning to Leifur, who'd been chatting to Olafur.

Astrid felt Leifur stiffen next to her.

'I'm sorry,' Leifur said. 'He asked me to see if there were any jobs going, but I haven't had a chance to talk to you about it.'

It made Astrid sad that Leifur felt the need to apologise for his brother.

'No problem at all,' said Jonas. 'He's a nice guy who's had a run of bad luck, by the sounds of it. Anyway, I said I'd keep him in mind if anything came up.'

'Thanks. I appreciate it.'

'I hear you had engine trouble today.'

'The filters were clogged. All sorted now, but we had to get a tow into the harbour, so there'll be a bill for that heading our way. And we had to offer the guests a tour tomorrow, which means some guests will need bumping over. I spoke to Siggi, and he was going to sort all of that out this afternoon. I said we'd do an extra sailing on Monday to help out.'

'I appreciate that, and I'm sure Siggi did too. Makes it a bit easier to sort out.'

Thor climbed onto the stage and stood waiting for the crowd to notice him and quieten down a bit. Astrid and Leifur sat down at their table.

'They're about to start,' said Sol, slipping into the seat next to Leifur. 'Thor introduces the acts, and he'll sit with us because the bar won't be so busy once it starts.'

'Welcome!' Thor said, his voice coming through the speakers and causing everyone to cheer. 'We're going to start with one of your favourite acts. Let's hear it for Ned and Brun!'

Ned Nokes and Brun came onto the small stage, both carrying guitars and grinning.

'Good evening!' Ned said, and everyone cheered. 'We're going to kick off with one of our favourites. This song was born here, and we always think of you guys when we play it.'

Everyone cheered as if they knew what was coming, whereas Astrid and Leifur looked at each other and shook their heads because they had no idea. But when the song started, they recognised it. It was a beautiful love song that had been popular a couple of years ago and had been a sensation amongst Icelandic people because some of the lyrics were in Icelandic.

Astrid felt Leifur's hand move onto her thigh, under the table. Without hesitation, she took it and gave it a squeeze. She didn't need him to say anything to know that he felt the same way as she did; sat listening to the first love song they'd heard together, but for the last time.

When everyone clapped and cheered at the end, Astrid leaned into him and said, 'That's our song.'

He nodded and smiled, and Astrid wondered how she was going to leave him without looking back. He was everything she never knew she wanted in a partner. She was throwing away the only love that had come her way so far in her life, and for what? Okay, for an amazing opportunity to work on a significant research project that would hopefully lead to other opportunities in the future. However she span it, however she talked herself in and out of staying in Iceland, the fact was that she didn't want her career to end on a whale-watching tour boat at thirty-five. She'd loved it, had been surprised at how much she got from the interaction with the guests and how good it felt to share the knowledge she'd built up. But deep down she knew it wouldn't be enough for her. And she didn't want to risk the day coming where she'd resent Leifur for being the reason she chose it. That's exactly why he'd told her not to look back, because he didn't want that either.

So at the end of the night when it felt like the most natural thing in the world to walk back to her apartment hand in hand, they said goodbye and Leifur headed off to *Brimfaxi* for another evening in the forward berth.

'He's not staying at yours tonight?' Sol asked. They were walking back together while Thor stayed behind to close up.

'No, I'm leaving on Tuesday for a new job in Costa Rica.'

'That's such a shame. We've only just got to know each other. And what about you and Leifur?'

'We're not going to do long distance,' said Astrid. 'Reykjavik isn't really my home. I thought it could be for the summer at least, but I don't know if I'll come back after this job finishes.'

'Not even to pick up with Leifur again?'

'It's too much to ask him to wait when I don't know when I'll be back. We decided it's better to have had a great time together but call it a day.'

'Oh my god, that sounds so thought through. Aren't you going to miss him like mad?'

'Yes.' Her heart ached thinking about it. They only had three more days on the boat together.

'I've been meaning to explain about the pregnancy tests in the toilet cistern.'

'Sol, you don't have to.'

'Months ago, I thought I was pregnant and I was worried Thor would find the test so I hid it but then before I could take the test, I got my period and then forgot to take them out.'

'Are you guys trying?'

'Not really. We've talked about it but we're not trying yet.'

'I can't imagine knowing when the right time would be.'

'I know. That's part of the problem. So you and Leifur, is it the real thing?'

'It's the closest I've ever got.'

'I'd never be able to leave if I felt like that, but then I've never had a career like yours. Do you think you'll ever settle back here one day?'

'I've never really thought about it. It's hard to know in this career where you're going to end up. It could be teaching, it could be working in a research institute or for a charity. Until now I've taken the next step when I had to without planning ahead but now, I'm starting to realise that if I want to settle down anywhere, I need to make some longer term decisions.'

'Probably,' Sol agreed. 'It's hard falling in love and then having to leave, especially when it's someone as lovely as Leifur.'

'It is, but it's harder imagining staying in one place for the rest of my life.'

'You're doing the right thing then.' Sol linked her arm in Astrid's. 'You'll never be happy if you compromise on the things that are most important to you. You love Leifur, but going all in and giving up your career based on knowing him for a few weeks is crazy in anyone's world.'

Astrid nodded. Sol was talking complete sense, and in her heart she knew she was doing the right thing, but that didn't make it easy.

29

The last days on the boat before Astrid left were wonderful and dreadful at the same time. They saw the fin whale again two days in a row, and Leifur loved seeing how excited she was about that and was thrilled she was leaving on a high. Eva was hesitant about taking over the commentary from Astrid, but she'd done the middle tour two days in a row while Astrid manned the galley, and it had gone very well.

It was heartbreaking knowing that this was what he was going to be missing when she left. She was the reason he looked forward to coming to work. She'd been part of *Brimfaxi* since the boat had had her facelift, and there was going to be a gaping Astrid-sized hole in his day, every day for as long as he could imagine.

Worse still, Jonas had had no luck finding a suitable replacement for Eva and had suggested they use Isak. He was waiting on the quay on Saturday evening when they got back to the harbour.

'We need someone, he needs a job and if he's anything like you, he'll get stuck into whatever needs doing,' said Jonas.

Leifur didn't feel he could disagree, especially since Jonas had already said he had run out of options and they needed an extra person before Tuesday.

'He'll have to be happy with running the galley then,' Leifur said.

'It's up to you to decide what you need him to do,' Jonas said, not realising that would be easier said than done. 'And the great thing is you've worked together before, so he should slot into the team more easily than a total stranger.'

Astrid strolled over and caught the end of the conversation. 'Oh, you've found someone! I don't suppose there's any chance they can start tomorrow, or even on Monday for the extra tour. I'd love to help out with getting them up to speed before I go.'

'I doubt he'll be able to start that soon,' said Leifur, wanting to prolong the inevitable.

'Let me give him a call,' said Jonas, pulling his phone out and walking away.

'It's Isak,' Leifur said to Astrid, knowing that's all he needed to say for her to understand.

'I'm so sorry,' she said, reaching out to touch him but pulling away as if perhaps she thought he'd reject her. 'Is he going to be happy doing Eva's job?'

'I doubt it.'

'He can start on Monday. At least he'll have one tour to see how you guys do it,' Jonas said.

'Jonas, Isak —' Astrid began.

'It's fine,' Leifur said firmly, laying a hand on her arm. 'Unless you're planning on staying, this is the best option.' He knew he was deliberately playing on the guilt she was already feeling, but he didn't want to get into the details of his relationship with his brother with Jonas. It wasn't Jonas's problem. All he was trying to do was help. Leifur knew it was up to him and Isak to work things out so that they could get along. 'Thanks Jonas. I'll pick up with Isak about it.'

'Great! That's worked out for everyone.'

'Why would you put yourself in that position?' Astrid

asked later when Eva had gone home.

Letting Astrid leave without showing her how heartbroken he was was taking all of his energy. Working together for these past few days had been a battle with himself not to beg her to stay every time he thought about what it would be like without her. And now Isak was coming onto the boat instead, it felt like the final thing that was going to beat him into submission. Over the past weeks, he'd gone from having nothing but a fishing boat to now having a share in a thriving business, a smart tour boat and the girlfriend of his dreams. Battling against Jonas's plan to employ Isak was something he had no energy for. He knew if he said anything, Jonas would probably listen to his views and try to find someone else. But at what cost? At least this way they didn't have to stop operating while they found a new person. Maybe having been out of work for a few weeks, Isak would come into it grateful that he had a job and be willing to be part of the team.

'I don't have any choice,' he sighed. 'We need another Eva, but most students will have their holiday jobs by now. And whatever I think of my brother, perhaps he'll be different this time. I have to give him the chance to prove himself instead of telling Jonas what he's been like in the past and having him be judged by that. It isn't fair.'

'Okay. But promise me you'll tell Jonas at the first sign of anything you're not happy with, the same as you would if it was anyone else.'

'I promise.'

'What are you doing tonight?'

He shrugged. 'Nothing. Going home and sitting by the fjord with a beer.' Part of him hoped she was going to suggest doing something together, but when she didn't, he knew that was probably best.

'That's a good idea. I might do the same on my balcony.'

'You may as well get the use from it while you can.'

'Speaking of which, I had to pay for my apartment for the whole six months, so if you want to stay there instead of sleeping on the boat, you can. Anytime.' She handed him a key.

'Are you coming back to pack it up later in the year?'

'I'm not sure what will happen after Costa Rica, so I'm going to pack everything but leave a key for Gudrun, and she'll pick my stuff up if I can't get back.'

'Thanks, it might be useful sometimes.' He put the key in his pocket knowing he'd never stay there. It would be like ripping a fresh wound in his heart every time he went there, and she wasn't there. The apartment was all her, the same way she said his house was like him.

Now that the nights were drawing out, there was plenty of daylight left when he got home to be able to grab his tarpaulin and a beer and sit down on the shore to enjoy watching the water. The wildflowers and heathers had begun to bloom amongst the moss, making him realise how long it had been since he'd done this. It felt as if the time from when he'd first seen Astrid in her boat to now had been a dream, which it sort of had. The time he'd had with Astrid was so brief, it felt like he'd grasped something magical only to have it fade with the same speed as a dream.

He watched a small boat round the peninsula. He stood up, squinting to see because the sun was lower now and behind the boat, which made it hard to make out. But when the person in the boat waved, there was no mistaking who it was. He waved back, his heart full of the memory of the first time he'd seen her do this. He put his beer down, propped up against a mossy rock and walked along the shore, tracking the progress of the boat until he had to climb the path where his bay ended and the next began, and lost sight of it.

He climbed down the rocks on the other side to the small

sandy inlet and looked up to see Astrid coming towards him. He pulled the boat in as far as he could. She stood at the prow.

'You're looking for whales? Still?' He had to make a joke because he couldn't let himself believe that there might be another reason.

'Last time I did this, I wanted so badly to get out of the boat and sit on the shore with you for a while.'

'You could have.'

She smiled and shrugged. 'I'm not very good at being forward.'

'Neither am I.'

'Kind of a miracle we got to where we did, then.'

'Want to sit with me now?' He held out a hand. She took it and jumped onto the sand. They held hands and walked back to where he'd been sitting. 'Take a seat. I'll get you a beer.'

He grabbed a couple of beers from the fridge and headed back outside. He stood for a moment looking at Astrid with the sun behind her, hair lifting off her shoulders in the breeze, and wondered what on earth he was doing letting her go.

'Here.' He passed her a beer and settled himself down next to her.

'Thanks. And just to say, I'm not here for anything except to watch the sunset with you in the place where we first met.'

He put his arm around her and pulled her to him. 'That's perfect.' It was good to be clear about where they stood. And a relief to know there was a line drawn, because when they'd made love on the boat the other day, it had felt like a goodbye and he had accepted that. Since Astrid had got out of the boat here, he'd been anxious that this might turn into the same thing, and while that would have been wonderful, it opened him up to too much hope that this equally might not be the last time. He couldn't cope with endless goodbyes, and he loved Astrid all the more for coming here and understanding that.

'We didn't do enough of this,' she said, snuggling into his side.

'We would have. We've only had a couple of days off since we met.'

'I think it's a good sign that we managed to work together and not get fed up with each other,' she said.

'I think so too.' Although who knew how it would have gone if they'd had longer. Maybe they would have seen too much of each other. Perhaps work would have been the only thing they had in common, the only thing they talked about. He could tell himself these things, but he knew it wasn't true. The truth was, they had so much to discover about each other, and they'd barely started. He was greedy for every conversation, every moment they could be alone together and every time she smiled only for him.

'Will you be alright with Isak?'

'Of course. I have to give him a chance, and maybe it'll be different this time because the work is different, less pressured.'

'I hope so. I hate the thought that I've put you in this situation.'

He hated it too, but he didn't blame her. Isak was family, and Leifur would always feel an obligation to him, or at least to their mother, to help him out if he could.

'It will go one of two ways. He will either embrace the opportunity and be the perfect employee or he will take advantage. I hope he proves me wrong because I'm not the only boss he has to answer to anymore.' He took his arm away from Astrid, put his beer between his thighs and leant back on his elbows. 'Let's not spend our last evening talking about Isak.'

'Thank you for not hating me for leaving.'

'Astrid, I'll never hate you. I know it's the wrong time for us. And I also know that the right time might never come and it wouldn't be right for either of us to wait. I think we had something very special. Something I don't think I will find again, but if you had the chance at that with someone else, someone who is where you are, you should take it.'

She turned her head slightly towards him, but kept her eyes on the water. 'I won't find anyone else like you.'

'You don't know that.'

'I know that better than anything, Leifur. But I also know I can't stay because of you. I never thought I'd have to choose between two things that I love.'

It could have hurt him to hear that he had come second, but he knew how much her work meant to her, and he couldn't be angry about that. And it wasn't as if he was willing to change anything about his life to make things work.

'I'm doing the same, but staying here instead of being willing to take the risk and come with you.'

'I wouldn't want you to do that.'

'I know. But that's why I understand, and that's why you have to go.'

She leant over and settled her head on his shoulder. 'I wonder if we'll always love each other because of that?'

'Falling out of love with you is going to be hard work. I might not start right away,' he said, planting a kiss on the top of her head.

'Ditto.'

30

The end of the season was almost upon them. It was hard to imagine now how different things would be if Astrid had stayed because the time she spent on the boat once the tours were actually up and running was such a small part of the summer in the end.

Eva had taken the commentary job in her stride after a slightly rocky start. The biggest hurdle they'd had to overcome was finding a rhythm again once Isak joined them. Leifur knew Eva had found it hard to work with him to begin with, and he'd thought it was quickly going to become apparent that Isak wouldn't work out. He'd seen it coming, the way he had been reluctant to learn from Eva on the last tour they did with Astrid, his only chance at having a proper handover from her. With him being older than Eva, she didn't feel able to challenge him about his attitude, but when Jonas suggested to her that she ought to as the more senior staff member between the two of them, things changed. Eva grew in confidence, and Isak continued to arrive at work on time — something unprecedented in his days on the fishing boat, and he was fun, pleasant to be around and began to play a supporting role for both Eva and Leifur.

Jonas had called a staff meeting to discuss the plans for the end of the summer. After the tour on Tuesday evening, Leifur drove the three of them to Jonas's house.

'Do you think he's got someone to take over from me?' Eva said. She was due to leave for Canada in a few days and was worried about leaving them in the lurch.

'You mustn't worry about it,' Isak said. 'I've heard you say enough stuff about whales that I could take over from you.'

Eva laughed. 'I'm still not sure you know the difference between a minke whale and a dolphin.'

'That's fair,' said Isak. 'But most of the guests don't either. I reckon I can get away with it.'

Leifur smiled to himself. He and Isak were getting on better than they had in years. Perhaps because the jobs they had on the boat were different and Leifur didn't need to be Isak's boss. Isak, much like Astrid, had discovered that he enjoyed the customer-facing part of the job. He was a naturally charming and attentive host, which surprised him as much as it did Leifur.

Leifur pulled the truck up outside Jonas's house, and the three of them climbed out.

'Nice place,' said Isak. He knocked on the door, and Jonas answered almost instantly.

'Come in,' he said. 'Go through to the kitchen. We'll eat and then have a proper chat.'

'Hi,' said Rachel, who was already in the kitchen. 'I hope you all like curry.'

'Lovely,' said Eva, going over to the stove to have a look.

'Beer for you guys?' Jonas asked.

'Or we have wine,' said Rachel.

'Wine's great for me,' said Eva, while Isak and Leifur opted for beer.

'How's the whale-watching?' Rachel asked. 'Is there any difference in what you see compared to the start of the summer?'

'Not really,' Eva said, looking at Leifur, who shook his head in agreement. 'I think we could carry on, maybe reduce to two tours a day once the prime tourist season is over.'

'What do you think about doing northern lights tours out in the bay?' Jonas asked.

'So we're not waiting until after we've eaten for the business talk?' Rachel said.

'You know how it is,' Jonas said, shrugging.

'I should do by now.'

'It's a good idea,' said Leifur. 'Not many companies are doing that.'

'And you don't need me for those,' said Eva.

'We could put one of the team on board to do the northern lights talk,' Jonas said.

'I wouldn't mind learning that,' Isak said.

'Actually, that would be great because sometimes we struggle to cover the existing northern lights tours if Brun or Siggi are away.'

'You need to take the opportunity to have a break,' said Rachel. 'You've been working almost seven days a week.'

'We've had time off for bad weather,' Leifur pointed out.

'Rachel's right,' said Jonas. 'You've all worked hard over the summer. It's easy to think we could carry on at this pace, but it's important to take the opportunity for some downtime.'

'Do you have anyone to take over from Eva?' Isak asked.

Jonas shook his head. 'No. Which makes it the perfect time to stop for a while.'

'Altogether?' Leifur was used to working at the pace they had been. Harder even when he'd been fishing. 'The bad weather hasn't hit yet, and there are still whales to see.'

'We only put dates on the website until the end of August. We could have loaded on more dates, but I wanted to see how things were going. And I think we probably can keep going in some form over the winter, whether it's whale watching or northern lights trips, but now that the summer's over, let's take a different pace.'

'Let's eat,' Rachel said, putting a pan of curry and a bowl of rice on the table. 'Dig in.'

Leifur spooned some curry and rice onto his plate. Although the full days had been a blessing, taking his mind of missing Astrid, perhaps it made sense to take stock of the summer and work through the winter at a slower pace. He knew he'd paid back almost all the loan he'd had from Jonas, and that was despite the wage bill being bigger than they'd planned. It had been a good season.

Rachel, Isak and Eva went into the lounge after dinner, leaving Leifur and Jonas to talk.

'What do you think about having some time off and starting back up in November, on a much-reduced schedule?'

'Honestly, I'm not used to having time on my hands and I'm not very good at it,' said Leifur. 'I'd rather keep going even if it's just a few trips a week.'

'Okay. Let's make a plan.' Jonas opened his laptop and found the scheduling spreadsheet. 'When Eva leaves, that's the end of the whale-watching season for us. It's hard to find a marine biologist willing to work seasonally, and we can't afford to have a permanent one on the payroll.'

'Agreed. But if we run any tours, we'll need another pair of hands.'

'I'll find someone to help out,' Jonas said. 'Shall we agree on three northern lights trips a week until November? After that, the season really gets going, and we'll have a feel for whether we want to increase it to six or seven times a week over the winter.'

'We're more likely to get disrupted by the weather at that time of the year.'

'Exactly. It gives us a bit of room for manoeuvre. And you

and Isak will still be paid the same amount over the winter,' said Jonas, still looking at his spreadsheet as if he hadn't just made the most generous offer in the world.

'We can't accept that.'

'You can. You've both given everything to the company over the summer. If we worked out your hourly rate, I bet it would be a pittance.'

Leifur knew that wasn't true. 'I'd rather we were paying the loan off.'

'I'm not going to be moved on this, Leifur. You run the boat and the tours with little interference from me. The business side of things is my call.'

'Thank you.'

'Besides, you think your brother would be with you on that?'

Leifur laughed. 'Definitely not.'

They heard a knock at the front door, and Olafur appeared in the kitchen. 'Am I interrupting?'

'No, we've just finished.'

Jonas dished out another round of beers, and they went to join the others in the lounge.

'Honestly, Rachel, you need to speak to this woman who brought her felted placemats into the shop today,' Gudrun was saying. 'She's got a studio and is up for you taking tours there, and she could do workshops for you.'

'That sounds amazing,' Rachel said. 'I need to start planning for next summer. I'll pop in and get her details from you.'

It was the first time in a while that Leifur had seen Gudrun. He'd been avoiding her. Astrid's three months had been up around a month ago. They'd not kept in touch over the summer, after agreeing it was best not to, giving them both space to move on. But part of him had thought she would come back after the summer, and the fact she hadn't was something he'd tried not to think about. But seeing Gudrun, he'd have to ask how Astrid was. And then he'd know whether she was still working and that's why she hadn't come back, or if she'd met someone else and that's why she hadn't come back to Reykjavik.

'We haven't seen you for ages,' Gudrun said to him.

'The weather's been good recently, so we haven't had much downtime.'

'Have you heard from Astrid?'

He shook his head, bracing himself for the blow. 'I guess she's finished in Costa Rica now?'

'She's in Tromsø, staying with her friend while she waits for her new job to start.'

'She has a new job?' Suddenly he wanted to know.

'Yes, it's a three-year contract working in Greenland over the winter. I can't think of anything worse, but she's very excited about the prospect of living in a wilderness for a few months.'

'What's she doing up there?' It was easier to ask more, now that he'd started.

'I don't know. Something to do with narwhals.'

'Narwhals?' said Eva. 'Wow. That's amazing.'

'So she won't be back to pack up her apartment?' Leifur asked.

'Aren't you two in touch?' Gudrun said.

Everyone was looking at him now. 'No, it was better to have a clean break.'

'That makes sense,' said Isak, to Leifur's surprise. 'If she's always working away, you'd never see each other.'

'She almost stayed,' said Gudrun. 'It's the longest she's been back for years, and I know she misses it.' She looked at Leifur, telling him in one glance that it was him she was talking about. Astrid missed him.

And he missed her. The ache in his heart was there all the

time, and he'd learnt to live with it. But now, having thought about her, which he tried not to do too often, it grew to an intensity he hadn't experienced since they'd said goodbye.

He drove Eva and Isak back into town and, for the first time since Astrid had left, headed to her apartment. He kept the key in a zipped pocket inside his coat, and it had been untouched since she gave it to him. Leaving his truck on the road outside, he unlocked the door and headed up the stairs.

Although she'd said she was going to pack everything up, she'd left the bed made and some cushions and blankets on the sofa. It was enough for him to feel like she could walk through the door any minute.

He sat on the sofa and grabbed a cushion, giving it a quick sniff to see if there was any trace of her. He laughed softly to himself. What was he doing? Nothing had changed. Their situation — the very reason they couldn't be together — was exactly the same as before.

Except he knew she wasn't coming back now, and he knew that until tonight, he'd been harbouring a hope that she might. Sighing, he got up and ran the tap for a minute before filling a glass and drinking it down in one. Since he was here, he might as well stay the night. It was late, and he had to be back on the boat in a few hours. The bed here was definitely more comfortable than the berth on *Brimfaxi*.

In the morning, he made the bed and let himself out of the apartment feeling like it was yet another goodbye, but this time, he had more of a sense of closure.

He drove his truck to the harbour, parked and headed for the boat. His phone vibrated in his pocket, so he pulled it out, wondering who would text him so early in the morning.

Astrid: Sleep well?

Leifur: How did you know?

Astrid: Sol. This is the first time you've stayed?

He felt as if she was asking, why now? After four months?

And it was hard to answer that in a text. He typed out a couple of messages and deleted them. Then, before he could talk himself out of it, he called her.

'I heard you're going to Greenland, so I know now you're not coming back.'

'You weren't supposed to be waiting for me.'

He exhaled. 'Well, I guess I was.'

There was silence for a moment.

'It's okay,' he said, once he realised there was nothing either of them could say that changed what they'd known four months ago.

'I miss you,' she said.

If he'd had to imagine what Astrid might say in his dreams, this was it. He missed her desperately, but it just made him feel worse knowing that she was still out of reach for him and they had no future. They couldn't both spend years waiting until the time was right and nothing else was going to be in their way. If they wanted to be together, one of them had to want that enough to compromise, and it seemed obvious to him that neither of them was willing to take the risk.

'I went there to say goodbye,' he said. 'I didn't realise until tonight, but I have been waiting for you and I can't do that anymore.'

He heard a muffled noise, then she said, 'And you mustn't. I'll always love you, Leifur.' And she ended the call before he could say anything else.

31

Astrid had been in Nuuk, the tiny capital of Greenland, for a week. Her new contract was with the government of Greenland, and she was part of a small team of scientists monitoring the narwhal population of West Greenland.

Until now, most of her work had been with humpbacks, which were more common below the Arctic Circle but the narwhals were a huge part of what drew her to come to Greenland for this job. They were otherworldly, with their long single tusk, like a unicorn for whales, and their numbers were decreasing. She was going to spend the winter studying them in the West Greenland polynya, an area of sea that historically doesn't freeze over in the winter because of the warm sea currents in that area.

She had been given a tiny house on the edge of a fjord in the northern, old part of Nuuk. The view over the fjord was breathtaking, and Astrid felt a sense of peace as soon as she stepped into the house. It was an enormous relief, since she would be here over the worst of the winter, perhaps snowed in for days at a time. The plan was to collect data before the worst of the weather arrived, at which point she would review and write up the results. The winters in Iceland when she was a child had prepared her for what it would be like to some extent, but the little town of Nuuk was not Reykjavik, so she was planning to accumulate what she could in the way of supplies over the next couple of months in readiness for the days when she might not venture out.

While the weather was still good, cold but bright, and with light evenings, she took advantage of where her new house was and sat outside watching the water as much as she could. It reminded her of Leifur's house, although she'd already seen an abundance of marine life in her fjord; humpback, fin and minke whales had all made an appearance, but she was yet to spot a narwhal.

The tiny deck that faced the water had become her favourite place to sit, and she sipped a hot chocolate while she watched the calm water of the fjord for signs of life. As well as wildlife, there were boats that sailed past regularly. Not only fishing boats, but larger vessels like cruise boats and sailing ships. Today, an elegant sailing ship came into view, and she watched it as it cut through the glassy water at a leisurely pace, the ripples it created lapping at the rocks beneath her. It slowed right down, and she watched as a small wooden tender was lowered over the side of the boat, followed by someone climbing into it and setting off. Towards her.

She squinted her eyes, but at this distance it was hard to see the figure in the boat, but for some reason she needed to. She held her breath because this boat seemed as if it were heading deliberately in her direction rather than anywhere more logical, like the quay in town. As the boat came closer, she had a feeling about why it was coming this way, and once she could make out the figure sitting next to the tiller, she could hardly believe it. Leifur.

So many questions were running through her head as she watched him approach. The main one being, what was he doing here? But as he got closer and she could see his face, could see the smile despite it being hidden by his beard, her heart filled with the love she still held for him. It had taken everything she had not to head straight back to Iceland to see him when she got back from Costa Rica because she already knew then that she'd be coming to Greenland. It would have been so easy to go to Reykjavik and stay in her apartment for a month but she knew she and Leifur would have picked up where they left off and it wasn't fair to either of them when she was only going to leave again.

The boat came close, but it wasn't like Hafnarfjörður where the sea gave way to a shingle shoreline. Here, the coastline was rocky, and there was no way Leifur could disembark or even secure the boat to a mooring, but it was so wonderful to see him. That was almost enough.

'Do you ever see whales in this fjord?' he asked, killing the engine as he spoke.

'Yes, it's teeming with whales. Is that why you came?'

He tipped his head as if considering his answer, and Astrid wanted to laugh, but she waited, enjoying the anticipation.

'I came to see if you'd be willing to welcome a weary sailor in for a bite to eat.'

'I could rustle up some soup and bread.'

He laughed. 'That's just what I was hoping for.'

'Head down the coast. I'll meet you on the quay.'

He saluted her with a big grin, started the engine and puttered off towards town.

Astrid ran into the house, grabbed her coat and ran down to the centre of town where Leifur was securing the boat to a mooring post. He climbed out and, once he'd clocked her, started striding towards her, his arms ready to catch her as she flung herself into him.

There was no better feeling in the world than this.

'You're here,' she said, pulling back to take a proper look at his face. 'I've missed you so much. This is a terrible idea.' She laughed and wiped a stray tear away.

'It's the best idea I've ever had.'

'Did you sail that boat here?'

'I hitched a ride. Navigating these waters isn't for the fainthearted.'

She beamed at him, wondering if she'd ever be able to stop smiling. He came here just to see her and that was the most romantic thing that had ever happened to her. Even if it would break her heart all over again when he had to leave, it was already worth it.

'Come on, let's go home.'

Tempting as it was to fall into bed without a second thought, Astrid prepared soup and bread for them both, and they sat at the small table, gazing at each other as they ate. Then afterwards, she made tea, and they went out to sit on the deck.

'This is incredible,' said Leifur. 'The most beautiful place.'

'It is.'

'So you're here for three years?'

'Yes. Although I do have four months off in the summer months.'

'I know, Gudrun said. And that's why I'm here.'

Astrid frowned. 'I don't understand. Nothing's changed. We can't have a summer romance every year for four months. That's not fair on either of us.'

'No. But things have changed for me. We're operating a different schedule over the winter, and with Isak on the team I don't need to be captain of *Brimfaxi* all the time.'

'It worked out with Isak?'

He nodded and grinned. 'Isak's great. He's part of the team now, and it made me realise I can make different choices.'

'So you're here because you think it can work?' She could hardly breathe waiting for him to answer. Please let him think it could work.

'What would you say if I stayed here with you for the winter? And what do you think about coming to work on the tours over the summer? Every summer.'

On the face of it, it sounded like a near-perfect plan. 'You want to come here for the winter? What would you do?'

'I'd like to fish. In the traditional way. And I'm going to knit Lopi sweaters. I've thought about this a lot, Astrid. Isak being willing to take more responsibility made me realise that I need a break from that. My whole life has been dictated by my job, but now that I'm partners with Jonas, it doesn't have to be like that anymore. He's fine with Isak taking over for the winter and me having a break. Then Isak has the chance to take off if he wants to when I get back.'

'You're going to live with me for the winter and fish and knit?'

'If you'll have me.'

'Of course I'll have you.' She hooked her arm into his. 'You want to knit?'

'Yes. I loved it when we learnt at school, and my father used to knit gloves for the men on the boat in the days before you could get technical fabrics. And it's very relaxing. I need more relaxation in my life.'

'I love the thought of you sitting out here knitting while I'm looking for narwhals.'

'And the summer tours? Do you think it could work? Then there would only be a couple of months at a time when we're not together.'

'I can't believe you've come up with this. It's the perfect plan. I took this job thinking I'd find something else for the summer months, or maybe I'd go somewhere warm for a holiday, but I never thought about working in Reykjavik for the summer. I thought you'd have someone else by now.'

'When Eva went back to Canada, Jonas decided not to look for a replacement, so I asked him whether he'd support my idea. And he did.'

'So, everyone's okay with the whole plan? You have everything aligned, and you just need me to say yes.'

'Only if you want to. If you don't, I can catch a ride back to Iceland in a couple of days on the boat I came on. I don't want to push you into anything. It's your decision.'

It seemed like the easiest decision in the world. She could see it working for her.

'You're the one doing all the compromising. It doesn't seem fair. And what happens in three years when I need to look for another job?'

'Three years is a long time. Who's to say that even if we lived in Iceland year-round together, we'd still be together in three years?'

'You don't believe that.'

'No, I don't. But you have to know, this isn't a compromise for me. It's the opportunity of a lifetime.'

She didn't say anything, just looked at him until he carried on.

'I thought I'd be tied to Iceland my whole life, and I was happy with that. I wanted that. But these past four months have shown me what else there is to enjoy about life when you're not the person who has to keep everything going all the time. It's given me a chance to breathe, see that sharing the responsibility with other people, Jonas and my brother, makes life easier. It's fun being part of a team, and they're all behind this.'

'You don't think it'd drive you mad not being out on the sea in the winter?'

'Not if I'm here with you.' He reached out and took her mug, putting it down so that he could pull her onto his lap. 'This place is incredible. There's a different pace of life somewhere like this, and I'm ready for that. Hibernating with you over the winter isn't going to drive me mad. Living without you would.'

'It's too good to be true.'

'I'm glad you feel like that because I was so scared you would think it was a terrible idea. I thought you might have moved on and not looked back.'

'Like you told me to.'

'I didn't want you to do that.'

'I know. And that's why I'm still in love with you, Leifur. Because you love me enough not to make me choose. Even now, you're not making me choose. You're giving me everything I want in the world.'

He kissed her like she'd never been kissed before, and it wasn't until they came up for air that they realised it had started raining.

'We should go in,' Astrid said, picking up the mugs.

They stood in the kitchen and pulled off their wet clothes.

'My bag is on the boat,' Leifur said, standing in her kitchen in his underwear.

'You'll have to stay here until your clothes are dry then,' she said, moving towards him, revelling in the moment their skin would touch and she'd feel his warmth against her. And she'd have this for the whole winter.

'I'll pick my bag up tomorrow,' he murmured into her neck as he began kissing her.

'You're staying. For the whole winter.'

'The whole winter, my love.' He picked her up and carried her into the bedroom, laying her on the bed. The rain lashing at the window made the idea of being in bed together even more tempting.

'I love you more than narwhals.'

32

Six Months Later

Leifur stood on the quay, staring at the road that led to the harbour car park, waiting impatiently for Olafur, Gudrun and Astrid. The rest of the Iceland Adventures team were on board *Brimfaxi* waiting for the other three to arrive so that they could set off for the dry run for the new season of whale watching trips.

After a long winter in Greenland which had been some of the best months of Leifur's life, they had parted ways for a couple of months while he came back to Iceland to take over from Isak and Astrid went on a trip to Australia to see her friend from school.

'Bet you wish your reunion wasn't on the boat with everyone else here,' Isak said, coming up behind him. He looked tanned after a month of island-hopping in the Caribbean, and Leifur had been surprised to find himself looking forward to working with his brother again.

'I don't care, I just can't wait to see her.'

Isak clapped him on the back. 'Well, you have all summer now.'

Leifur had a lump in his throat. It was hard to believe how

far he'd come in a year. As well as starting a new business, he'd found the love of his life and a relationship with his brother that he never thought he'd have.

'Yes,' he managed, keeping his eyes firmly on the car park. 'Here they are.' He walked over to where Olafur pulled up the truck and watched Astrid climb out of the back seat. She was wearing the very first Lopi sweater that he'd knitted in Greenland and it warmed his heart that she wore it, even though it wasn't perfect. She looked amazing. The Australian sun had lightened her hair and dusted a few freckles across her nose and cheeks. She was grinning at him as he took her in his arms.

'You look wonderful,' he said, squeezing her to him.

'So do you.' Her eyes were shining, and any worries he might have had that she wasn't looking forward to being back here for the summer disappeared.

'Nice sweater.'

'Knitted with love.' She reached up and touched his cheek and he wished more than anything that they didn't have to spend the afternoon with everyone else.

'Are you sure you're ready to launch straight back in?'

'I've been looking forward to it from the moment you turned up in Nuuk.'

'There's no pressure to work today. It's turned out to be more of a team outing than a dry run, so you don't need to worry too much about finding whales.'

'Stop trying to spoil my fun.'

Olafur and Gudrun had already headed over to *Brimfaxi*, giving them a precious moment alone before they had to do the same.

'I can't wait for tonight,' Leifur said, kissing her again, hardly able to believe that they had the next four months together.

'Neither can I. I'll put my stuff in your truck later.'

They were going to live at Leifur's cottage. It was more convenient to have a place in Reykjavik, but they'd decided the short commute was worth it for the beautiful summer evenings they could spend looking out at the water.

'And no Eva this year?' Astrid put her arm around Leifur's waist as they walked to the boat.

'Actually, she's sharing the galley job with Isak. She's writing her dissertation, so it suited her, and he's working for the wider team now, so it's worked out well for both of them.'

'It's like I never left.'

He put his arm across her shoulders and squeezed her against him.

'Not at all. This has been a long time coming.' He kissed the top of her head and then stepped aside to allow her to board *Brimfaxi* first. The entire team was waiting on deck to welcome her, and Leifur loved seeing her reaction.

'Welcome back,' Jonas said, hugging her. 'Sorry for throwing you in at the deep end.'

'Oh, it's fine. I'm looking forward to it. I can't wait to spend the summer with lots of guests after a winter with narwhals.'

'And Leifur? It was that bad?' Jonas laughed.

Isak was in the wheelhouse and started the engines. Leifur let off the ropes, and they set off.

After Astrid said hello to everyone on deck, she went below and found Eva in the galley.

'Astrid! It's so great to see you.' They hugged each other. 'How were the narwhals?'

'Incredible. Don't tell Leifur, but I can't wait to get back there.'

Eva laughed and handed her a glass. 'It's a non-alcoholic cocktail. Everyone else had one when they came onboard.'

'Thanks. And how's the degree going? Leifur said you're writing your dissertation over the summer?'

'I've been working with the Marine and Freshwater Research Institute here to look into how their database of humpback whales could be expanded to create a global database.'

'Wow, that's amazing.'

'If it hadn't been for last summer, I wouldn't have come up with that idea. I hope I can work in that field, identifying individuals, when I graduate.'

'Can I get a glass of water for Rachel? She's not feeling well,' said Gudrun coming into the galley.

Astrid filled a glass. 'I'd better come up with you and get started. Is she seasick? It feels calm.'

Gudrun followed Astrid up onto deck, but got waylaid talking to Iris. Astrid found Rachel leaning over the bow, looking determinedly at the horizon while Jonas rubbed her back.

'I don't think looking at the horizon is going to help,' he was saying to her.

'It usually does,' said Astrid.

'Perhaps not if you're pregnant,' said Rachel.

Jonas looked at Astrid and grinned. 'We were keeping it a secret, but I guess with a sea as calm as this…'

'Congratulations! Hey, Gudrun!' Astrid called her sister over.

Rachel turned around and sipped the water. 'We're having a baby,' she said to Gudrun.

'No! Are you?'

'Yes. By spring you'll be an honorary aunt,' said Rachel.

'That's wonderful, congratulations,' Gudrun said to Rachel and Jonas, who were beaming.

'I'd better start looking out for some whales or Isak's going to be halfway to Canada before we know it,' said Astrid.

After a successful couple of hours of whale watching, with Isak at the helm, they headed back into port. Leifur joined

Astrid on the stern as she watched the water behind them while everyone else had headed downstairs for drinks and food.

'It's like you were never away,' he said, smiling.

'I'd forgotten how much I love it. If I see a whale in Greenland, most of the time there's no one to share it with. Unless we're on the deck at home.'

The winter had been an amazing experience. One that bonded them and made them realise that if they could live together for two weeks while they were literally snowed into the house, they could live through anything together.

'I know what you mean. It's great to have the immediate reactions of everyone around you. I didn't realise how that was until Isak took the wheel.'

That evening, at the cottage, after Astrid had unpacked her things into the drawers that Leifur had cleared for her, they headed down to the shore with a beer each, for old times' sake.

'I can't believe Rachel's pregnant,' said Astrid.

'They looked so happy.' Leifur gazed at the water with a smile on his face. 'Do you want kids?'

'Yes, do you?'

'Yes, with you I do.'

'I used to think that by the time I was ready to have kids, I'd have reached the point in my career where I'd be happy to give it up. And now that I'm with you and we've worked out how to be together, I'm scared that wanting kids on top of that is too much to wish for.'

'You're thinking of it in the context of what you're doing now. Think back a year and you'd never have thought we'd be where we are now. Who knows what things will be like in another couple of years when your contract in Greenland finishes.'

'We have two more winters to discuss this endlessly, I

suppose,' she said, laughing.

'And there are other things we could do before we have kids,' said Leifur.

'Like what?'

'Like get married?'

'Are you proposing?'

'Yes, very badly.' He stood up and pulled something out of his pocket. Then he knelt on the damp moss in front of her. Taking her left hand, he pushed a ring onto her finger, keeping his hand over it while he said, 'Astrid, will you marry me?'

'Yes.'

He moved his hand to reveal a silver ring with the most perfect piece of blue sea glass in a claw setting.

'Leifur, this is beautiful.'

'I found the glass when we were on the beach together. I know we don't know what will happen after Greenland, but I know we'll always work something out so we can be together.'

'Me too.' She shifted so that she was on her knees too. 'I love you so much,' she said, embracing him as hard as she could.

'I'm sorry,' he said, laughing as they lay down next to each other on top of the tarpaulin. Each of them propped up on an elbow and facing each other. 'It was more romantic in my head. I didn't mean to blurt it out tonight. I just —'

'It was perfect. More than perfect.'

'Maybe I'll surprise you sometime and do it properly.'

'When will we get married? Oh my god, we're getting married!'

He laughed and kissed her. 'Let's have a summer wedding.'

'On the boat.'

'We don't have to do that.'

'I want to. Without *Brimfaxi,* we might never have fallen in love.'

'That sounds perfect.'

The End

Other titles in the Icelandic Romance series

Snug in Iceland

Hideaway in Iceland

Stranded in Iceland

Ignited in Iceland

Also by Victoria Walker

Croftwood Series

Summer at Croftwood Cinema

Twilight at Croftwood Library

Festival in Croftwood Park

Wild Swimming at Croftwood Lake

The Island in Bramble Bay

Sign up to Victoria's mailing list at
www.victoriaauthor.co.uk
to receive a regular newsletter, with
information about new releases, special offers
and exclusive content.

Author's Note

I can't remember when I decided this book was about whale-watching trips, but once I did, I felt an irresistible urge to go on a whale-watching trip in Iceland. It was booked and planned on a whim but I had the best time. Besides the amazing whales, I loved being in Iceland at a different time of year. I'd only ever been in the winter before so it was a joy to see something of what lies beneath the snow and ice. I'd already written half of the book before I went but the second half was a dream to write once I'd sucked up all the Icelandic vibes, and found some new places to write about.

I was lucky enough to be able to grill the marine biologist, Annika, who was the guide on our boat, about things like the rarest whales she's seen in the bay off Reykjavik. She told me the story of the blue whale that visited the bay once and also that she'd been lucky enough to see fin whales. Her life outside of working on the trips gave me the inspiration for how Astrid's career might play out. She was an excellent and informative guide and made our trip unforgettable! Her information was so valuable in making *Brimfaxi* and the trips realistic, and any mistakes in my retelling are my own.

And a shout-out to Lee-Anne who gave me some great ideas of places to go on the trip, a few that have made it into the book. She shares her Icelandic knowledge generously and is wonderfully supportive.

There's a good chance that if you're here, you've probably read the other books in the series and I'm thrilled you're part of my Iceland gang! It shocks me in the best way every time I get an email from someone telling me that they went to Iceland and visited some of the places from the books or have Iceland on their list of places they want to visit. One person even found a copy of Snug in Iceland in their apartment while they were in Iceland on a yoga retreat!

Thank you as ever to Berni Stevens for another beautiful cover. Thanks to Catrin for editing and to James for proofreading and Claudia for being my marketing and social media guru as well as giving me honest advice on the story. Thanks to Jake for buying my Garth Brooks tickets. And last but not least, thank you for choosing to read my book. Reviews mean such a lot to writers, so if you have time to leave a review for this book, or any book you've enjoyed, it makes all the difference.

The best way to keep in touch is to sign up to my exclusive mailing list at victoriaauthor.co.uk. I send a newsletter every couple of weeks to keep you up to date with what I'm up to, as well as any special offers, new releases and exclusive content. You can also find me in all of these places:

Instagram @victoriawalker_author
Facebook Victoria Walker - Author
TikTok @victoriawalkerauthor

Printed in Dunstable, United Kingdom